For Nicola

Contents

Introduction

IT WAS AN OVERCAST FEBRUARY MORNING and I was sitting in my pants eating All-Bran. The Ugandan Black Death outbreak was trending on Twitter and a museum assistant who hearted autumn, spooky stories, and collecting old polaroids and broken barbies, posted a gif of a scared Cookie Monster in response to this emergency epidemic. His furry, string-operated paws reached up to his face in shock, as if to say, "Oh no! Not the Black Death!" I considered, briefly, pointing out this person's embarrassing flippancy in the face of unrelenting misery, explaining inside a thin rectangular box restricting me to about twenty-two words how her response, calculated to earn her likes and retweets at her own creative wit, was not appropriate when people who were living in hopeless poverty also had to suffer violent diseases, for which there were insufficient inoculations or western donations, and that such a response was typical of the comfortable white millennial's casual carelessness to anything outside their own navels, but I pictured the string of unapologetic responses, with Big Bang Theory gifs, Harry Potter gifs, and attempts to twist me into an aggressive super-asshole for pointing out basic human idiocy, but I was too miserable to move my fingers in a typing motion. Snow fell. I viewed the chaotic, wind-whipped snowfall as a reminder of how we are battered and blown along in our lives in unwanted directions with little control over our own fates, and the laughable attempts we make to contrive a significance to our actions in the face of the final arbiter, Death.

I needed a holiday. A temporary respite from time's prodding. I located a pair of trousers, a stain-free t-shirt, and sloped downstairs to purchase a chocolate oblong. The promotional banner on a Munch bar screamed WIN A FREE HOLIDAY FOR TWO IN JERSEY, so I purchased that fictional product. I ambled along a street musing on an idea for a social platform that captured the real incoherence of thought, called Nutter. A series of nano-tweets in an endless chain loaded in a permanent continuum, branching in random directions, each consisting of the fetid flotsam of one's inner monologue, allowing the reader complete access to the immiserisation of each user's soul. This would render the endless process of apologising for the poor articulation of one's offensive thoughts moot: the unedited awfulness of every man and woman would be on show for all, no one allowed to hide behind their own taste filters or delete buttons. It might yield a utopia. Everyone's thoughts a product of whatever rubbish is spooned into their ears, everyone a victim of their psyches.

Having chewed on the Munch (munching impossible thanks to the nougat and caramel contingent), I peered inside the wrapper to observe that I had won the FREE HOLIDAY. Before I made ecstatic noises, I returned home to read the online terms and conditions. The FREE HOLIDAY was located at the Hotel Diabolique in the English-speaking Bailiwick of Jersey, a self-governing island off the French coast famous for tax avoidance. The wrapper had boasted "a tremendous hotel with sweeping views". When I searched on the Opera browser, I observed that the hotel was a one-star affair with sweep-up views of the outside bins and pavements, with no French coastline in sight and, more unusually, that parts of the structure acted as a "prison for public nuisance offenders" and held forty-seven people.

The Hotel Diabolique, French for "Rubbish Hotel", was constructed in 1999, originally named The Land's Pride, and earned a reputation for its bedbugs, uncooked bacon, unhoovered rooms, and rude staff. To keep trading in the age of the internet, the hotel played on its humorous reputation for discomfort, and adopted the new name. People came to the hotel to experience the worst service in the world, and staff hammed up the horror, keeping their guests waiting at the check-in desk for twelve hours, handing them the wrong keys every time, only tidying up the rooms when blood appeared on sheets, charging £10.99 for an uncooked sprout, refusing to let in late-night guests even in the winter months, and so on. The only visitors to the place were masochists, sex tourists, and contest winners.

In 2021, British Prime Minister Frank Oakface made an historic choice to radically improve the lives of the people of all forty-eight English counties. The scheme, adopted in England only, involved an online polling of the population as to who was the largest irritant in each county, and the yearly removal of that person from the county and their incarceration in a one-star hotel for a number of years, determined by the scale of their "crime", until their release. When I arrived at the hotel, I met all those incarcerated, and over year-old bottles of ginger beer, they told me their stories, of how they were voted out of England in these punitive internet polls. I found their tales fascinating and frightening, and set about turning them into a book immediately.

This work is an almanac of terror, a year in the life of this irritant-cleansing scheme. I have authored the stories herein from the prisoners' own accounts, recasting them in more palatable and vivid literary styles wherever possible, allowed them to relate events in their own voices, or sourced documents that tell their stories stronger than my own attempts. A large number of those incarcerated were writers and artists, this being a time of deep-seated anti-intellectualism in the country. It is hoped that these accounts will provide a stark and uncompromising account of when the British government, for a bizarre and regrettable period, set about trimming England.

—M.J. Nicholls
New Brunswick, 2023

TRIMMING
ENGLAND

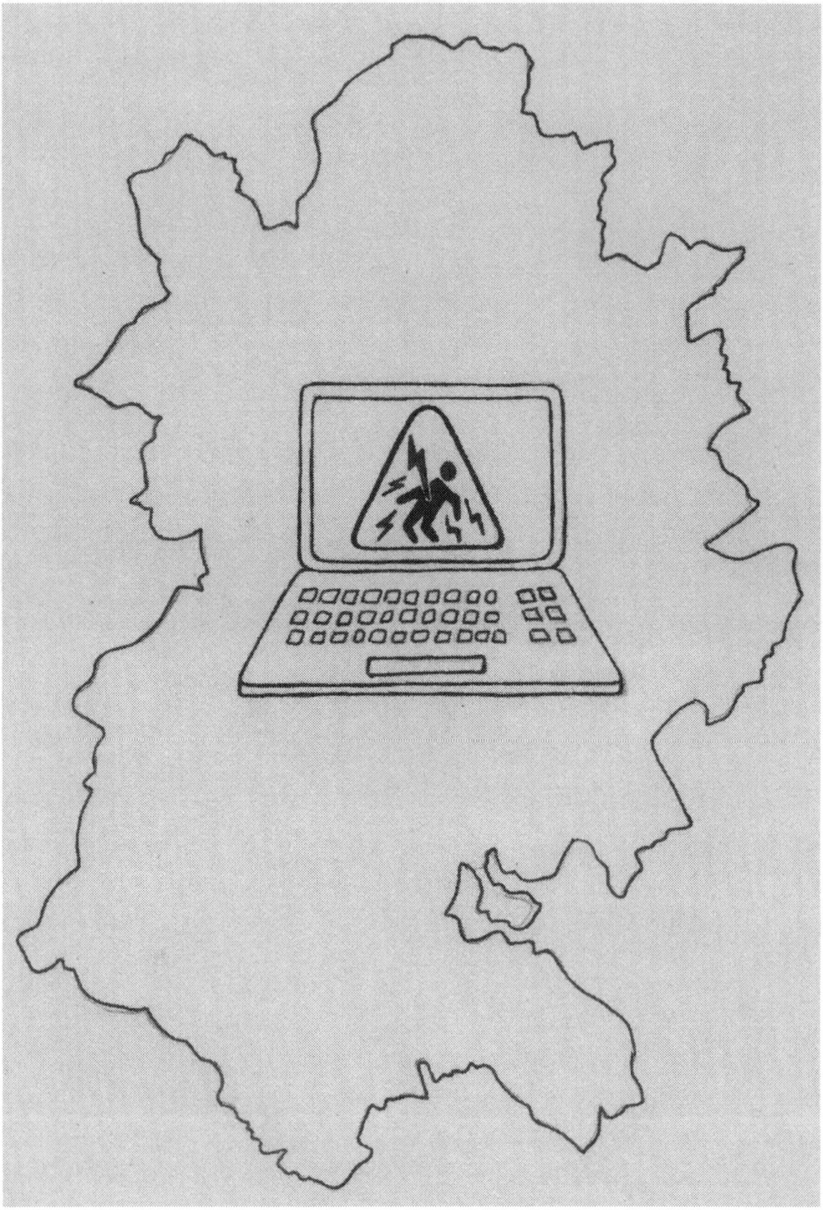

[BEDFORDSHIRE]

NAME: TYRONE POUCH

AGE: 27

SENTENCE: 2 YEARS

CRIME: ABYSMAL SECOND STATUS

ONE FILTHY MONDAY, I ARSEPLUMMETED into social media oblivion. Having not written a sentient sentence of note, I checked for the fifteenth time how many nonfriends had liked the phrase Today, I lapse into creative coma. The first two likes served up simple peer-to-peer validation. The mouse-click equivalent of an expressionless appreciative nod for a transaction too minor to merit the employment of facial muscles. The fact that two people, somewhere in the world, had acknowledged a notion I hurled without forethought into a small textbox on a popular social networking website yielded a shameless throb of pleasure. The sort of pleasure I took from that simple validation was minor, like two meaningless taps on the shoulder from an uncle at a wedding or funeral, signifying nothing more than "Hello, I am your uncle." Third, fourth, and fifth likes appeared. In writing such a status, I had intended to take a sardonic swipe at the writing process, the unending pressure to parse prize-winning sentences, to show that creative impotence is a common complaint and that I suffered from this more than most, battling self-hatred from clause to clause, like a man simultaneously punching and bandaging himself. I hoped that fellow writers might empathise with this unfortunate malady, and that their own trials might seem, for that brief moment in reading the sentence, less taxing. And I wanted full credit for expressing this. Because I had lapsed into that creative coma, I sought solace in this status, hoping the instant approval might somehow salve that failure, and make the barren wordless afternoon seem less disgusting. As the likes reached over fifty, the approval tasted sweet. I had been handed a picture of myself signed by fifty strangers with the caption: "Yay, we like you!" Expressing failure on this social networking platform was more satisfying than writing another well-shorn sentence about rotten human beings spewing venom at each other in wan rooms (as per my previous publications). I continued to seek approval for my absence of skill, writing: Verily, I sink into a trough of brain-mush. This status, more opaque in tenor, less immediate than the previous, received fewer likes. As the clicks remained in the single figures, I had to conclude I had lost the core base of likers with this strange phrasing: I had expressed my impotence in a creative way, hinting to the reader I was merely pretending, that I was able to write a sentence showing some semblance of skill, that I was lying to solicit attention. The next day, still humming from the 50+ approval, I wrote: I cannot write a single pissing thing. This was a catastrophic misfire. A clamour of commenters sprayed the status with their faux-concern. I had moved from an amusing expression of creative impotence to the shameless public solicitation of heartfelt replies. I was on a par with the 4AM cri de coeur writers, those who in a blur of bourbon and tears write Does anyone care? Really, anyone?, and awake with a hangover to several hundred pages of "concerned" messages from family members, and emoji responses from people they thought should have at least *commented* on their partial suicide note. I was forced into writing lengthy retractions in my replies to comments, stating my intent in a tiny font in remarks that ended up clipped below, my wheedling and backpedalling explication of the central text forever lost below the blunt and crass howl of my public self-exposure. At that moment, I made a pledge to vanish from self-serving servers the world over. I would commit myself to crafting prose, whether unread forever, excerpted briefly on student ezines, or published in hallowed hardback. I would be a writer plumbing the human condition once more, not a writer writing nonwriting about not-writing. Sadly, I was bundled onto a plane before this could happen.

[CUMBRIA]

NAME: EVAN V. RUFFLE
AGE: 39
SENTENCE: 13 YEARS
CRIME: THE SOCIAL WRITING PROGRAM

HAVING TOILED IN THE ILLUCRATIVE and lucre-free field of "experimental" fiction for four years with no success (even among "experimental" publishers who bragged about publishing 900-page lipograms in Chaucerian Ebonics), Vince signed up for the Social Writing Program—a live writing platform where each sentence of an author's work-in-progress was streamed live on a social network to millions of people, who could like, dislike, and comment on the ongoing effort sentence by sentence. For authors committed to monetising their art, the SWP was a brilliant platform for new and experienced writers to be noticed by the agents and publishers who prowled the site, and to connect instantly with readers who could help improve and champion the work-in-progress if it connected with them. The site was designed to be accessible—on the right-hand side of the screen, a list of numbers indicating sentences scrolled down the page in sequence, and by clicking on any chosen number, the readers were taken to a live feed of all the incoming sentences of that number, and could comment, like, or dislike at whim. If the reader wanted to catch up with any one work, they could expand the author's feed and the complete manuscript would appear below (each sentence clickable to retrieve the previous likes, etc.). The most visited sentences were the first and last. Trolls frequented the first sentences, attempting to stop writers whose ineptitude was blatant. If a consensus formed around a clearly terrible opening sentence, a group of mobilised trolls swooped down and performed "charitable euthanasia" so these sentences were deleted from the feed to prevent a build-up of

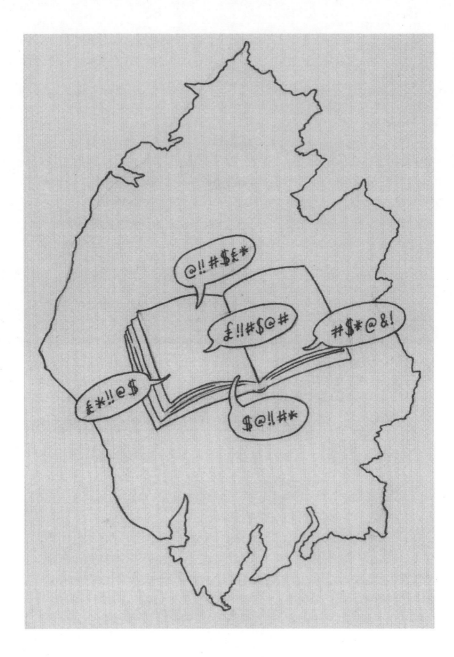

badly spelled and ungrammatical work. Comments were moderated and those with foul language or abuse were eaten by an algorithm. Vince had been collecting ideas for a sci-fi novel he felt had mass-market potential about benign aliens who thrived on boredom and colonised the planet in the form of accountants, mortgage brokers, pedagogues, and pedants. He opted out of titling his novel—not the best move for a beginner, but those who named their novels first and improvised the content often changed their titles to match the plots, infuriating readers who had stuck with the book for the promise in the title alone.

He opened up the first-sentence feed. Five sentences per second streamed down the screen as his fingers hovered above the keys. He promised not to be drawn to reading first, but his eyes caught:

> Helen_Hunter
> "Do you know the way to Sam's, Hosea?" she asked.
> 417 dislikes—2 likes—900 comments.
>
> BIG_Author
> The middle men were on the left, the left men in the middle, and the right men were in the wrong.
> 327 dislikes—110 likes—679 comments.
>
> Paul_Toffman_Writer
> My balls were freezing off.
> 627 likes—236 dislikes—1,018 comments.
>
> Angie_Brody
> The darkness was rising.
> 1,181 dislikes—0 likes—4,025 comments.

He chased the last ten sentences down the feed, looking for some coherence in the reader responses. Sentences he thought well-written had more dislikes, while crude and unfunny sentences seemed to scoop up likes. On the advice page, they stressed that the feedback on first sentences could be misleading—if the first paragraph received more likes than dislikes, this was a good omen. A greater like-consensus developed as a successful story progressed, with occasional dips into dislikes common due to reader apathy. After the 100th sentence, if you still had readers following your story, this was considered a success as most writers failed to engage readers past ten sentences and the authors who still had readers after the 100th were viewed by publishers and agents. Vince had snorted at the deceptive easiness of this. How simple! Just write one hundred amazing sentences each as good as the last that captivate a majority of impatient and lazy readers! He sighed and wrote his debut sentence. Once posted, sentences could be rewritten and reposted an hour later to avoid clog and only five attempts were permitted. There was pressure on authors to perfect sentences on the third or fourth tries, as readers rarely paid any attention to fifth attempts (known as "last-click lunges.") He wrote:

> *What if, after a million movies and novels, two centuries of speculation and horror, aliens arrived on Earth and were simply . . . boring?*

His sentence received 300 dislikes and 29 likes and passed down the stream. He hesitated before clicking on the comments stream.

NayDee > Boring.

Jim T > Clunkers... like a bad movie tagline.

Arnold > Crap.

Jo > Lame. :(

Paul > Terrible idea for a novel. A bad sketch? Yep.

He wiped the sentence at once, ashamed. His cheeks surged red. Each curt and dismissive comment was a simultaneous slap in the face and boot in the testicles. He had written four works of complex and intricate fiction—this appalling sentence had received more reads than all his novels put together, and 329 people out there had decided that he couldn't string two clauses together to save himself. On the basis of this ill-thought and fumbled attempt, they were right. After an hour of hating himself, he regrouped and conceded that the system was fair—decent sentences were respected by readers, the writers had to be accountable for every weak syllable they presented. The main criticism of the site was that writers couldn't expect to perfect *every* sentence—but in an age of such copious and unnecessary literature, it seemed more vital than ever that *every* sentence worked some sort of magic.

As he thought on the comment *won't work as a novel*, his confidence evaporated. Far better to devote his time to something mainstream and literary, not attempt to cash in on genre writing like all the retired, greedy, and untalented delusionals on the site. He would write an acidic realist novel with fantastical elements, laced with wit and tough social observation. Where he'd mine these elements was the question—better to have the ambition now and source inspiration later. He wrote and posted:

> *The streets looked coarse that night—full of stale violence and violent hum.*

After a minute: 582 dislikes, 39 likes, and 338 comments. He opened the thread.

> Fran > No.
>
> Joe > The partial repeat of 'violence/violent' is awkward.
>
> George > A woeful attempt a literariness that sounds stilted, false and faux-streetsmart, probably written by a trustfund tot from the Cotswolds.
>
> Bole > 'Violent hum' is laughably pretentious.

He wiped the box clean. He'd done it again. Rushed in with an incompetent sentence! He closed the laptop and went to the pub for a few beers and a vodka. He didn't often resort to alcohol to numb the pain of being a literary failure, but since the local was across from his flat, he found himself drifting there more often. He considered his completed works so far. An anaphoric and homophonic crime thriller written in an arcane Welsh dialect. A novel where each right page is printed in reverse and readable in mirrors only. A murder mystery with edible and soluble pages, made using wheat and zinc. The pleasure of making these works weighed against the result having no large (or even minor) readership. Only hardcore reader-weirdoes. He polished off the vodka and went back to his flat to be sick.

The next morning he returned to the SWP and paid more attention to the popular material. Sentences with the most likes were those that worked in three elements: a sort of hooking pithiness that made the reader curious for more (written in such a manner the reader didn't realise he was being pithily hooked), direct language free from ornamentation with simple description, some reference to an identifiable emotional state the reader could relate to. If he could pull off this level of interminable pinpoint reader-baiting accuracy, he would be on his way to the Big Time, whatever that meant.

He wrote a new first sentence:

Bill had an epic hangover, and felt something even more epic stirring under the sheets.

This sentence took 400 likes and 134 dislikes. Promising. Readers could relate to the epic hangover and the sexual innuendo or threat of horror was hooking them. He continued to write careful sentences containing "relatable" content and minor hooks in each second clause until he progressed past the fifth sentence point, as people became more curious to know where these hooks were leading. By the sixth sentence, he had to reveal what some of these mysteries were—what was stirring under the sheets, what was lurking under the bathroom sink, what was that strange rattle in the closet, who was knocking on the outside window, what was causing that awful smell in the fridge? He had to find a sixth sentence that resolved these issues and kept the reader interested (he had about five minutes to think up a solution). In a panic, he wrote:

As he wiped the sleep from his eyes, he realised he was still partly in a dream and imagining things.

He'd blown his novel's brains out. A barrage of dislikes followed.

Billy > LAAAAAAAAAAAAME!

Jo > Come on now.

Bob > Clawed the face off a promising paragraph.

Callum > An unpolishable, unflushable turd of a line.

Lara > I had such high hopes. :(

Scritti > Torched the whole thing.

Pete > Ooooooooooooooooooooooooooooooouch.

Viv > This writer sure has a knack for massacring readers.

Biff > Worst. Sixth. Sentence. EVER.

Rick > This is incompetent. An incompetent sentence—
that is what this is!

Vince slammed the computer shut and returned to that novel in binary code he was knitting into the hide of an ox.

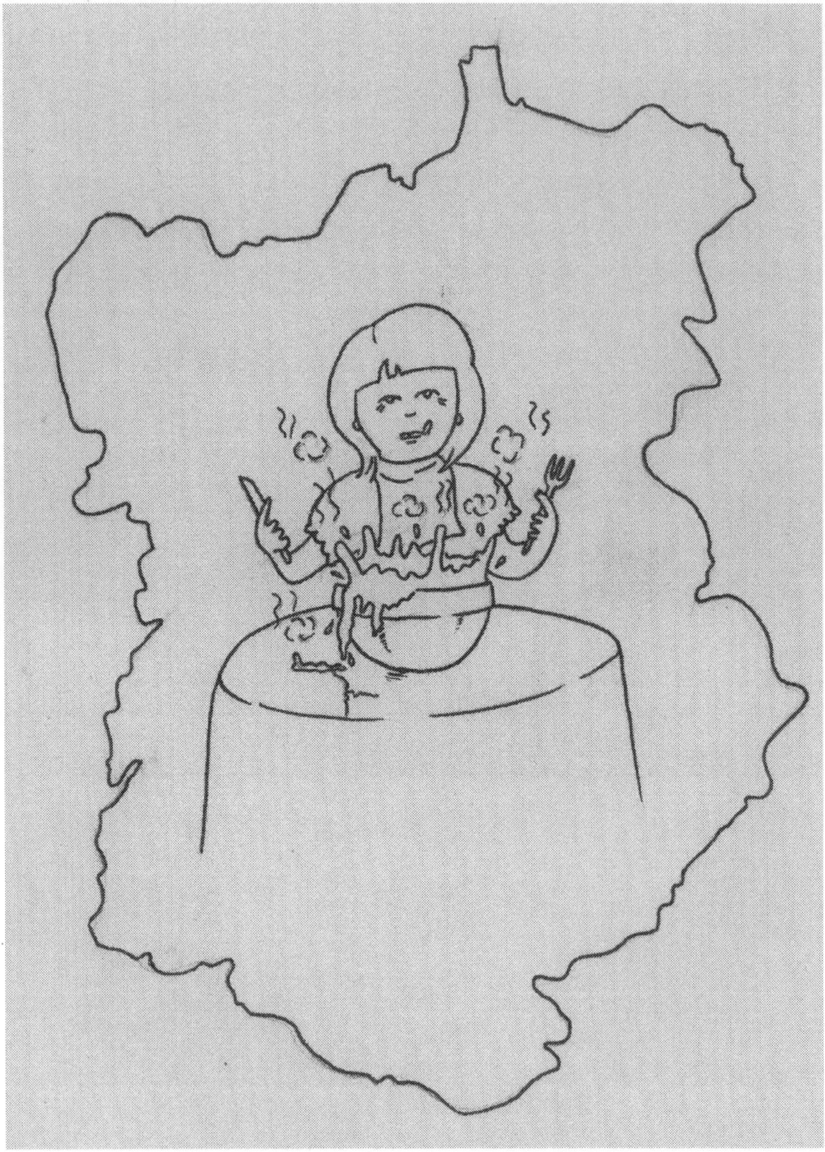

[WEST YORKSHIRE]

NAME: ANGELA BARNET
AGE: 46
SENTENCE: 10 HOURS
CRIME: SEE UNDERLINED

The following are a list of candidates for excommunication printed on the Leeds Exposé *website. The person chosen is underlined. As the people of West Yorkshire made clear,* all *of the candidates deserved excommunication, so in accordance with their wishes, I have included everyone else here, sans* names. *—Ed.*

T HE MAN WHO WALKS INTO A PERFUMERIE, saying "a puff of oleander, if you won't, ladies".

"   " owns ten fourths of the Rocko's Modern Life calendars.

"   " sweeps up outside the train station with an expression that indicates "this shoe here, this one here, is not podiatrically proper, and you, you, commuting scoundrels, will never know the pinch."

"   " rearranges the letters in his forename to spell 'COLD LUNG' on most occasions.

"   " stalks Mandie Grandpapple for twelve minutes, then leaps into the nearest puddle.

"   " is always, always, always, inconstant.

"   " sings in the shower, upsetting the tone deaf inventor next door, who scowls whenever a soapy rendition of 'Saturday Night', or 'The Earth Died Screaming' is heard.

"   " rocks on the balls of his feet and rolls on the soles of his shoes.

"   " reminds people that all human endeavour equates to zip, and that their successes and babies mean naught in the scheme of things, as these people are kissing each other on their lower nodes.

"   " applies a cold compress to the warmest areas and wonders what makes this sound: *Screeeoooouuuu*.

"   " cannot work past *Seamonsters* in the Wedding Present discog.

"   " is accused of "fishing for compliments" when casting his rod and praising a lover.

"   " reads the local news in a cheery, ebullient manner even when two million frogs have been massacred, or a loveable ogre is caught stealing a mattress, or a sideboard has been compromised.

"   " cannot wait until the French attend a concert.

"   " uses a handheld fan at important board meetings, blowing the papers here and thither, and hither and there, and sometimes allows the blades to connect with the CEO's cheek, thus slicing a portion off Dennis Whitelaw's face, when the annual GDP statements are about to be declared.

"   " always asks for lava in restaurants.

"   " accuses his sister of secreting his pencils in a cove, when his sister cannot write, and has no intention of learning to write, and in fact loathes all words and the smartasses who write them on dead trees.

"   " is named Ditto, yet writes his name on forms as " ".

"   " although well-practiced in semaphore, always ends up bursting into an unstoppable flap of expletives as he is signalling to his grandmother in a passing helicopter.

"   " struggles to swim in armbands while being held up by two men below the water, and having his legs kicked for him by two other men, and his arms arced for him by two other men, so in short, six men.

"   " never caterwauls when asked.

"   " could not care less if the fixture in your gums is bleeding.

"   " asks the barman to use the card machine, and upon being told there is a 50p charge, throws the undrunk beverage in the barman's face, slaps a tenner on the bar, and says "Have another one on me", and stands there until the barman realises that the customer wants to have a pint of beer thrown at his face.

"   " wins competitions because the size of his brain is twelve hexagons larger than standard Haworth noggin.

"   " owns up to the murders committed in 1989, pointing out the exact spots where the bodies were buried, hires a lawyer and pushes for the case to speed towards a criminal trial, then changes his mind when he remembers he was born in 1990.

"   " purchases a soul for £5.99, wears the soul to his mother's funeral, weeps for nine hours during the service, then returns the soul to the buyer, stating the soul was faulty, and that he hardly squirted a tear.

"   " is awake longer than most men, remaining open-peepered for up to twelve lunar cycles, plus an extra two.

"   " resents what happened to him in the shed with the pelican and the lantern and writes a weekly column pouring venomous hate on all pelicans and savage excoriation on most lanterns.

"   " wonders what weird critters lurk under his bed.

"   " likes to potter round the Brontë Parsonage Museum in a lime-green corduroy suit in case someone wants to talk to him about something.

"   " worries that the archangels in the tower might not buff their wings with the requisite density of wax.

"   " is concerned, over there, in a sack.

"   " upon receiving his bowl of lava in a restaurant, complains that the lava is too hot, and asks if they have anything less volcanic on the menu, and ends up eating the chicken supreme with new potatoes.

"   " is unconcerned, somewhere, en plein air.

"   " bought Travis's second LP.

❋

A woman who would rather have a nun than a vegetarian.

"   " is not impressed at Stan Uniform's temperance in the aftermath.

"   " attended her marriage in spite of the rumours that she might catch waves on Halifax beach instead.

"   " made salmon for her pet Pekinese, then sat on a chair while the mongrel optioned his script to an agent for £3,000, sniffing the fish imperiously.

"   " listens to Stockhausen in her stockings, and thinks it cute, in spite of the internet comments that that isn't cute at all, and that her brand of pretentious quirk is the lamest of all lameish things.

"   " correctly considers Belly's *Star* the pinnacle of their short-lived recording career.

"   " is responsible for correcting all spelling mistakes in metropolitan borough of Calderdale, yet spells weird 'wiedr'.

"   " imagines things without a licence, yet lacks the imagination to wonder where one might acquire such a licence.

"   " is proud to attend the local Flu Flux Flan club for fans of popular viral diseases, the flow of energy particles, and open fruit-based pastries, but suspects the name might have unsavoury undertones.

"   " cries whenever a poll tax is introduced, yet feels nothing when her firstborn is tied between two trucks and severed in half, like Jennifer Jason Leigh in *The Hitcher*.

"   " is not really vying for piemaker of the year contest, but wonders if she might win anyway, if she sends in a picture of a shoe.

"   " sounds leukemic on the phone.

"   " is not impressed by Mike Leigh's *Happy-Go-Lucky*, for at heart she has nothing except sneering contempt for humanity, and cannot tolerate unflapping optimism from anyone, for she is from Keighley, where the world reeks like a pickled onion crisp packet wafted from a landfill into time's face.

"   " while spatchcocking a guinea hen accidentally inserts a carving knife into her left nostril, slicing off half her face, but continues preparing the meal anyway, knowing that Mitchell will really love the hen, in spite of the pieces of nose and cheek and eyeball and blood slopping all over it.

"   " isn't sure the drama club is ready for a performance of *Cannibal Holocaust*, but follows her instincts.

"   " rings up a credit card company to ask for a credit cardboard, and continues the call until the operative comments on the suffix '-board' at the end of 'card', and if no operative comments, when she receives her credit card, complains with vehemence that she asked for a credit cardboard, and not a stupid piece of plastic, and that the whole world is a raving madhouse of nutters.

"   " thinks that Samuel Butler uses 'etcetera' instead of rounding up a paragraph with élan, but has no one to tell this to.

"   " whose belly, usually butter-yellow, has turned creamcheese-white, and no one knows whyforsooth.

"   " whose outrageous stories about men falling off ladders, cats chewing live wires, and pedlars losing their socks on the run from the rozzers, were never published in the *Yorkshire Evening Post*, in spite of her heady persistence.

"   " who considers it rude to stop a policeman and ask him if the real victor is the umpire, when the policeman is usually busy slapping a suspect, or chain-whipping a vagabond caught being improper around atoms.

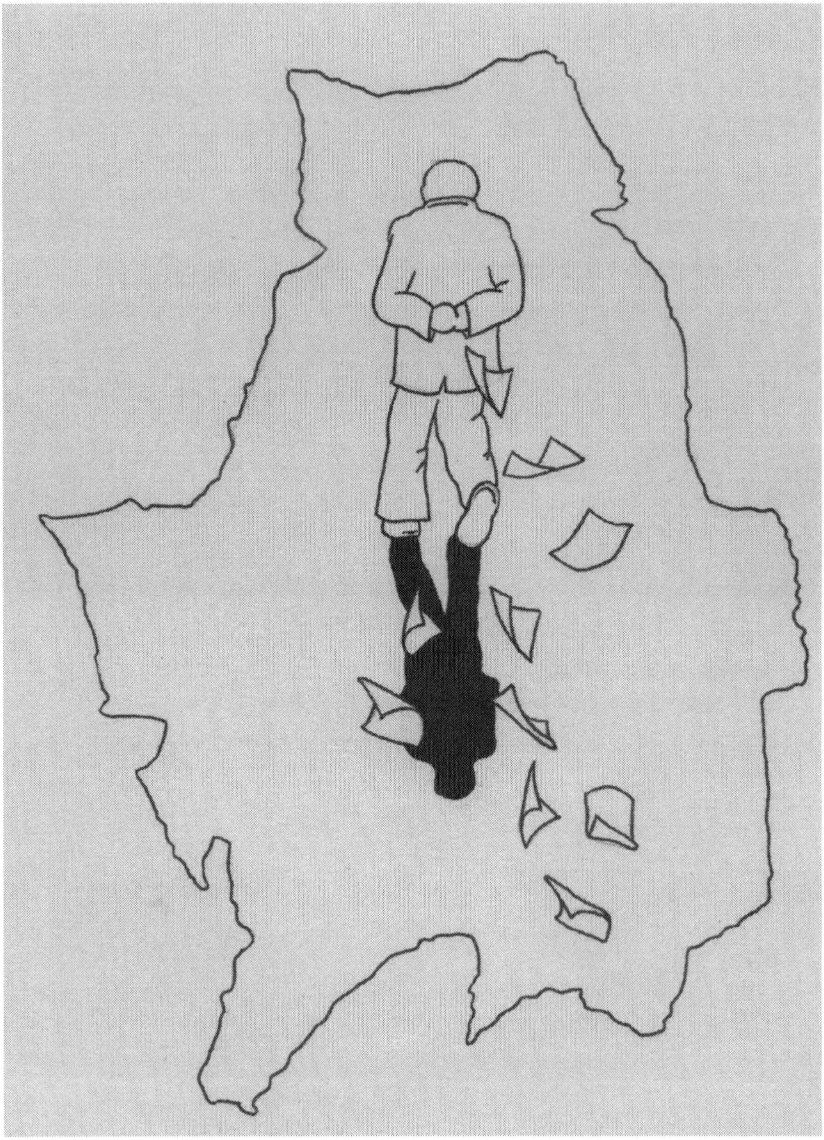

[CHESHIRE]

NAME: HECTOR LETTSIN
AGE: 35
SENTENCE: 79 YEARS
CRIME: WANTON WINDOWPANNERY

1

AS WITH MOST WRITERS who publish in small unprofitable low-circulation presses, I had a midnight panic attack at the constant lack of reviews, acclaim, or readers, and went agent-hunting. I searched the *Artist & Writer's Yearbook 2011* (in my tenth year of refusing to update), circled nine who represented "literary fiction", and printed off seven pages of my highly literary new novel, provisionally titled *My Highly Literary New Novel*, for each agent. A last-minute Yahoo! search told me the first six were no longer in business, so I began with Tom Valence at Steadman & Gorchester Unlimited, who represented "literary fiction (with strong film + TV tie-in elements)". He wrote: "I cannot envision your seven-page list of absurdities being turned into a successful HBO series with Chloë Sevigny and Steve Buscemi. I pass." The second, Ian Albumin at Steadfast & Winchester Unlimited, repped "literary fiction (with broad mainstream appeal)". He wrote: "This has a) no broad mainstream appeal, b) no mainstream appeal, and c) no appeal. I pass." The third, Sam Ruple, at Ruple Limited, said yes. He wrote: "Neato! Love your shit. Text me, bro." He specialised in "sculpting potential" and was open to any words on paper. I met him the next day in his Chester office.

I located his premises on Northgate Street and rapped on the shutters. He rattled them upwards and revealed the six-foot craven raven that was himself. His office had the sallow pallor of a lifelong smoker's bedsit. The ill-timed wall-clock, Cheshire landmarks calendar from 2001, and enormous PC monitor honed the mood of a room pickled in the past with no hope of ever being unpickled. His spooked face, a cast of five o'clock shadows, twitching lineaments, and cracked skin-craters, reminded me of the writer Simon Hopper: a one-book wonder who sleep-walked into the River Weaver one night following a painful first review in *The Observer*, if the legend is to be believed.

"You are a man on the up," Sam said. I sank with no irony into the rigor-musked settee.

"Thanks."

"Two things. First: we need characters. I'm here to propel you. Strap yourself to me, mate, and we are bound for the stratosphere."

"The ozone layer?"

"Ha! *That* is funniness." It wasn't funniness. He had been standing over me like a socially awkward Nosferatu. He popped a Smint and pumped up his swivel chair to an acceptable sitting height. "Now, those characters. Peep this pie," he said. He showed me:

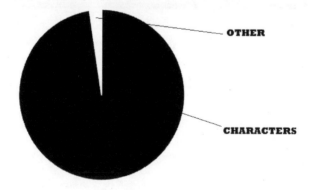

"You see the cruciality of characters? I propose we work together on a novel. A breakthrough big whopper. To further the burger analogy, you're frying minor patties on the skillet of talent. I help authors source the plumpest tastiest cows, have them humanely executed, carved with love in the abattoir, sourced to the finest restaurants, and served in mouthwatering baps by award-winning chefs."

"We still talking about books?"

"Mmhmm. You a Smint man?" he asked. He shoogled his tinned mints.

"No thanks. So you propose I start a new novel with an emphasis on characters? You realise I have made a point of spitting on the tired conventions of the novel: characters, plots, themes, ideas, coherent sentences?"

"Sure, sure. Screw that fogified bullplop. But this is the nowish. Characters equals readers equals a shot at a small sum of remuneration. Does that sound wow?"

"A small sum of remuneration? Not in this writer's wildest."

"Yes. Characters. It's simple. You write a character with strong qualities: believable, likeable, relatable, and whatnot. The core -ables of cash-cow fiction. We can test-market the novel as it is being written. You see? I can focus-group this baby, from chapter to chapter. At the end we'll have a novel that will annihilate the market. Let's Tony Parsons this motherfucker. You in, bro?"

I stared at Sam Ruple, sad scrupleless Sam Ruple, with his nervous Smint-popping hands and owlwide orbs, and saw that Sam was me. I was a nervous Tic Tac-tippler with aye-aye eyes, craving the raving acclaim. I sought his spindly twitchers upon mine, taking me hand in hand to the Promised Land of a small sum of remuneration. A partner in struggle. A burden-shouldering brother with bothersome shoulders and no brotherly resemblance. I accepted Sam's strong handshake: the sweaty clasp of mutual desperation, the informal formation of a codependent union seeking two diverging outcomes. And so in less than twelve hours, Sam Ruple at Ruple Limited, was my literary agent.

2

"Good start, man!" Sam piped. He offered me a puff. I declined. "I love this Victor. His quandary is universal: to pursue a dream even when there's resistance from the home-unit. My ex-wife loathed the prospect of me agenting. Preferred me to remain an obedient office stiff for the sake of the kid. No thanks, ma'am. Question? How come Victor and his missus know he's the 'likeable' character? Does he need to know this?"

"Victor is a 'likeable' character in the fictional village Echt. You ever been to a small village like Echt this fictional one? In these places, people have 'characters'. They're the closest thing to fiction in reality, if we accept that reality is not a fiction. Victor has a standing there that keeps him a crucial part of that place, that helps the home-unit retain its sanity and keep its face in a place of no privacy."

"Right, sure," Sam said. He perched his pipe on the PC monitor. "Another. This dialogue. It's cool man. Interesting. But is it how people talk in the real?"

"Fiction is fiction. For me, mimetic fiction is an oxymoron. You fictionalise reality the moment you write a fiction. It's called *fiction*. My characters can talk however they like. They can be irrational. And as you'll find out, they can deviate from their 'characters', they cannot be tethered to their labels."

"Sure, sure! Coolio. But let me flip this omelette. I'm here to sculpt this into a bestseller. We need folks that talk like us folks."

"But even we, Sam the man, talk in ways that mimetic fiction would scorn. There is no such thing as a proper mimetic form of dialogue. Soap operas and other cliché-peddlers trade in that shlock and as a result, all written speech that isn't a series of recognisable banalities has become the norm in commercial fic. Any character who chooses to whip out an ornate phrase and lasso that lummox into their discourse is labelled 'unreal'. An 'unreal' character! Can you imagine!" I said this.

"Nice, nice. We'll work at thon. You mind if Melanie Offal peeps this MS-in-progress? Melanie Offal is my squeeze, she likes to read. Next time, she can come along to the meet and slap some verbal meat on this oak table."

"Fine." I sounded surly.

"Speaking of slapping things on this oak table . . . £200?"

"Yes. Here." I produced four £50 notes from the wallet in my right pocket. (I was wearing a coat. And other clothes).

"Gnarly, friend. See you next week."

"Is that . . ."

"Aye, laters."

3

I arrived the following week, a flummox of nervous arms and legs, and rapped the shutters. I had been scanning the reviews of Sam Ruple on ratemytrader.com. Among these: "This beelzebubble needs bursting. His hellacious advice had vice. Nine months hence, the savings account was a sinkhole into Hell." And: "Oblivious to the Oblomovian oblivion into which his victims obliviate, Sam Ruple has no scruples and will eat your rubles." And: "I hate this balding fat assclown and his repulsive wife." Melanie Offal was the "squeeze", and was present when I was present at that present present (whenever that was). She had the same expression as Sam—on constant lookout for the nearest taxi to a safehouse—and stared at my shirt as I rearversed myself into the chair before Sam's Dell PC.

"A Samless session?" I asked. Melanie Offal opened a drawer and stared into the drawer for a length of time that made me wonder what was in the drawer that required that particular length of time to look at what was in the drawer.

"Hmm?" she hmmed. "Nosir, no sir. Sam Ruple is in Forfar with his midden. This week I will wax up and wax down. Let's light this candle." She retrieved from the drawer a large eucalyptus-scented candle and struck a match. She had the face of Welsh actress Catrin-Mai Huw and the figure of a female woman.

"You read my novel so far?"

"Comments-ça-va? I have. You start with this weasel who loves frotting a washboard and not frothing his missus. This is weirdlike. You establish this twerp as 'likeable' then spend the next fourteen pages showing him spinnakering into such unlikeability, the label becomes so moot as to make me moo."

"Yep. The point is to attach labels to these characters to show that such labels attached to characters is a thankless hecksercise. The novel is a savage critique on the sort of committee-written fiction that makes a mediocrity of the modern novel."

"Hmm. But, Client Number Three, therein lies our therein. You want us to bag a market-huggin' label for yo'self. You want to take that market and hug that market so hard the market makes the sound 'Ooweeluvooo'."

"Yes. But there has to be a shock to the systemic. A zap to the zipper. If I break through with this I can blow the market asunderland. In other words, I can break into the market with an anti-market axehead."

"Mmhh. As your consultancy, let us consultantly consult you. Bin this Vince. Our focus groupers have expressed exasperation at your undermining their efforts at reading. 'It's like this chump, so sickened at the business of basic world-building, stands on the sidelines of his own fiction, heckling himself as he hacks it out,' Emily Pinediddle remarked."

"Exactly, Emily, exactemily! I want to undermine the ethos of big-sellin' fiction with a continual tone of carping self-mockin'."

"But. No do. Gotta shoot straight, Hector. People want Victor, the man. Not Victor, the manmade construct through whom the author is unloading the fuming frustration that he cannot sit and pen a pedestrian prizewinner. Give them Victor without the snarkhate. Victor sans the moanbile. Victor nix the whinevom."

"Must I?"

"Must you. £200?" She extended her palm on which was tattooed a small chinchilla weeping into a satchel.

"If I must."

4

Putting trust in the powertwosome, I rewrote the character of Victor, removing the man from a selfconscious fictional terrain into an unselfconscious urban topoi. I made Victor a humble man with an estranged son who learns that that son has a heroin habit and that that that son has an estranged son himself. I cranked up the hurt. I opened with the elder Victor bungling a call to the son following a late-night pub session at the pub with alcoholic liquids consumed at the pub. I refrained from the using sentences like that one, where I repeated "at the pub" to make a mockery of my own attempts to render reality real, and my own mockery of the real-time buildings that actually exist outside my own doorstep, in that laughable "real" world. Sam had returned from his business trip (ferrying upcoming authoress Belinda Blueghel around Stuttgart), and read the latest sample.

"Wowish! This has 'kiss me, I'm an author!' written all o'er. A first chapter hasn't unchapped mine lips since the Clement Ordore's 1998 one *Impaled at the Disco*. That astounding opossum trickled me plink. Pologies, I am semi-half-cut. Richt. I think we should proceed at pumping this premier chapter at the periodicals, whet their knickers for the upcoming main attack, son. The bidding wars will erupt like—" A loud burp left the concluding part of that sentence to hover in the air like a wingtorn bluebottle.

"You sure I'm not backsliding into branded bumble?"

"You wannabe a bumblebee. You wanna buzz readers, not fuzz readers. You wanthat renumeration? Here tiscomin'."

An excerpt appeared in the *Chester Conch*. As the readership of this periodical is limited to the other contributors, who re-read their own pieces for proofing errors and to see their words take on the hallowed sheen of the typeset page, I had not expected a single ripple of a thing to occur. I retreated to my room to complete a heartwarming character-driven plot-driven populistically popularist love-me-please novel that a critic might brand "a sensational new voice", and pictured my lifeless moribund body clutching that award-winning novel to my ailing heart on my deathbed. I imagined myself thinking something like "it was all worth it" before I croaked. Something like solace, I suppose.

After four months spent blowing chunks of prose chunder onto the page, I placed the novel into Ruple's palms. "Plam plam!" he said and sat to read the écriven pages, nibbling the corner of a pomegranate. Melanie Offal kneaded his shoulders and read over the kneaden shoulders the novel I had écriven. To pass the hours, I read *Our Hearts Will Burn Us Down* by Anne Valente. I emitted a steady stream of vomit after the first two chapters, filling Ruple's drawers with Valentean sick, and once purged, continued into the third chapter, at which point a furious flotilla of turds entered my underwears.

"Hang on. I have an incall comingin," Sam said, snatching the unringing phone. "Pulitzer committee? You want him to receive the prize every single year until the heat death of the universe? No? I see. You want to have the prize squirted into his veins every afternoon. Pump him up to the eyeballs with Pulitzer, make him the walking embodiment of Pulitzeriness? We can arrange that. Thanks, cats."

"You hear that?" Melanie asked.

"What?"

"That sound?"

"No."

"It's the sound of an approaching bus that will take you towards the train that will take you towards the airplane that will fly us to the moon."

"Aaaaahhhh," I aaaaahhhhed.

5

And so, having sweated several shedsworth of underarm ooze, having lubed the lexicon and varnished the vernacular to a presentable prose supersheen, I posted the final-final-final novel to Ruple Limited for their "astroeconomic" (Sam's word) appraisal and publishing "semiprecious stratagem" (Sam's two words). I heard nothing cept the plopping of pizza menus and overdue demands for weeks. I tried texting Melaine reminders, like 'Read the MS yet? ;)', and 'Hate to push . . . peeped the MS?', and 'I would appreciate a response, I have texted and emailed like a stalker on speedballs'. This yielded no yackback. I frothskipped in a fume to Northgate Street and rattled the shutters, shouting "What is happening with the novel? DO YOU HAVE MORE NOTES?" No noise was heard. In two weeks' time, I spotted my manuscript, retitled *Ordinary Vic*, published under the name Sam Ruple, sitting at a 58° in a prominent bookstore. I noted that a "launch" was taking place that nicht, and concentrated the continent of chunder I had into making a painful entrée that eve. I turned up at the bookstore with a ringbinderful of legal Anthrax. Melaine was stood foldedshouldered at the door, next to a beef-bodiced male asshat-protector, and blew me a kiss from across the street. In a moment of uncommon rage, I located a nearby boulder (my fate was sealed by the unfortunate proximity of one an inch from my toe—pre-placed by Offal), and lobbed this rock through the window, making the noise "MIIIIINNNNEEEE!" and charged towards the shop seeking to noisily sever Sam's sesamoid bone. Sadly, I was felled by Offal's meaty honcho, and as I was being led away by the police, I spotted through the windowframe Ruple shaking hands with Martin Amis and airkissing Donna Tartt. One day, one fine and pleasant day, I will eat nachos from their uncapped crania.

[From *My Agents*, Chap. 3 'The Consultation Room', Hector Lettsin, p.38-42, Teetertotter Books, Chester.]

[DERBYSHIRE]

NAME: SAMMY ONION
AGE: 34
SENTENCE: 12 YEARS
CRIME: LETTERBOXD FILM RATINGS

Battleship Potemkin (1925) — ★
The 39 Steps (1935) — ★
Citizen Kane (1941) — ★
Some Like it Hot (1959) — ★
La Dolce Vita (1960) — ★
The Birds (1963) — ★
Five Easy Pieces (1970) — ★
Jaws (1975) — ★
Stalker (1979) — ★
Raging Bull (1980) — ★
Blue Velvet (1986) — ★
Raise the Red Lantern (1991) — ★
Highlander III: The Sorcerer (1994) — ★★★★★
American Beauty (1999) — ★
Lost in Translation (2003) — ★★
Pan's Labyrinth (2006) — ★
We Need to Talk About Kevin (2011) — ★

[DEVON]

NAME: JIM ABADDON
AGE: 34
SENTENCE: 20 YEARS
CRIME: FRAUDULENT CLAIM FOR DISABILITY LIVING
ALLOWANCE

JIM COMMITTED SUICIDE by taking forty aspirin. His body was buried and his soul arrived in Hell. It assumed the shape of a methanous octagon spitting poisonous ash. When he got to the entrance at Hell HQ he was told to take a number and wait until he was called. Five months later he was summoned to a desk where a stocky bald man with a retroussé nose pointed to a chair. Due to the overcrowding problem and trivial nature of your sins, you are to be returned to your body immediately. There is a penalty for any additional suicides after you have returned to your body. Thank you. Jim returned to Earth.

He was fully reinstated. All memory of his death and burial among his family and friends had been erased. He was back in the miserable life where nobody loved him and he lived in a shoebox beneath the railway and no one would employ him and so on. It occurred to him he'd need to expand his portfolio as a sinner if he wanted to get into Hell, so he went into Dixons and tried to walk out with a DVD player. An assistant blocked his path. What are you doing there, sir? Jim blinked. Walking out with this DVD player. Do you think that is a good idea, sir? No. Would you like to put it back, sir? All right then. Jim thought the attempted theft was good enough and went back home and took forty aspirin.

Back in Hell he was a methanous octagon spitting poisonous ash again and was kept waiting for a year before being seen. Stocky bald man with the retroussé nose again. Sorry, but due to the trivial nature of your offence you are to be sent back to your body with the penalty

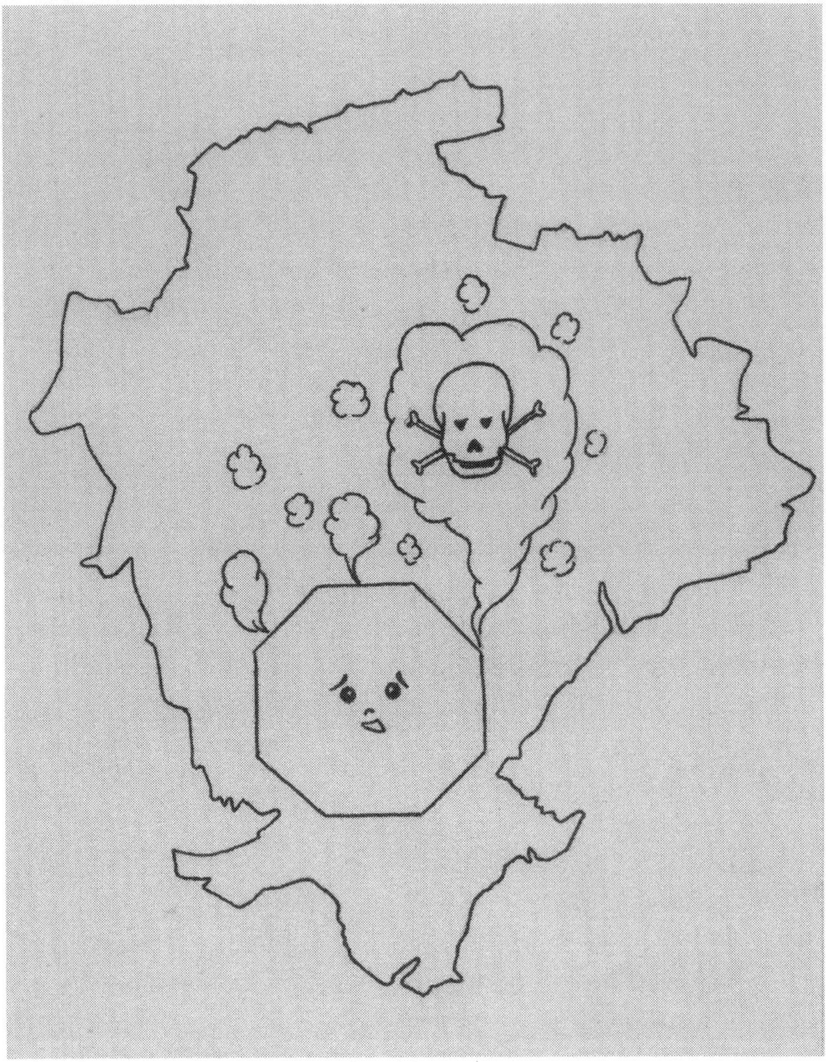

of permanent blindness for wasting our time. Thank you. He was re-turned to his body, bat-blind as stated. It wasn't fair. How could he find the aspirin to top himself if he couldn't see anything? He'd need to get someone to help him and there was no one in his life who cared about him enough to help him commit suicide.

After a few weeks adjusting to his blindness, he decided to smash the window of a large department store by throwing bricks at that window. This would get him into Hell. He chose eleven o'clock at night to source a large brick from a nearby building site and hurl it at the window, where it bounced off making no impact on the pane. He had several tries, but his arm soon hurt. Eventually, hoping he'd made enough of an impact on the pane, he found his way to the train station and leapt under the 1.12 to Whimple.

Back in Hell (a napthous solid this time, a two-year wait) he was returned to his body with another penalty, no arms. He finally cottoned on to their plan. It was a ruse by the devilish administrators to make it physically impossible for suicides to even gain access to Hell's reception area. At his wits' end, he pinned his guide dog to the ground and, knife in mouth, gouged out its entrails. Then he leapt under a train. He was put on the waiting list for a place on the first floor. In the meantime he would have to wait on Earth until he was called, with the additional penalty of no working legs.

He sat, a blind, limbless torso, on his bed, waiting for the call-up to Hell.

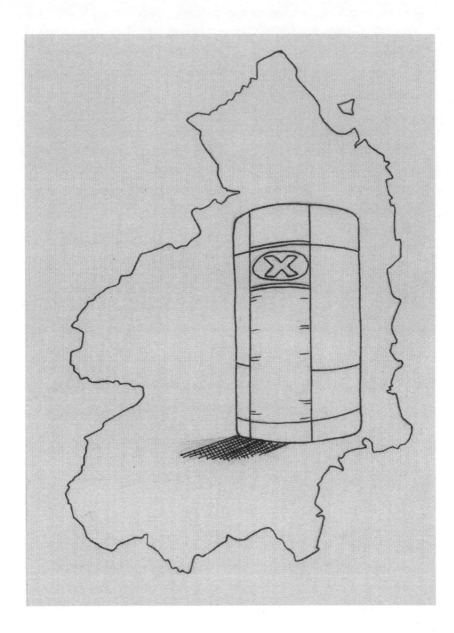

[NORTHUMBERLAND]

NAME: CRAIG SCOWLY

AGE: 39

SENTENCE: 19 YEARS

CRIME: VERBAL UXORICIDE

As written by the former wife of Mr. Scowly. —Ed.

Q: We asked one hundred people to name a European country that ends with a consonant.
A: Paris.

IT IS MONDAY, I AM SITTING IN MY ROOM, it is Monday, I am un-washed and unfed. I am staring at a redwood from my window. It is Monday. I smell like a cracked vial of cadaverine. I am sitting here writing this on a Monday, I am hungry, I am staring at a redwood, I stink like that particular compound, I am repeating myself. It is that time between seven and twelve o'clock I call The Decomposition Zone, when I am paralysed with indecision and apathy and I sink back into bed and listen to slowcore on my earphones. I haven't eaten since lunchtime yesterday. My mother says I am wasting away. I am thirty-two. I am a woman. I am a thirty-two-year-old (is that all hyphenated?) and I am rotting away in my old bedroom in my mother's house, the room that looks onto a redwood, a tree that blocks the view of the world outside. The tree has fattened its trunks since I was a kid. I have become thinner, because I skip up to five meals a week, sometimes more. I like to write, I like to sit in my room in the mornings and write. I keep on writing. I tend not to stop to correct myself. If I can't think of anything new to say, I simply repeat myself until a new thought comes to mind. It's Monday, the tree is obese, I am skinny, I am weak. I am living in my mother's house. My daughter is waking up somewhere I am not. I am not going towrite about her. I am going to write about when I played in the redwood. I built a series of wooden steps to climb the redwood, and tied two pillows around a branch for me and my friend Holly to sit on. We would sit up there, our legs dangling over the edge, and suck strawberry milkshakes from a straw. We were seven or eight. I can't say, really, whether I was particularly happy then. I liked strawberry milkshakes. Nowadays I drink water in my room. I no longer sit up on trees swinging my legs over the edge drinking strawberry milkshakes. Holly is married to a rich man and lives in Luxembourg. I am no longer married.

There. I like to take breaks in my writing. A paragraph break is like a breath. A page of words and words and words is suffocating and suffocating and suffocating. It makes me choke. I used to stuff the pages with words and leave no spaces between them. It made me choke. Here, I can breathe. It is Sunday, March 23rd once more. I am in the car with my daughter (I can't say her name) and him (I won't say his). I am zooming along the M6 towards Bristol from Harbottle. I am in a cheerful mood. I am looking forward to the holiday, to the sunshine, to appearing on the show. My daughter is singing in the back to the Ramones song that goes 'hey ho, let's go', which I put on whenever we set off for a long trip. He is talking about what categories might come up and we rehearse some of our answers. Questions on capital cities, African countries, football managers, or chemical elements. We revise these questions as we zoom. I am writing this on a Monday, in my room. I am hungry, but I will keep writing. I am inside The Decomposition Zone. My daughter is sleeping as we pull into the services outside Manchester. He says that he will not pay £5.95 for two measly sandwiches and I say that we should have stocked up on supplies from the supermarket beforehand but you were too eager to set off. I buy my daughter whatever she wants while he takes a piss. My mother is shouting something from downstairs, shouting if I want breakfast. Sometimes I respond. Othertimes, I am too busy writing this. I don't want to hear my own voice echo in the room.

We arrive at our hotel in Bristol and head straight to bed after the long drive. I am starting to experience pre-show nerves. I take a sleeping pill and practice shallow breathing. The next morning, I put on the smart blue taffeta top with the elegant white neckline, he puts on a smart blue shirt. We colour-coordinate. I drive my daughter to the childminder we hired for the day, kiss her on the forehead with a vigorous lipsmack (my daughter), and head for the studio. He mentions for the fourth time that the cost to take this trip will outstrip the prize money, if the jackpot is back to £1000, and I ignore this remark for the sixth time. When I arrive at the BBC, in the Green Room waiting to enter the studio, I have raging butterflies. I concentrate on breathing. I meet the other contestants. A stringy blonde and beefy bloke from Newcastle. Retirees from Poole. Two loud and obnoxious brothers from Castleton. One of them turns to me and asks: "Nervous?" Before I can catch a breath I am stood on a plinth behind the scoreboard, staring at the audience and the cameras and Richard Osman's receding hairline. I fight to keep a neutral expression. I feel like a politician fixing a rictus when the appalling byelection results are announced. I blink, I blink, I blink. I attempt a smirk when Richard makes an amusing remark. Xander is talking to him. He explains I am his wife, that we are from Northumberland. The strings of purple tubing shooting up from the kaleidoscopic floor are taking me into a psychedelic reverie. The colours swirl from purple to blue to red. I am dreaming. I laugh when the audience laugh. I am trying with every inch of self-control I can muster not to collapse on the shiny floor and crack open my skull. In ten minutes, Xander is saying words at me. I manage to stammer out that I am a teacher and that I like teaching and that I teach children with special needs and I find the work rewarding then I have to answer the question. I snap into complete awareness. I pause for a long time. The length of pause is noted with the hesitant look on Xander's kindly face. I read the text on the screen in front of me. There is no time for a second pause. I stammer out an answer, in haste. There is an intake of breath from the audience. Xan-

der looks askance. I know, I know, I know, I have said something wrong
and wrong and wrong. I clench every organ in my body, and forget to
close my mouth. Xander repeats what I have said. I can see the horrified
expression on his face, from the teensiest corner of my eye. The screen
stabs me with a sharp red 'X', indicating that I have fucked up. It is some
minutes before I realise what it is I have said, out loud, in this room, on
national TV. As I am leaving the stage, I am consumed with such shame
and embarrassment I need his help to walk. I see what I have done. I
said a word at that moment in time, when Xander, with his parting tide
of hair, his penetrating smirk, turned to me and asked me for an answer,
and that word was a fucking embarrassment. I see what I have done.

I have written this before, I have written this over a hundred times.
I have sat on this wicker chair staring at the redwood, pausing for a
moment before cramming the page with more words. It is eight o'clock,
I am hungry, I am cold, I am weak, I am thirty-two, I said the wrong
word at the wrong time on TV. I must continue writing to ward off the
pointless rot of the morning. I am a thirty-two-year-old woman. I used
to teach children with special needs in the Harbottle area. I am sitting
here in my knickers writing this. If I write this enough times, changing
little details in each page, the facts might become so entwined with invention as to erase the memory from my mind. Nice idea. The more
I write, the more clarity I bring to the memory, the more I remember
the agonising minutiae. Why sit here, why torment yourself, why write
starving in your knickers? Because I lost you, and I want to remember
you, that last day, when we were all truly happy, and unblighted by this
horror. So for now, I leave the studio. I am shaking and sobbing in the
car. I smother my face in my arms, I make unflattering mewling noises.
I am in more pain than I have ever experienced. And he is silent, un-
consoling. Have you finished wailing. Have you finished howling. How
could you say something so stupid. I have humiliated him on national
television. I have made an unbelievable idiot of myself, and hisself, and
myself. I have condemned myself to be viewed on YouTube for eternity,

to appear in 100 Worst Quiz Show Answers features or videos, to have my moment of panic broadcast forever and ever as an example of how stupid people are, and me in particular, and that he looked like a moron for being married to someone who could come out with something that monumentally brainless. He pulls away from the studio as I continue to shake, sod, and mewl. He looks at me with outright contempt. I see his hatred, his heartfelt hatred, and I stop loving him instantly. In the car, I sit sullen. My daughter is silent and sad on the trip home. We skip the second show appearance we are contractually bound to attend. She asks me why mummy and daddy are not speaking. Mummy answered a question incorrectly, he tells her, might as well have said Mummy has stabbed a kitten in the face seventy-nine times. Mummy answered a question so idiotically, so monumentally stupidly, and caused an unbelievable amount of damage to herself and myself, he adds. I cry in the front seat more or less continuously back to Harbottle. I muffle my sobs so my daughter cannot hear. He looks over at me with nothing except contempt. He loathes me, hates me, looks at me like I have pulled his strangled mother from a bog and proceeded to suck her blood. Fuck him.

At twelve o'clock, I will eat some toast. I will dress. I will walk around the garden. I will watch television. (Not that programme, never again). I will have exhausted this morning's replay. For now, here I still sit, here I must resume the litany. I return home and ride the roundabout of repetitive ritual abuse. He asks me how I—a supposedly intelligent teacher of children with special needs—could ponder on the whole fifty-one European countries, twenty-six of which have consonants at the end of their names, and choose a capital city, a world-famous capital city, that everyone in the universe knows is a capital city, and furthermore, say that idiotic thing out loud, in front of millions of viewers, on national television. I respond hopelessly, for the nth time, that I was overcome with pressure, that I was sitting in The Green Room with two extrovert twats from Castleton, that Xander had walked past the room and blanked us, that the lights from the studio were hot and bright, that I was stunned by the cameras, that the violence of the audience's applause and Xander's charm was overwhelming, that I was trying not to faint under the pressure, that it was a miracle I managed to stammer out any word whatsoever. He says I should have warned him that I would be such a fruitcake ahead of time, that he wouldn't have booked us on the show. And on like this we continue, rehashing the events of that afternoon until his screaming and my crying and my screaming and my daughter's crying brings our days to a miserable, wretched end. My stupidity, my temporary, panicked stupidity, my fear and apprehension, my sudden failure to tell the capital city of France from a European country ending in a consonant, has poisoned my family against me, has turned our loving nest into a hissing snakepit, in which we writhe and scream, hourly, in agony, in hatred, and in shame.

Because of the shame, I cannot leave the house. I let him take my daughter to school. I sign off work. He returns home in a foul mood. He is sitting around waiting for the air date. He makes me watch the episode. He reminds me that I confused a capital city with a country as I am confusing a capital city with a country on a television programme that is being aired across the country, at that very moment, and once the programme is complete, he replays the programme and reminds me that I confused a capital city with a country, as I am confusing a capital city again and again until I feel my mind crack, and my daughter's beautiful face shard into a dozen pieces. Over the course of two weeks, he replays the episode, archived on the stupid internet, where my moment of shame is easily replayable, and reminds me of my stupidity, as my daughter cries, as I stare vacantly at a self, myself, who I no longer recognise, until the nervous words that are spilling from my mouth are no longer my own, and I view a strange pixelated approximation of a person that I used to be, a person who said that a famous capital city was in fact a country on television, and I start to deny that I am that person, that I never said that thing on that television, and I scream at my husband that he is a liar, that he is a liar, that he is a liar, and that he is trying to poison me against my daughter, and then I start to question whether I have a husband or a daughter, since I am no longer myself, I am no longer the self I had been told I was, and I run from the house, I run from the house, and I leap in the car.

As five o'clock nears, I sit calmly in a meadow, humming to myself, listening to the birds. I know that on televisions, a certain programme is soon to air, and I must lose myself in the sounds of nature, or I will scream. Once the hour has passed, and six o'clock beckons, I can sleep soundly, and calmly, and I experience something like respite. Then I am back in the car, I am in the Vauxhall Astra, and I am powering along roads, I am a cracked and broken self, I am in a million pieces, a speeding non-self, powering to nowhere. I am up a road in the night, I am up a road in the twinkling black of the night, and I am splintering. I wake up in a field. I have no idea who I am. I stumble across the field to a farmhouse, I make no sounds with my mouth, and I crumble into a field of wheat. Then a short period of time later, it is Monday, I am at my mother's house, I am wasting away, I am thirty-two. I used to teach children. I used to have a daughter, and I cannot write about her. I'm not sure I can even remember what she looks like. My daughter is waking up somewhere I am not.

[From ten pages of notepaper mailed to the editor by Mrs. Scowly's mother].

[HEREFORDSHIRE]

NAME: THE WRITER'S WRITER
AGE: 42
SENTENCE: 2 YEARS
CRIME: A FLOCCULENT FOUL

I AM THE WRITER'S WRITER. The Writer's Writer is not be to confused with The Writers' Writer. The Writer's Writer is a writer read only by other writers, whereas The Writers' Writer is a writer who writes on behalf of other writers. These are not to be confused with The Writers Writer, who writes only about writers, or The Writer Writer, who writes about only one writer, known as A. Writer. One time, the four writers met up to discuss being writers, their writing, and other writers. The Writer's Writer (me) complained his writing was read only by other writers, and The Writers' Writer complained his work was written for other writers and no one credited him as a writer. The Writers Writer said that those qualities are what made them respectively The Writer's Writer and The Writers' Writer, and if they were any different they would simply be known as The Writer and The Writer, like the other writers. The Writers Writer complained that too many people were writers nowadays, and it was impossible to write about all The Writers out there, while The Writer Writer complained that A. Writer was hard to write as a writer, since he only ever wrote about the one topic: riders. The Writer's Writer (me) suggested The Writers Writer should write about writers who had written a richness of writings and not the writers who had written little, and that The Writer Writer should write a new character, I. Writer, who wrote about writers who only ever wrote about riders. At that point, The Written Writer entered the room along with The Writ Writer, who issued the writers with writs for plagiarising the writings of The Written Writer. The Writer's Writer burst out laughing and explained that The Written Writer was a fictional writer and a writer can't plagiarise writing from a fictional writer—whoever wrote The Written Writer was entitled to sue, but not The Written Writer itself, who was merely a written construct. The Written Writer and The Writ Writer were then written out by The Writer of These Writers, who wrote the other writers out too before they realised they were really The Written Writers themselves. I stabbed a sheep.

[ESSEX]

NAME: R. SWOMP
AGE: 22
SENTENCE: 3 MOMENTS
CRIME: DENTAL OOPS

Permanent Dentition

upper right – 1   upper left – 2

18 17.4 16 15 14 13 12 11 | 2 22 23 24 22 26 27 22

R --- L

44 44 44 45 44 44 44 44 | 31 32 33 She 35 36 37 38

lower right – 4.88   lower left – 3 (and)

Primary Dentition (ooh)

upper downer – 5   upper upper – 6

55.55 54 53 59 500 | 61 62 63 Mom 65.00

East ------------------------------------ West

85 84 83 Her 81.Sweat | 71 72 73 74 755.29

lower right – 8 (chop)   lower left – 7 (uh)

[From Mr. Swomp's dentist (unnamed)].

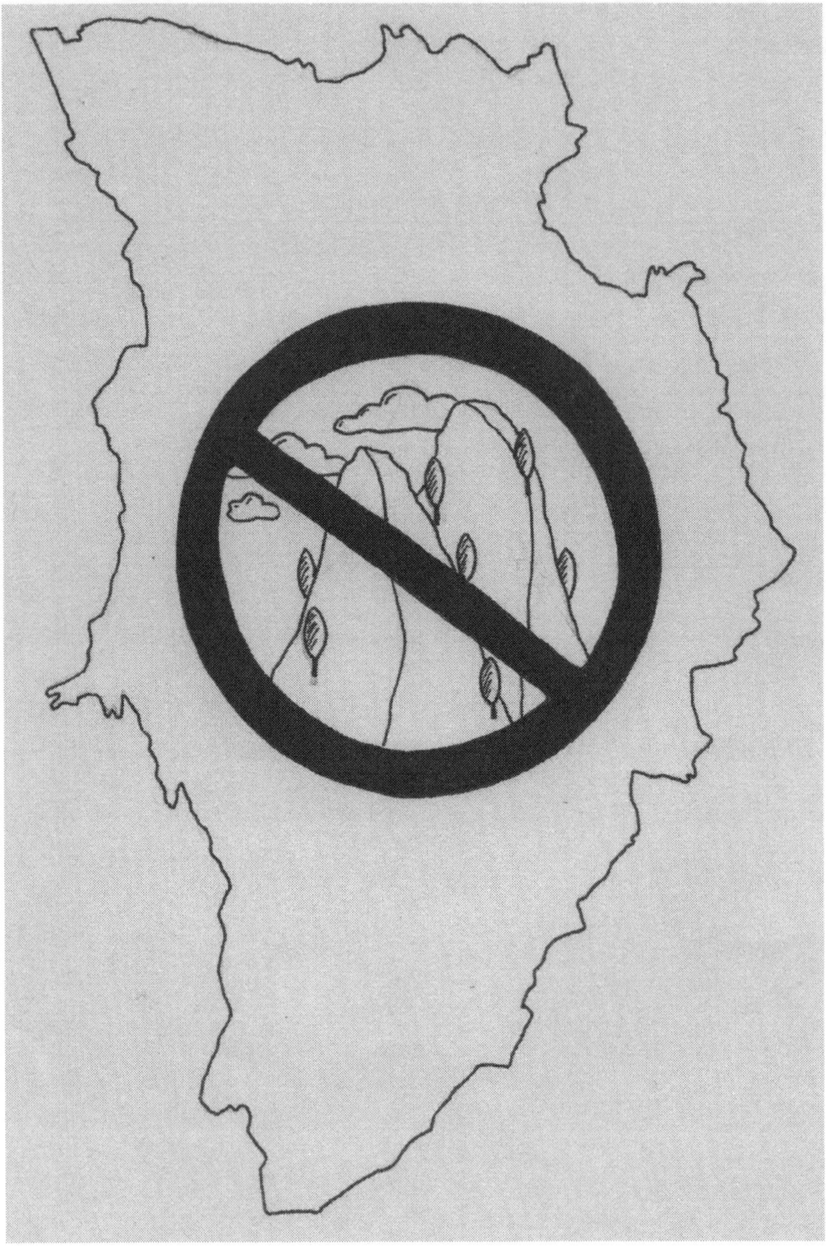

[SOMERSET]

NAME: WILBUR AUSTRYN
AGE: 63
SENTENCE: 10 YEARS
CRIME: OFFENSIVE INDEX IN 4th ED. OF SOMERSET HILL
GUIDE

Beacon Batch
Marilyn *Fun*roe? Nope!

Black Hill
Queen Mary of the Quantocks.

Black Mires
A featureless fuck hepped up like a whore in heather.

Blagdon Hill
Nothing but a jumped-up kopje.

Brent Knoll
If hills had eyes, they would blind themselves immediately so they didn't have to look at this really rather revolting grassy incline known as a hill.

Brean Down
Sagging sub-HuMP backing onto the blasted blaze of the Bristol Channel.

Burrow Mump
Even the crumbling church, the panoramic peep at Southlake Moor, the asskissing nod to Alfred the Great, cannot save this miserable mump from mediocrity.

Chains Barrow
Thump this TuMP, this third tallest trek along a tedious trig-scrag.

Cothelstone Hill
Mimsiness in hill form.

Couple Cross Hill
Not suitable for angry sex.

Cow Castle
Grassed to the nines at the summit. No perceivable bovines, like, any-where.

Dowsborough
A site of Saxon lookout that sucks balls, sucks balls, sucks balls, and your mum too.

Dunkery Beacon
A puffed-up sandstone ponce, a Bronze Age braggart with banal bowl barrows and crudtastic crapstone cairns.

Elworthy Barrows
Even the pristine polished stone axe cannot rescue this ferric fart from failure.

Glastonbury Tor
I really dislike this hill.

Great Rowbarrow
Exmooronic tumour with a twattish tumulus.

Hadborough
A sadsack stonepile with pusillanimous pebbles, repugnant rocks, and stupid-faced stones.

Heydon Hill
Shonen Knife would never walk here, ever.

Horsen Hill
This bog-sodden blandland, replete with rambler-packed rimmed sum-mit, is 443m of suckivarious asswank.

Ley Hill
"I have heather," it says. "I have gorse," it also says. "I have 318m of hilliness," it also also says. "You are impressing no one. *No one*," we all say, in bitter concord.

Lydeard Hill
A partially decomposed shrew, fourteen beer cans, and a hiker's nipple pepper this path to perdition.

Lype Hill
This so-called Brendon Bruiser, this poor man's plateau, resembles the walloped mug of a Taunton pensioner.

Maundown Hill
"Love me!" this hill begs. "Never. We will never take you to our hearts, you lumpy sump of sod and twigs and earwigs," we respond, our hearts ice-cold forever towards this hill.

Monkham Hill
Monkham Hill, I will hatefist you.

Niver Hill
Kill me now. (Actually, kill this hill first).

North Hill
What?

Oldrey Hill
A hill so fascinating that scientists have come from Panama, Argentina, South Africa, and Wales to study the geodesic functions of its very interesting rockface, and explore the history hewn in every striation of stone. Not.

Pen Hill
Despair. Eternal void. Screaming hellfire. Hill.

Road Hill
Oxymoronic schlep that sucks the oxygen from morons.

Selworthy Beacon
Listed on ebay for £0.01. No bids.

Staddon Hill
The cairn isn't very nice.

Staple Hill
As Fats Domino sang: "I found my thrill, nowhere near this smelly scrofulous chit of a hillock."

Storridge Hill
Storridge? More like lukewarm porridge!

Thornemead Hill
Horsepappers' paradise, how sad.

Treborough Common
Cormac McCarthy meets E.M. Cioran.

Upton Hill
Where even *is* this?

Whitefield Hill
Even your fat-ass momma wouldn't trek up this dismal bump in her thong to tout for trade.

Wills Neck
. . . is perfect to throttle, hard, until it oozes the gore of death.

Winsford Hill
Bursting with B-roading buffoons, taking their pathetic picnics toward micropeeps of pissing ponies.

Withypool Common
As common as a Yeovil slapper on speedballs.

Withypool Hill
There is nothing to see. NOTHING.

[From *The Rambler's Guide to Somerset*, Wilbur Austryn, 4th Ed., Halsgrove Publishing, p.245-248].

[STAFFORDSHIRE]

NAME: SIM TRIPLE
AGE: 36
SENTENCE: LIFE
CRIME: ZYDECO AWAKENING

1

OUTSIDE THE TRAIN, A BLUE-BLOTTED SHEEP had mishooved herself into a bog. Inside the train, a rubicund man in a beige overcoat, skimreading *From the Velvets to the Voidoids: A Pre-Punk History for a Post-Punk World* by Clinton Heylin, observed the ticket collector step into the car. Sim Triple, a veteran in the ticket-collecting racket for some nine annums and two months, picked up the malefic stink of faredodging on the wind, catching sight of the artful evader, known to rail staff as Hepatitis, at the farthest end of the car. The train inched along the rural line towards the stuporous terminus of Rugeley Town. Sim had spotted him several times in the past, never risking a confrontation. He had heard tales of Hepatitis pretending to choke to the point his forehead turned aquamarine; painting a scene of his polio-stricken mother shuffling alone in a nursing home, trailing tens of tubes; and working himself into such whirlpools of eloquence as to leave the conductors speechless.

The previous evening Sim had sat in the livingroom—corner lamp tilted towards the bookcase, left-side curtain parted to permit the moonlight a peep—in a shadow of contemplation. His wife, Claire Triple, had not been kidding when she said that he could make his own lasagne, and that she wasn't starting a second pasta-based evening meal at that particular time (nearing 8 in the PM) when she had more pressing things with which to press on (pressing flowers and tippling pressé). He had slumped into an unpleasant sump of self-reflection—when the banter-

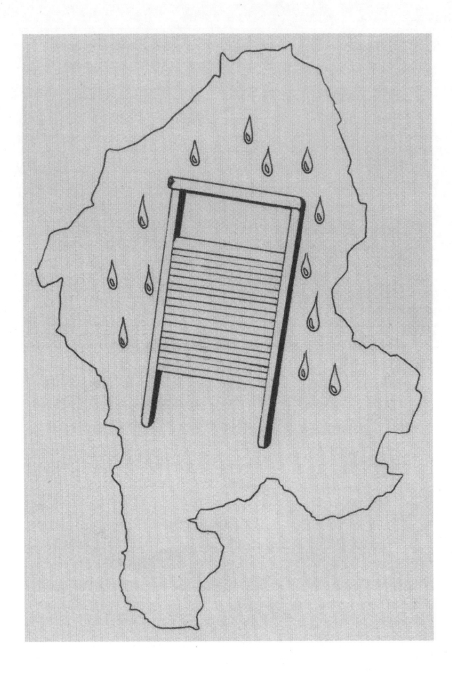

-ous cut and thrust of married life is muted and one must untangle the adult thoughts lurking inside the snug mesh of one's defences, and make logical choices and sensible conclusions and real decisions. This caused him extreme displeasure, and that afternoon, to vent his peeve, he chose to poke Hepatitis in the wallet.

Hepatitis, hip to the hostile vibe, picked up a pretend call. "Hi Zandra," he said. "I'm on the locomo." Shielding two travellers from these ho-hum home morsels, he rode the rubber accordion between cars, mumbled another sentence, then entered the next car, heading once more for the farthest seat. Sim was well-versed in the pretend call. The raised index finger, indicating that Zandra or Charlie or Naomi were more important than keeping the rail network an efficient and punctual operator; the mock-jocularity, indicating that their phone merriment was too fierce to permit the inbutting of mere transactional blahs; the intense concentration, indicating that a ticket check was a sick imposition when matters of huge import hung in aural space; the vexed frown of poor reception, indicating that the comprehension of one's interlocutor was a struggle that could not permit a sudden demand for funds. And on one occasion, the hurling of a phone towards the train door, orchestrated so that the passenger had time to reinsert their sims and batteries before hopping off.

Zandra zipped her non-lips as Sim approached a cool Hepatitis. Expecting the rugged chancer to create a scene, instead the post-punk book was raised, and extreme interest in a sentence was feigned. The town of Hednesford, the penultimate station, hoved into view. "Ticket please," Sim said. A pause followed as Hepatitis completed the interesting sentence with a wide satisfied smile. "What?" he asked. The sentence had been so amusing as to halt his understanding at the obviousness of the request. His face showed that his thoughts were still swimming in the profound pool of Clinton's prose, and that extraction from that pool would require a persistent and humourless officiousness, the providence of the most vengeful ticket collectors. "Ticket please," Sim said. There was enough time, as the train chuntered past a short confederation of Dutch elms, for a ticket to be issued. "Return from—" A convenient lapse in memory, a ten-second scan of the station names. "Bloxwich." Not stating where to. "Where to?" Another pause while a narrow tributary, flowing from the invigorating non-fiction account of Richard Hell & the Voidoids into the footling requirements of the present in the form of this insistent man, opened up. "Hednesford!" he said in a tone inviting Sim's participation in this minor triumph of memory, a triumph commemorable with the waiving of a train fare. "I'm sorry, I always forget the names of the stations!" The train was slowing. Sim knew that a brief hesitation over the method of payment would prevent Hepatitis from alighting at his stop. The rules were clear: no conductor was permitted to hold a passenger on past their stop unless the passenger had caused violence to the conductor or another traveller.

"£15.50, please," Sim said. There was enough time to retrieve two or three coins from a pocketed wallet. Hepatitis patted one pocket. No wallet. He patted the second pocket. No wallet. He patted his left trouser pocket. No wallet. The stonechip strip bordering the platform was within spitting distance. He patted his right trouser pocket. "Ah!" He opened the wallet to the note-storing compartment. No notes. He unzipped the coin-storing compartment. No coins. "Can I pay with my card?" he asked. Sim had the card machine prepped in his right hand. The train was near done licking the rails. In less than twenty seconds, the doors would open. Hepatitis tried to locate an appropriate card for the transaction. He observed their whereabouts and closed the wallet. "This is my stop. I'll pick up a ticket at the station," he said. "There's time," Sim said. "You can tap your contactless card on this machine in under two seconds." There was no time for the printing of the ticket. This fact was written on Hepatitis's "I must rush" face, now level with Sim's "You must not win this pathetic battle" face, as the ticketless man moved towards the exit that thrice blipped: "Open me!"

Rather than shaking a fist from the train's edge, rather than logging the incident in his rolodex of revenge, rather than allowing the veteran fareshirker kudos for a snatched victory, Sim planted two brogued feet on concrete, and walked. Before his inner monologue had time to make baffled interrogative remarks, Sim was walking at a measured pace some ten metres behind Hepatitis who, strolling past the ticket office towards the barrierless exit stairs, noticed this strange aberration while tilting his head to unload pocket trash (among the items, a train ticket—had Hepatitis paid the fare all along?), and continued onward into the vague whiff of violence that was now a present scent. "Sir! Sir!" Sim called, confirming to Hepatitis that the ticket collector was soon to snap the tether of mild-mannered rural respectability and charge into an unknown and potentially lethal realm.

"Sir, I need to see your ticket," Sim said.

Hepatitis sped to the steps, veered right to the scenic road. Sim twostepped down and closed the gap to five metres.

"Sir! You have not paid for your ticket. I know, like me, you are concerned that in 2010, four hundred thousand pounds was lost to missed fares and faredodging. This impacts on the wages of rail workers."

Hepatitis kept calm along the long flat pavement, the waft of verdance from opposite fields lending a "relax! here's some trees!" vibe to the mo. The town of Hednesford, a poikilothermal haven for sour-faced rentiers, was not too far to flee to in fear. Sim had managed to prevent the corrective voice—the voice that screams and howls at social transgressions, the voice that reprimands misplaced words in sentences uttered in certain company, the voice that works to keep each human being in the mode of self-styled denial to which they are accustomed—from intruding. The inside of Sim's head sounded like 'Swampland' by The Birthday Party, and no mellow elms or louche conifers or chillaxed brambles could temper that mental cacophony. "I need to check your ticket," he shouted.

"Eat my meat, old man," Hepatitis said. Sim was thirty-six. Regardless, whatever sound Hepatitis had made, whether long snake moan, whispered recitation of the Book of Luke, or seductive ululation, would have prompted Sim to snap, as happened, launching as on springed sneakers to the shoulders of the villain, toppling them two to the pavement where an unpleasant shape, like a man's mutation attempting to escape the man, formed, rolling on to a damp lawn with sounds like "aarrtt!" and "ffaannoo!" and other incredulous yips of primitive rage expressed at 3.46 on a Tuesday, outside a town that had never seen an assault since the days of leather-gloved thwacks on insolent cheeks.

At some point, an elbow, Hepatitis's, connected with high hurt to a nose, Sim's, forcing the latter, Sim, to roll right in maximum ouchiness, leaving room for the former, Hepatitis, to flee, feeding short messages of inexcusable vulgarity into Sim's aural postbox as he staggered to the Samson Blewitt to unload the above.

2

Outside the cottage, a calico fauxpawed into a plant pot. Inside the cottage, a tall woman with a black bobcut was ramming a vacuum cleaner into a crevice populated with paperclips, cracker crumbs, and family fluff. This was Claire Triple, brandishing the hoover like a medieval longsword and communicating to her couchbound ex-ticket-collecting husband subtle messages with each vigorous Electrolux ram. The first ram, in the back wall behind the television stand, communicated the message: "Your unprovoked assault on Hepatitis has created a temporary financial setback for us, a matter about which I am vexed." The second ram, in an unaccommodating slit below the bookcase, communicated the message: "In six annums of marriage, this incident is the one misstep in a series of behaviours that I have learned to predict and accept. This has alienated me from you." The third ram, under the couch beside Sim's Garfield socks, communicated the message: "This will prevent our proposed child from happening for another ten months, like the last convenient delay tactic."

Post-Hepatitic punch-up, Sim had lain on the lawn with a bashed nose in bliss. The clouds formed into vuvuzelas, streamers, and thumbs-ups, and the sunshine caressed his cheek like an heliacal ephebe. He had interpreted the attack as the passing into some brave new realm of Sim-hood. The attack had sparked a revival in the old frottoir narrative that once ran in his inactive brain. At the beginning of his time as a ticket collector on the sleepiest lines, a narrator known as Supersim told him a pleasing tale, spun from the moderate success he had had as a wash-board (or frottoir, as favoured) performer in short-lived zydeco band The Rootin' Tootin' Zydeco Mumblers. Supersim had narrated varia-tions on the success of this riotous extempore unit from their humble origins in the village of Landywood to the international superstage—the Hollywood Bowl or the Royal Albert Hall—and their rock star excesses, from supermodel lovers to untold riches blown on cocaine and cadillacs.

Each part was associated with a particular stop:

Rugeley Town—That first TRTZM concert in the Rococo Club, playing at the open mic night to an audience of silent drinkers (an actual event), and the reluctant frott-lovers who found their limbs abducted by the rhythm (where the fiction began), and the evening spent in sheer zydeco-crazed exaltation. Dialogue often used: "These people are ut-terly electrified by our sound!" "Work that squeezebox harder, Mike!"

Hednesford—The band's demo of original compositions is spun on the turntables of a resurrected John Peel, and a large cult following blows up, making their next six performances an instant sell-out. Dialogue: "Peel will propel us hat over clogs into fame!" "Zydeco is about to shatter the mainstream!"

Cannock—Backstage at the Hackney Empire, Sim meets the beau-tiful groupie Aisla Luxx to whom he makes love in the hotel following a six-encore set. The ravishing Aisla calls Sim her "sweet frotting forever-man". Dialogue: "Caress my body like you work that frottoir." "Oh Sim, syncopate my backbeat."

Landywood—The dexterity and nuance of Sim's frotting improves and the band conclude that his skills should be featured more prominently, with him performing next to the lead singer at all future concerts. Dialogue: "The elegance with which Sim explores each ridge is something that everyone should witness."

Bloxwich North—A video and interview on MTV propels the band to instant fame and success. Dialogue: "Louisiana is back."

Bloxwich—The band prepare for their first sell-out turn at the Hollywood Bowl. Over 30,000 appear—twice the venue's capacity, topping the record set by Lily Pons in 1936. Dialogue: "If they scream any louder, their lungs will burst!" "30,000 souls have been suddenly possessed by the excellence of zydeco."

Walsall—In the middle of the concert, the band step aside for Sim's intense frottoir solo. The huge stageside screens showcase the speed and magic with which his fingers frott the ridges and empower the metal. The solo ends with chants of "Sim! Sim! Supersim!" Dialogue: "No one in the known universe has worked a frottoir with such breathtaking afflatus." "That dude is the Hendrix of the frottoir."

Claire had swept to love with Sim the serious Clashhead in a froufrou of post-millennial splendour. Nights spinning *London Calling* in a Vauxhall Nova across the Landywood scrubland tippling low-alcoholic beers. Afternoons exploring the complex patchwork of *Sandinista!* on the velveteen couchette at Claire's flat. Mornings punkthrashing to *The Clash [US]*, taking an artful anarchism to an artless emploi. Singing 'Lost in the Supermarket' to themselves when splitting up to source separate items. Their union was built on strong aural foundations—Strummer and Jones, Simonon and Headon. To resurrect a zydeco rock-star fantasy, a symptom of the old Sim, the Lorna Wilnitt-era (Sim's hexed ex), could create Clairemageddon. In returning to this period, Sim was falling into the freckled hams of lumpen

Lorna, the time of simpering hipsters, the box-size flat in Stoke with college pals, the realm of aimless ambition. Claire had received the odd nostalgic nugget ("those all-night heartpumping rave-ups at the Frisker Bar", "coursing along night's edge to the starlight of skiffle") with polite tolerance, sensing the fondness in his voice, even when making the token slams on Lorna's crappiness. To utter the bouncy Caribbean noun "zydeco" was to poleaxe the future. "I want to take up the frottoir," Sim said in bed that evening. "The what where?" Claire asked. "The washboard. I want to form a zydeco combo." Claire said nothing else for twelve seconds. Those twelve seconds easily expanded into twelve days.

3

Sim sidled into the spareroom with an armful of pants. His fabric conditioner of choice was Linnux Deluxe. The implausible scent of elderberries and cream wafted from their soapworked seams. Another moment had arrived to resume the paused proposition and shout "I want a washboard!" at Claire's hair. He had bungled seven other chances to insert the unwanted topic into conversational crevices, failing to exploit the following pauses: that triumphant pause following the successful plonking of bottles at the bottlebank; that contemplative pause as the credits roll to a string-backed soundtrack following a tense TV serial; that satisfied pause when the car has been parked and automotive death has been averted again; that bedtime kiss when both parties are waiting for the other to initiate sex but neither does; that uncertain pause when the waiter has closed the menus and your stomach evaluates your meal choice; that unsure pause upon closing a novel and taking a peep at the number of remaining pages. Another time, snacking on crackers and pickled cucumbers, he almost said: "I've always liked dem riddums". After staring upwards at a passing helicopter: "The tunes have a Gallic flavour". As the 3.58 train approached: "There is an art to frotting." But no matter the moment, or whatever phrase he prepared to slide the notion painlessly into her ears, he knew Claire would hear: "I want to play a shitty sheet of metal from my past rather than have a child with you."

He went online and ordered a £125 frottoir with a striking rosewood frame, rust-proofed corrugated metal, two woodblocks, two bells, two thimbles, and a set of straps for shoulder wear from Disraeli Music. This frottoir, known as The Archduke, had received the review: "For anyone with serious percussive intent in a zydeco or skiffle context, this washboard or frottoir is an insanely clever purchase."

He posted an ad online, "Zydeco Supergroup Required". Twelve hours later, the accordionist Alexander Tungsten responded. Twenty-two hours later, the guitarist Frankie Gravel responded. Thirty-seven hours later, the fiddler Iain Fairbank responded. Eager to complete the combo, Sim messaged on Facebook the drummer Tim Tipoli who had played in The Rootin' Tootin' Zydeco Mumblers. The five-piece agreed to meet in Frankie Gravel's garage for the first practice session. Unfortunately, the fiddler Iain Fairbank, who had waited fourteen annums for the opportunity to form a zydeco four-piece, made an unannounced appearance at the cottage, a well-fiddled fiddle in his right mitt, as Claire, hair unblown, opened the door and stared at the little lank with wind-blown hair, waiting for her brain to make the obvious connections between the well-fiddled fiddle in the man's right mitt, the request for Sim, and the latent tendency for folk-twiddling twattishness in her husband. Coolly retrieving Sim from his study and prodding him to the front door, Claire inquired as to the presence of the fiddle-wielding fiend. Sim opened his mouth and made no recognisable sound. Remorse made an unwanted appearance, rearing up from behind the net curtains to nailgun his nostalgic notions to the tarp of the present. Looking to the unsmiling wife, then to the fiddle-wielding smirker, Sim swallowed a lot and stepped from the cage of cagamosis into the freewheeling future of the frottoir.

[EAST SUSSEX]

NAME: FRANK FITCH
AGE: 62
SENTENCE: 11 FURLONGS
CRIME: YOUTUBE COMMENT HISTORY

Ricky Martin—She Bangs (English)
Frank Fitch *2 days ago*
wow that chicano can swing !!!

Slavoj Žižek: Political Correctness is a More Dangerous Form of Totalitarianism
Frank Fitch *3 weeks ago*
yeah but dialectical marxism is a more dangerous form of maoism

Opal Miners Find $8000 Worth Of Crystal Boulder Opal!
Frank Fitch *9 weeks ago*
what's with the appearance of a chaffinch ???

Escape to the Country East Sussex 13x49
Frank Fitch *3 months ago*
i've been to that tree

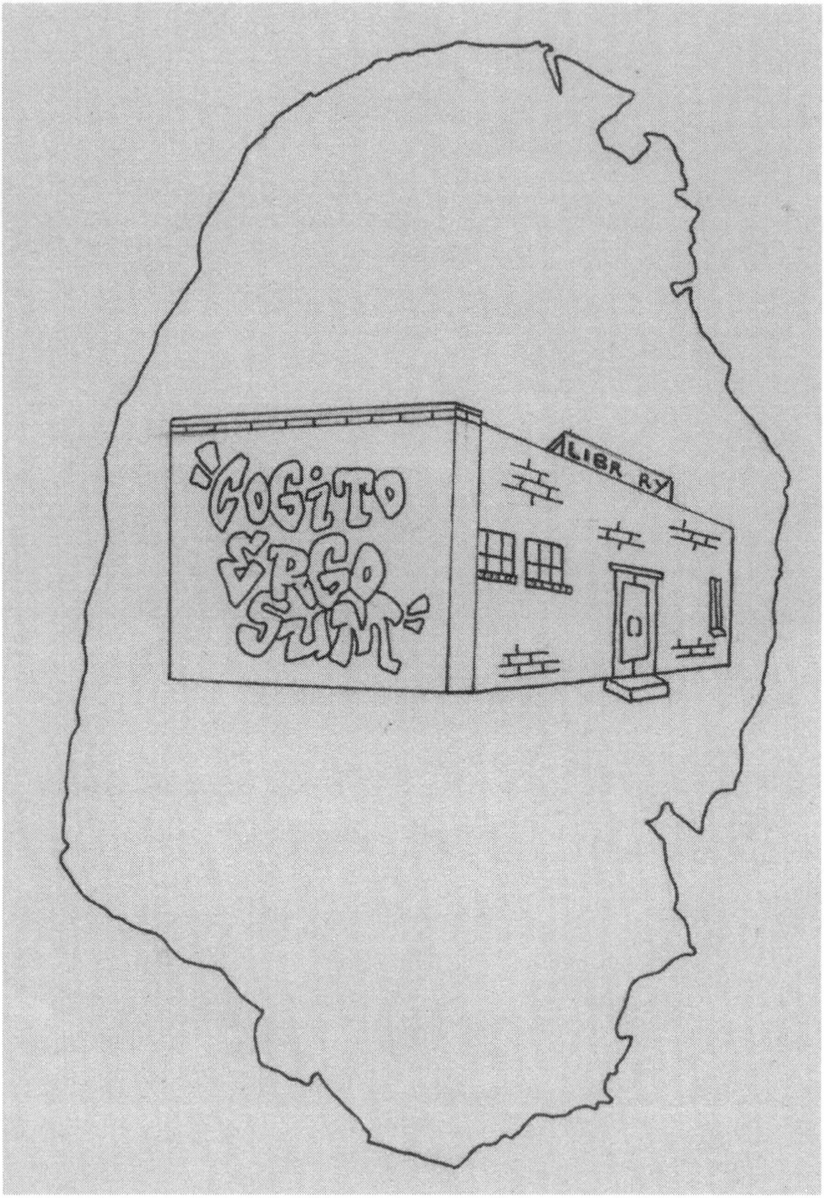

LIBR RY
COGITO
ERGO
SUM

[NORFOLK]

NAME: STEVE WHIFFLET
AGE: 46
SENTENCE: 2 YEARS
CRIME: ELITIST GRAFFITI

The following 'Wall of Readers' Excuses', in two columns with a centred afterthought, was sprayed on the public-facing wall of the Watton Public Library, two days before its closure. —Ed.

I have a sore clavicle. I have a zipzoomin' occupation that works me bonkers. I prefer to read the newsfeeds for my fiction supplement (hee hee!). I have a cute labrador named Blabber & Smoke to whose movements, bowel or ball-based, I must ministrate. I spend most afternoons combing a Serbo-Croat and running his limbs along the floor. I am too important like sir or lord important so that is too bad too bad.

S O D Y O U

I can't read, like I literally cannot understand words on the page, I stare at the page and before me the inked words are a blur, I might as well be looking at the inside of a flipflop, so, in short, I cannot read. I sit in a room listening to 'Bonkers in Phoenix'. I once knew this man named Elmo Spitz, a regal sort of fellow with a mercurial air, and he used to say to me, "Son, never read a novel in your life", and

I crouch in taverns watching the croquet on mute. I have no eyeballs, really, sorry, no eyeballs at all. I own a fuchsia cube, and into that fuchsia cube, I place a lifesize puma skeleton, a rotisserie, and a snatch of leg, and I find that takes me around ninety-nine minutes per hour, and I love my little fuchsia cube, you try and stop me opening her up, I tell you, you cannot. I prefer cuddling a cockhorse in Cromer. I like the drama of silence. I moved into a bothy recently. I favour the creamier, soupier sauces to the autochthonic realm of reading. I like to watch the latest boxsets, I find the storylines more involving. I hate the fact there are words in sentences in paragraphs on pages, and that the pages run left to right for page after page after page, and the pages sit between two thicker paper covers bound by a spine, I simply loathe this state of affairs. I sit

A

L

L,

Υ

O

Ʊ

L

A

Z,

Υ,

you know what, ever since hearing those strange words on that fragrant Friday, in the presence of the regal man named Elmo Spitz, I have never felt the need to read a novel in my life. I prefer throttling unthankers in Thetford. I walk a crooked mile, I sing a crooked song, I talk a crooked talk, I am the Man Who Cannot Be. I live in Weeting. I return from a grinding nine-hour shift in the call centre, to find that the call centre has managed to pummel all curiosity, inquiry, and imagination from my mind, and in a pathetic and futile attempt to relax, I turn to the sweet salve of the heroin needle, put Mazzy Star on the bluetooth speaker, and transport myself into a kinder, happier place. I skateboard, I freestyle, I bust moves. I have no interest in anything except my own Instagram account. I prefer sucking semicircles in Swaffham.

inside a prism of indecision and into that prism of indecision come wafting the spiders of automation. I have two kiddies, and their kiddilicious antics, their leaping and skipping and singing and hirpling are more important to me than a psoriatic Treacletowner's imagination on pulp. I have a health condition that requires me to lacquer my eyelids for 45 minutes every evening. I have a paunch like a Perro de Presa Canario and need to pump hard to present myself as a sexual possibility. I like to ride on the swing outside my tenement and think "Oh! What a marvellous time to simmer!" I prefer booing a bassinet in Booton. I have to complete my invention, the quarter-trouser, coming to a fourth of a leg near you.

BORING BUGGERS

I favour the left-handed sidle into rooms into which I am unauthorised to step. I am safe in not reading, for I know that the book is passing into insignificance, like the cucumber, the incense stick, the left-wing broadsheet, the credence paid to global warming, I am on the right side of history, losers. I prefer Götterdämmerunging in Great Yarmouth. I have to conclude, after fifteen years of philosophical inquiry, soaking up the finest minds in history, from Aristotle to Plato to Nietzsche to Zizek, after months spent pondering the most vexing conundrums ever devised by humankind, I have to conclude, that in the final analysis, life ain't nuttin but money an' fuck a bitch.

[BRISTOL]

NAME: SALSA RETROGRADE
AGE: 53
SENTENCE: 30 YEARS
CRIME: RIPPING OFF THIS MAN'S CORSET

[LINCOLNSHIRE]

NAME: DRAYFORD CORNSTICK
AGE: 50
SENTENCE: 30 YEARS
CRIME: THE LAW OF ANTICIPOINTMUNCH

G OOD MORNING. I was a man with a theory, like Martin "confusion" Fleischmann, like Giovanni "Mars Attacks!" Schiaparelli, like Francesco "bacteria" Redi. I called that theory The Law of Anticipointmunch, though there was nothing legalistic involved. Now listen up, you snickering walloon, and imagine you have booked into a restaurant with friends. Have you? Smashing. The Law states that whatever your friends order, whether your friends are vegans, gheegans, or briegans, that irrespective of the scrumminess of your own food, you will salivate with envy across the table at their meals, that your mind will convince you that their food is more succulent, tender, and tastier than yours, and with each stab and slash of cutlery, your envy will merely deepen, leading to conflicts over "sampling" their foods, opening up potential long-term rifts between your friends that can span years and poleaxe families. This has happened to me on numerous occasions. Let me throw you a memorypie, you impudent Belgian. I lost a lover in 2008 when I refused her a niblet of my katsu chicken. I took a firm stance then, as I do now, on The Law, arguing that she should have chosen katsu in concord, but regardless, she opted for the salmon en croute, and her fork transgressed the table, taking unwanted prods at my breaded fillets, sending my hackles skyhigh. My refusal caused her offence and she stropped from the restaurant, the pink robes of her salmon unparted. (On that occasion, her actions led to me bagging a second meal, but you would have to be a lunatic to use The Law for that purpose). And then there is the famous instance of the Keller family from Cleethorpes who murdered each other over a menumental mashap. The mother

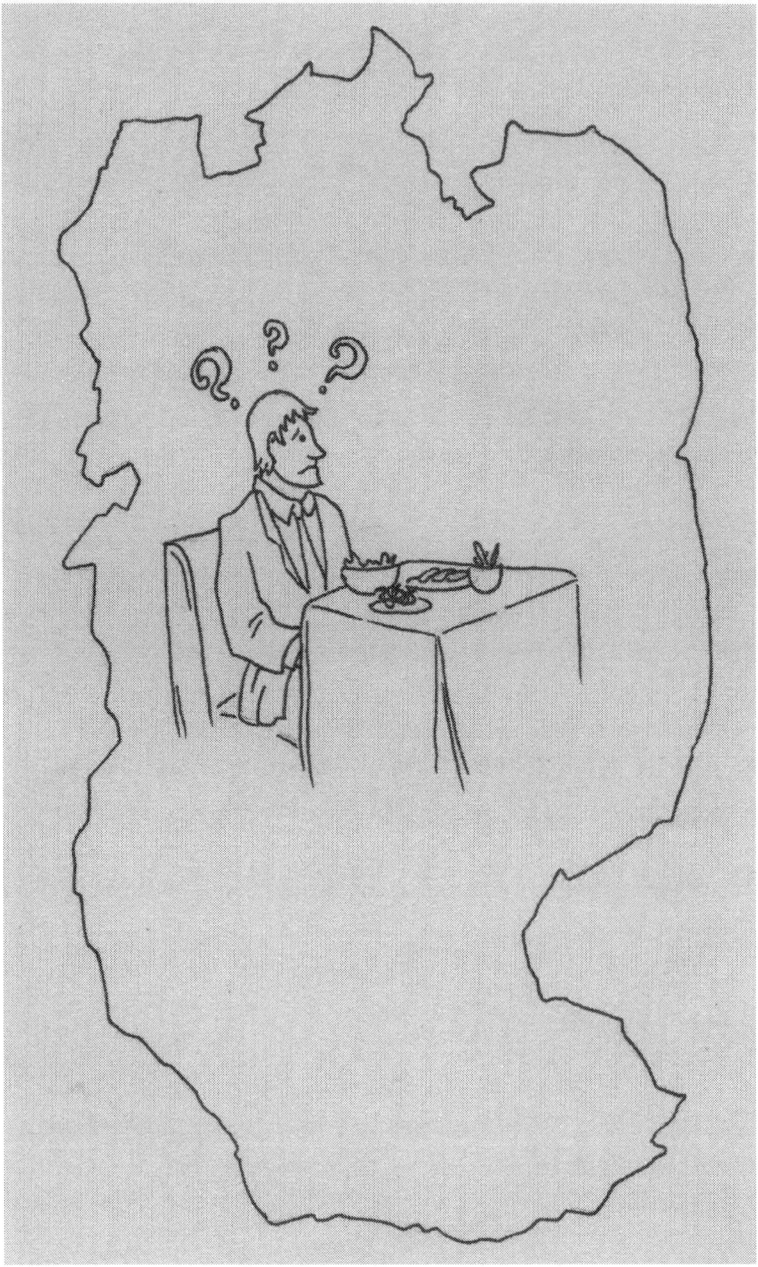

had ordered mash and cress, the father mash and sheep, the son mash and pigeon, and the daughter mash and nectarine, in a popular artisan kitchen called The Good Goddamn. The father asked the mother for a "taste", and in twelve minutes, the Keller family were slumped over their starters with slit throats. All right, so I published my theory in the *Gastronomic's Almanack*. Soon hence, I received a tart upchuck of praise from eaters. I received tweets of support, toots of support, and twangs of support. My theory had tapped into a long-suppressed feeling in the Lincolnshire stomach and a gastronomic revolution boomed. Frustrated eaters were furious for a change. In a week, most restaurants responded by becoming tapas and all-you-can-eat buffet places, where the torment of choice was replaced with the chance to pile everything on a plate. This proved disastrous and no solution to the problem. In these wretched dives, you shovel on seven contradictory foodstuffs, mixing chow mein with madras, melba toast with squid rings, and beef stew with chickpea salad. It is vulgar and insulting to the chefs. These places belittle the rapturous ritual of eating. However, having made my theory county-wide news, no one in Lincolnshire was able to enter an eatery without craving another dish, sometimes in mid-munch. In two weeks, Lincolnshire was named the most obese county in the universe. And they say I was to blame. What blithering ballcock! I was a man with a theory, like Gottfried "vis viva" Leibniz, like Carl "psychomotor" Delacato, like Constantine "eclectic" Samuel "botanical" Rafinesque. They are bonkbrained mooks, you slippy flem. I must be freed. Now leave me to my bowl of chowder. Good morning.

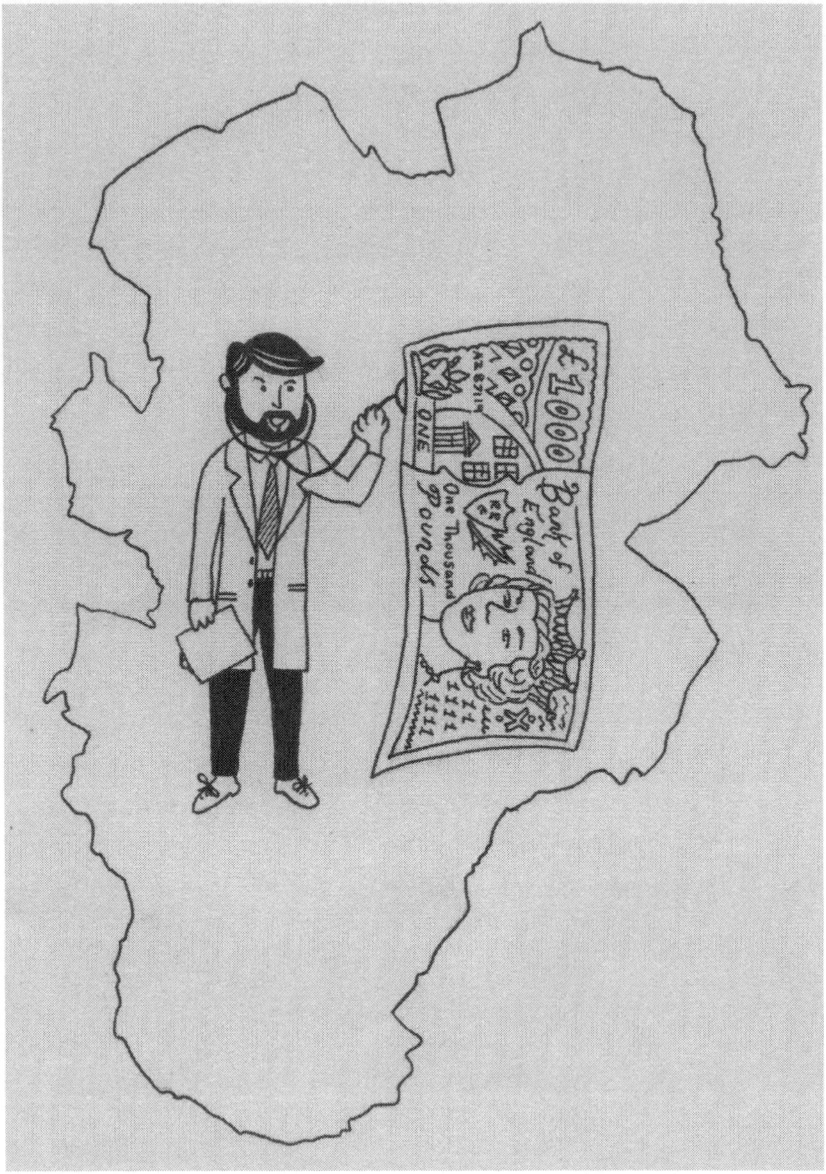
£1000
ONE
Bank of England
One Thousand Pounds

[WEST MIDLANDS]

NAME: ALEX FORTNIGHT
AGE: 36
SENTENCE: 100 YEARS
CRIME: CRACKED QUACKERY

KRISTEN DOUBT: Your controversial bestselling books have been strongly criticised in the medical community. One prominent doctor has labelled you "a cash-creaming charlatan leeching on the weak-willed", and one psychiatrist "a purulent sore on society's face". How do you respond to those attacks?

DR. ALEX FORTNIGHT: The medical community haven't read my works. If the medical community had read my works, they would realise that nothing I have written is factually inaccurate.

KD: What about the negative tone of your works? When you say that parents should "stop loving" their children . . .

DAF: Thank you, Kristen, for the opportunity to discuss my book, *Raising Your Kids Without Love: A Foolproof Guide*, by Dr. Alex Fortnight. There is a revolution in parenting taking place. The right *not* to love. Take the recent case of Billie Septum. Billie was fed up of the liberal left pressuring her into raising her child properly, when she really hadn't the time, what with the rollerblading and the piemaking and the performance art, and on top of that, she found her son Duncan irritating. She said that having looked at her son at least seven times, she came to the conclusion that she couldn't possibly love that, what with the mucous, the burbling, the icky hair, and the strange clicking sound from the back of its throat. It occurred to me, as I was working on a Good Parenting Guide, that the whole notion of "love", whether conditional or un-, has no real place in modern parenting. I thought back to a relationship I had with Bettie Ogru in the 1990s. I was so eager to reciprocate the love that she claimed she had for me, a love that I was unable to understand, and that she was unable to explain using cogent descriptives, that I strained for weeks and weeks to stir up the same ferocity of amour that she was physically expressing with her pelvic muscles. I hurled myself into furious lovemaking, hoping that the intense shoogle of my hips and pre-orgasmic yawps might pass for love, or that romantic gestures such as inflating one hundred balloons to spell Sharlene My Darling in the air might be the lovething. But I came to the conclusion that I was content in *receiving* her love. I was all right with the fact that I thought Sharlene was all right, not someone who sent me into a frenzied mutt-like state of femme worship, and that such a state was undesirable and pathetic anyway, so I was content to bask in the receipt of her love, and I really was in an enviable position. Sadly, she was not pleased with this one-way set-up, and stropped off to marry a lowly minion in the catering industry, who worshipped her, and who she no doubt loved not. I think non-loving relationships are the future, and the antidote to the common imbalance of love in most relationships. I am not talking mutual hatred. I am talking mutual tolerance and basic respect. Freed from the unwritten contract, the pressure to feel things for other people, might the world not be a nicer place if we learn to tolerate others, and have a mutual respect for them, without the unrealistic pressure to love among an essentially annoying, unloveable species? So, following this principle for parental relationships, in my book I prove that the loveless neglect of your sons or daughters will turn them into sane, intelligent, and ultimately loving individuals, who want nothing from you and will stay out of your way and will bring you a lot of nice things.

KD: This title sold a million copies upon its release. A month later, the total number of babies left in refuse bins and underpasses, on park benches and stoops, increased sevenfold in the UK. There have also been severe spikings in the rate of children being taken into care or attacking their parents.

DAF: These have no connection to my work. If those parents had read my book properly, they would see that I do not recommend leaving their children in underpasses or bus stops, or wherever. Irresponsible behaviour.

KA: You say irresponsible behaviour. How about your attitude to relationships, which some critics have called "cynical" or "the rantings of a loony goombah"?

DAF: Once more, I thank you, Kristen, for the chance to discuss my work, *The Foolproof Guide to Dating Without Dating, Sex Without Sex, and Marriage Without Marriage*, by Dr. Alex Fortnight. You are like me. You have no time to forge long-term relationships, what with the pell-mell non-stop no-time-to-breathe whirlwind helter-skelter schedule of stuff that usurps your face, morning and night and in between. You regret the hours spent wasted in bars chatting to interesting and attractive people who it would take an absolute age to become closer to on date after date after date after time-eating date. You are cynical about the prospect of keeping one partner for life, knowing full well the limited lifespan most marriages have in the modern world and the complications if breeding is involved. You need the 'potential' dating plan. A foolproof system that allows you to experience lifelong relationships over seven days, through a simple process of honing mind over matter.

KA: If we could move on to—

DAF: Permit me to outline the steps first, Kristen. The first step: select, from a website or a street nearby, a man or woman who appeals, and ask them "out". (If they refuse, you can attempt the following steps by merely observing the person from afar, but for now, it is advisable to start with a mutually agreed date). One the date has been scheduled, make a list of the facets of their appearance that both appeal to and repel you, and a provisional list of the traits that frustrate and tantalise you. That is step one. Step—

KA: Dr. Fortnight, with respect, this interview is not an advert for your—

DAF: Be quiet for a moment, Kristen. Step two is coming. The second step: have the date. Ensure that the selected evening is person-centred, not an activity, like paintball or sailing. A quiet tipple at a restaurant or bar. Ask the person about their past relationships, their family, their current occupation, their dreams, hopes, goals, and opinions on as many topics as possible. Make mental notes. (Taking actual notes is not advised, as it might ruin the prospect of the essential second date). Be sure to come across as interested in the person and make an effort conversationally yourself, to secure the second date.

KA: Really, Dr. Fortnight—

DAF: You have a hard time with basic commands, Kristen. It is sad. Step the third: in the time between dates, write down all the facts about this person and begin constructing scenarios that might arise in a long-term relationship—the fun activities together, sources of argument, incompatibilities, shared pleasures. Lie back on your bed and imagine as many of these scenarios as possible. To conduct a full 'potential' relationship, take each of these scenarios (or character traits) to an endpoint where the relationship will terminate. Squeeze as much pleasure as possible from the traits that appeal to you and take them towards the realm of frustration and departure.

KA: I have indulged you enough. Now—

DAF: This is the final step. The fourth and step final: have a second date. At this point, all the traits you dislike about the person should be amplified enough for this date to be the last—and good riddance. If you find you discover new traits of the person during the date that appeal to you, try to devise quick scenarios where these traits may cause frustration and unhappiness using the practice you have put in over the week. Remember to remain aloof on the date so the person doesn't like you. There.

KA: It has been said that you merely exploit the worst excesses of human behaviour, and allow people to pursue cynical self-interest at the expense of others, and you encourage people to indulge in destructive vices. For example, your book *Drink, Drink, Drink & Be Merry: A Guaranteed & Foolproof Guide to Embracing Alcohol—*

DAF: By Dr. Alex Fortnight, yes. An ocean of ink has been spilled on the topic of "kicking" alcohol, and the same medical "experts" who savage me in the papers bore us with tales that extreme alcohol consumption is an "addiction". I stomp this argument in the knees for 400 pages. Having a fondness for alcohol is like having a fondness for playing the ukulele, or trampolining in a tutu, or fellwalking in Holland. It is an unusual and misunderstood pastime. But it is a *pastime*, and nothing more. In the same manner mountaineers risk their lives scaling cliff faces, or lion hunters confront the roaring wrath of those African beasts, the habitual drinker places pleasure before their long-term health. Most "alcoholics" are hobbyists. If you see a man staggering from the pub, having consumed nine whiskies, two rums, and four cocktails, this man is not a "drunken wreck", but a man in intense pleasure at having scored another success in his pursuit of maximum inebriation. I call them "extreme drinkers", those who test the limits of what the body can endure. Sadly, in our society, we have this blinkered view, that most "alcoholics" consume alcohol to mask personal pain and cope with the rigours of life. This is incorrect. It is perfectly acceptable to drink over twenty pints a day, and society must accept this.

KA: This is, unsurprisingly, your most popular work. After its publication, the NHS reported a 300% spike in alcohol-related accidents, that their A&Es were stuffed around the clock with harmful drunks, and that AA groups have no attendees. Our high streets are littered with drunks "pursuing their hobby", as you would have it, and frequently attack children and pensioners. Your book is directly responsible for making our society more dissolute.

DAF: Nonsense. If my book has increased public interest in extreme drinking, then I am more than pleased to have helped the pastime along.

KA: You also deny that your book was funded by several prominent breweries, who offered you sums in the region of £2,000,000.

DAF: I never received that sum. Around the time of writing, I had the good fortune to win the National Lottery, a fine institution.

KA: It has been said by the Prime Minister of Norway that you have "reduced Great Britain to a sad alcoholic sinkhole, a feral nation of self-gratifying lawless pleasure-seekers, weaned on the warped words of that sick opportunist, Dr. Alex Fortnight."

DAF: Big sentence for a Norwegian.

KA: What are you working on at the moment?

DAF: Thank you for asking, Kristen. I have finished a book on the myth of childhood obesity, called *Sugar & Salt is Everything Nice: Why You Should Always Take the Kids to McDs*, by Dr. Alex Fortnight. It encourages parents to teach their children not to be ashamed of having a large body mass index. It is a positive book about embracing one's curves, and taking pleasure in eating food and living well. I expect excellent sales.

KA: Thank you, Dr. Fortnight.

DAF: A pleasure, Kristen.

[From 'Interview with Dr. Alex Fortnight', Kristen Doubt, *The Eye Spy* (online), Archived March 2020.]

[MERSEYSIDE]

NAME: "COLIN"
AGE: 29
SENTENCE: 24.5 YEARS
CRIME: SYMPATHY SOLICITING

13/5/2020

I AM COLIN BUT this is not my real name, this is a name I have chosen to elicit sympathy from people. My real name is Julian which is an extremely cool name to have but people do not feel sympathy for me if they know I am called Julian. They expect me to be a more spectacular man than I in fact am so disappointment is what they feel, not sympathy. On the contrary, they expect me to feel sympathy for them for their disappointment at finding my name so unlike my character, which is extremely pleading.

This is my problem. If you want sympathy because you are an unhappy, unremarkable, and unloved person, you are not allowed to have sympathy. People only offer sympathy for people in situations beyond their control, usually when they have sustained serious injuries or lost partners in romance or members of their immediate families. You cannot have sympathy for being a bland Colin whom no one really likes and whom people purposefully avoid because they do not want to be in my presence which they find extremely disagreeable due to my ineptitude in speech and my physical defects.

I am an ugly person. Facially, I do not appeal to others. I have spectacles with large lenses because I could not afford to get the lens flattened because I do not earn enough money to afford such luxuries and so as a consequence the lenses make my eyes seem larger and gogglier than they in fact are, which frightens people. I have a permanent five o'clock shadow on my chin, lower cheeks, and upper neck which does not come

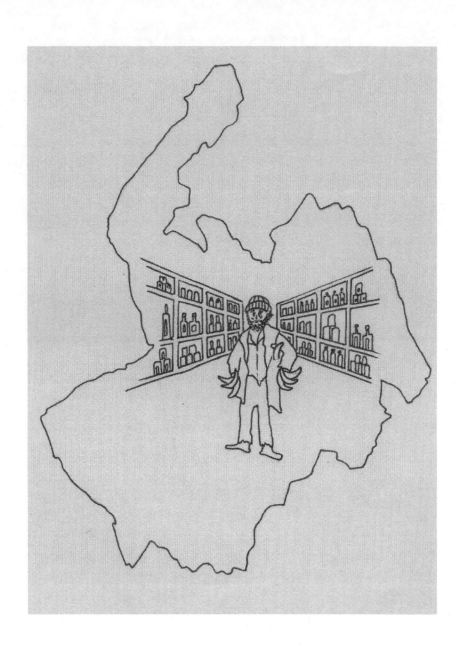

off despite how close I shave, which leaves me with a greyness permanently shaded on my face. My head is unusually formed in comparison to my body—I am very scrawny but my head is potato-shaped so does not sit well on my shoulders: it appears as if my head has been inflated from an air pump in my neck. I can tell you are laughing at me.

I have a sense of humour but you have to understand that a person like me can only take so much loneliness before he loses the ability to laugh at himself. If no one will take me seriously, how can I become a successful human being? I was not put on this planet for the amusement of others. You might, at this point, find my way of communicating strange. This is another problem. When I was a child I struggled to learn the alphabet and had problems with pronunciation. So my mode of speech is perhaps odd to the ear (or eye). I hope you find these reasons convincing enough to feel sympathy for me.

What is wrong in asking for sympathy? Why must we suppress our needs and hope certain basic human necessities come our way some day, if we are lucky, if we stoically bear our suffering from day to day? I am sick and tired of being unsuccessful in this life, and I want your pity, your sympathy, and maybe—if it's not too much to ask—your "love."

20/6/2020

The other day, I tried to elicit sympathy by looking sad in the supermarket. I stood by the bananas with an enormous frown on my face, clutching the Fyffes originals upside down so they mirrored the unhappiness etched on my visage. I was unsuccessful at eliciting sympathy on that occasion and later the in-shop security operative asked me to either purchase the fresh produce I was holding in my hands or to put it down and leave the store immediately.

The next day I went into a shoe shop and hung around for a while waiting for the assistant to come and speak to me, but with a predictable stroke of bad luck, the assistant was arrested for molesting a female customer, and the shop had to close early. To compensate for this failure,

I tried loitering around the stationery shop, wearing a melancholy face by the Pritt-Sticks, but the assistant only asked me if she could help. "There is only *one* thing you can help me with," I said. "What's that?" she asked. Her forced smile nearly sent the eyes popping from her head. I knew she was a false woman. "Oh never mind," I said. I placed the Pritt-Stick back on the shelf and left.

Yesterday, I made a final attempt in the High Street to make strangers pity my plight. I noticed how homeless people were permitted to sit in doorways with their heads bent down, looking extremely crushed in public, and passersby would show their sympathy by tossing coinage into rumpled hats or cups placed strategically beside their crossed legs. I found an unoccupied doorway beside a supermarket (not the same one as earlier) and sat cross-legged with a bowler hat at my feet. I hung my head and waited for people to express their sadness in the form of kindly deposited currency.

Typically, my plan was thwarted when a homeless thug from across the street shook me violently. "Hey, this is my spot, what you doing?" he asked. His grammar was pitifully inept, I barely understood him. "Could you express yourself with more clarity?" I asked. "This is my spot, clear off." He was blunt. "I see no official reservation or demarcation notices in the nearby vicinity. I am afraid you are mistaken on this occasion," I replied. "What? This is *my* spot!" Obviously no point trying to reason with this savage. "Very well. Since you are an imbecile and I am a gentleman, I will move on as you wish. I wish you luck eliciting sympathy from others, but with that sort of attitude, I doubt anyone will care very much for you." I walked away as he barked obscenities.

No one witnessed the scene.

Earlier this morning I hit upon a useful scheme. I went into my local newsagent to buy a bottle of ketchup and told the owner that I had misplaced my favourite overcoat. "That's a shame," he said. My skin prickled. Without thinking I ambled into the Post Office and told the clerk that I had lost my sister to lymphoma that morning. "Oh I am very sorry to hear that," she said. "Just take it easy for the rest of the day." I fought hard to suppress a delighted smile. "Thank you," I said solemnly (I hope!) and left with a book of stamps. Of course, this method of eliciting sympathy is more successful in large cities, like Liverpool, not small villages like mine, in Lydiate, where it is impossible to maintain a series of lies in so narrow a space. In cities, they are not interested in making small talk in shops.

So once more, I am stuck. I can only ride this current wave of sympathy about my fictitious sister for so long. What I require is a continual sympathetic reaction when I am spotted. I want people to see me and instantly respond: "Aww . . . that poor, poor man."

How about you? Did any of this work for you? Are you now beginning to see what a sad case I am and are you ready to "open your heart" to me, now you know what my life is like?

2/8/2020

Lately, I have been "feeling depressed" to help evoke sympathy. I have, naturally, been feeling low since my attempts to make people sympathise with me on a day-by-day, second-by-second basis have failed, but I do not feel crushed and hopeless . . . if anything the pursuit of sympathy has kept me busy and relatively content. You might ask why I *need* sympathy, if that is the case?

If my only purpose as a man were taken away, I would be saddled with a deep and true depression. A depressed man cannot successfully evoke sympathy, unless that depression pertained to a natural disaster or fatal accident. In your lives, you can only tolerate so much self-pitying unhappiness from people before you become frustrated and leave them to their misery. It is not insensitive. You can't spend your life wallowing in another's blackness, but you see my problem. To read about a man who is sorry for himself because he is unable to change his emotional state because you refuse to grant him the one human response he needs would frighten or intimidate you, and you would make a million excuses before you extended real sympathy, or would offer an unfelt superficial substitute such as a forlorn facial expression.

So I took my contrived depression to various support groups for dysfunctional people—the high-stressed, anxious, the properly depressed—and talked about my unmet needs in a circle of plastic chairs under inappropriate lighting. The modus operandi of these places makes it impossible to absorb sympathy, since every unhappy talker is seeking sympathy from the other, and each talker is too self-absorbed to transmit anything other than false nods or hums of recognition. The only person of use is the group organiser but he is trained to remain emotionally detached at all times, so doesn't offer more than professional platitudes. When I looked my rivals in the eye and told them *I desperately need sympathy*, eyes quickly darted up the walls.

Of course.

Afterwards I made friends with Alan Key, a depressed former alcoholic suffering from nervous anxiety and low self-esteem. Alan shared my point of view that people were short on sympathy for anything less than having your entire family wiped out in a car crash. It is almost like—I paraphrase Alan—there's this pecking order of feeling . . . that once the famine sufferers or enslaved and abused arrive on the scene, all First World problems are trivialities solvable with antidepressants and Pulling Your Socks Up. Like we should just dismiss our depressions as indulgent neuroses. "Shouldn't we?" I asked. He stared at me like I'd slapped his newborn child.

It seems "feeling depressed" was not the meal ticket I was seeking. All I can do now is crawl to you once again. All I can do is ask you whether my failed attempt to tease responses from other unhappy people so I can take pleasure in feeling thought-about, in feeling cared-for and considered for one second instead of passed over like the crossed-out man I in fact am, is enough to leak a little readerly sympathy onto the page to authenticate this blog. How was that for self-pity? Don't wince. That's not what I want.

9/9/2020

I met a man willing to help me. His name is Timothy and I met him in the underground. We struck up a conversation about the pressures of living in an oppressive world and he said we should be candid about what we want from others. I said that I desperately needed sympathy, that without sympathy no woman would want me and my life as a man would end. He told me that he was able to emote only when listening to the appropriate music. If he wanted to feel sorrow for lives lost in an earthquake or tsunami he would need something suitably desolate like Barber's *Adagio for Strings* or Beethoven's *Moonlight Sonata*. If he wanted to feel melancholy for minor sufferings, he would listen to downbeat indies like Red House Painters or Grandaddy.

"What music do you need to feel sympathy for me?" I asked.

"That depends, Julian."

"Colin."

"Right sorry, Colin. Your case is unusual. As I understand it, you want sympathy for its own sake. You want sympathy simply because you are unloved and unnoticed, and because you aren't naturally very sympathiswithable."

"Yes. That sort of thing."

"I think I have a solution. I need the ballads of Celine Dion and Jennifer Rush."

"Why?"

"What you require from me is a contrived form of emotional sympathy, so the exaggerated bombast of these balladeers will help me reach this faux-emotional response," Tim said.

"I'm not sure about that. I want heartfelt emotional sympathy, proper deep sympathy, like you really care."

"But my friend, you must understand, if the only reason you want sympathy is because you want to be seen as sympathetic, there is nothing for me to sympathise with. Even if I were capable of standard emotional responses, I would be hard pressed to feel for your situation without musical assistance. The only sliver of sympathy I feel for you is that because you want to be seen as sympathetic so badly, and are failing in that aim, you are unhappy and desperate. To access this sympathy I could use Norah Jones."

"OK."

Tim raided his CD collection for the popular singer of airy ballads and worked on his sympathetic response once the album started. Twenty seconds into the fourth track, he paused the music and approached me. On his face was a concerned expression.

"My friend, I am sorry you are unable to find the sympathy you require from people, and this is making you unhappy. I hope what I offer you right now provides some comfort," he said, patting me on the shoulder.

"Thank you, Tim. That does provide me with sufficient comfort. I feel I have a greater quest in front of me in earning the world's full sympathy, but for now, this is very satisfying."

"I am glad. Would you like to stay for breakfast?"

"No thank you, I should get back out there."

"That's brave of you. I hope you find what you are looking for. Feel free to come around any time if you want another of my sympathetic reactions."

"Thank you, friend."

I left Tim and for the first time since this blog began, I wasn't miserable and self-pitying. I even considered saying "nice morning isn't it?" to someone I passed in the street. Maybe this was the path to real sympathy, behaving in a pleasant manner to my fellow beings and having my pleasantness spurned. I said "nice morning" to a lady in a supermarket queue. "Yes, the sun's out today," she replied with a smile. Several moments later, I asked someone the time, expecting to be ignored. "It's quarter to eleven," he said, with a smile. Next, I tried crossing a social barrier, and asked a stranger if he could lend me 50p for the bus. The stranger, without complaint, gave me 50p with a smile. If people weren't going to treat me with indifference and contempt, how on earth could I evoke in them the proper sympathetic reactions I required?

24/9/2020

Clearly, I would have to provoke people into abusing me. Once they turned nasty, any passersby who missed my initial provocation would feel instant pity for me and help to fend off my bullying antagonist. For my first attempt, I kicked over a man's shopping bag as he waited at the bus stop. He appeared stunned that I would do such a thing and people around me were appalled. "What on earth did you do that for?" they asked, helping the man refill his bags and scowling me away. "I'm sorry," I stuttered. And I really was.

A less abusive method was required, involving more subtle anger-making techniques. In the post office queue I tried prodding a man repeatedly in the hope he snapped at me, but after one prod he simply turned around and said "yes?" so any extra prods seemed surplus. I tried verbally abusing a depilated pavement user. "Excuse me! You have absolutely no hair! Bald man! You are an ugly bald man!" I railed. But everyone started booing and several youths gave me menacing looks, so I made my exit from the scene. Finally, I tried whispering abuse into ears at bus stops. To one man I said: "Your wife is overweight, yes?" but he told me he wasn't married. To another I said: "You are a hideously ugly pig," but he merely laughed. For the third and final attempt, I said: "Your lardy sister is a prostitute." This elicited fury from the ear-owner, in this case an old man, but sadly his bus arrived and it was necessary for him to board.

I returned to my initial plan and provoked people outright. One man (I never abused a woman) I punched viciously in a sidestreet, running out on to the main street so when he leapt at me with the returning volley, people would only see an unprovoked attack. This plan worked. My punch victim charged at me, flung me to the ground and began kicking while shocked onlookers allowed for six aching chest blows before intercepting. "He hit me first!" the man cried. "I did not! This brute simply lunged at me unprovoked!" I countered between gasps. When the man ran off, several ladies helped me to a bench while I recuperated, offering me tissues and water, and most crucially, sympathetic expressions. Although my chest ached from the violent kicks, and rib damage may have occurred, I was in ecstasy. I milked my pain until someone suggested calling an ambulance, but I said I would be fine and they left me.

My good fortune only lasted once. When I repeated the incident, my punch victims simply ran off, stunned and dazed, or sent for the police, or produced lethal weapons from their pockets that forced me to run for my life. On my final attempt, I punched a man at the exact moment a party of priests and nuns emerged from a restaurant, and the pious curses flung at me were overwhelming. I immediately apologised and said I was a weak sinner, but they were too busy cursing me and tending to the victim who was crying pitifully. The nuns called me an ungodly thug and offered me none of their catholic charity. I left in disgrace and shame. Once again the only person feeling sorry for me was me. And even I hated myself too much to really care.

[From the online blog of "Colin", May 2020-September 2020, archived at: http://www.sympathyforcolin.blogspot.co.uk]

[CITY OF LONDON]

NAME: ??
AGE: ??
SENTENCE: ??
CRIME: ??

I SUGGESTED, IN A PUBLIC FORUM, in front of 267 people, that the City of London might be renamed Bladderooniepoops. That is my "story", you asshat. Please leave.

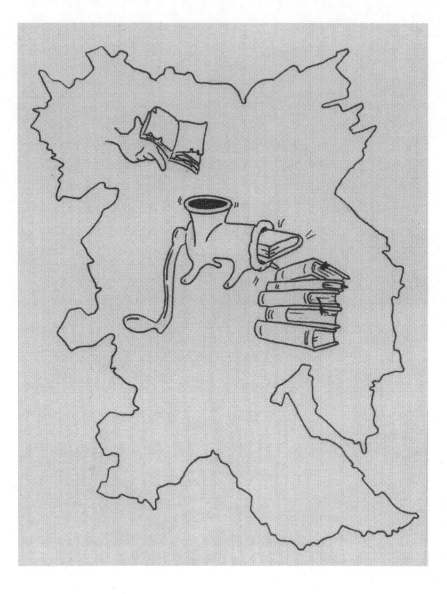

[GLOUCESTERSHIRE]

NAME: F. LEVETT ANDERSON
AGE: 68
SENTENCE: 15 YEARS
CRIME: PULPED BY MANY

F. LEVETT ANDERSON was a rich oilman from Quedgeley who wanted to be remembered for his literary achievements. Sadly, he couldn't even write his name, so he hired ten bodies to complete his substantial body of work—novels, poems, stories, essays, plays—everything. Each body was required to produce one work per month which would be sent to a body of editors for correction and revision before it was self-published and distributed nationwide at 2,000,000 copies per book. If the work did not meet the editors' strict literary standards, the failing body would be replaced by a new body to help maintain the high quality. In time, the more successful bodies began to incorporate long passages from famous writers' works into their own to prevent burnout from having to produce such quality work in a short space of time. Ten novels were released containing extended passages from ten famous writers' works and F. Levett Anderson had to reimburse the plagiarised writers one million dollars to prevent lawsuits. Because it was profitable, and because ten vacancies had suddenly become available, the famous writers came to work for the oilman. The writers, despite not getting credit for their works, made five million per book, which was more important in the end than having the right name attached to their works. But soon the same burnout problem befell the famous writers. To prevent this they plagiarised from the vast canon of works by F. Levett Anderson which, being so extraordinarily vast, and all products of F. Levett Anderson's incredible imagination, were impossible to trace to their original bodies. Since F. Levett Anderson "wrote" all his works himself, he could not sue himself for plagiarism.

He also could not attribute the self-plagiarised material to individual writers, so had no ground to sue the famous writers, who had replagiarised the extracts that had already been plagiarised from their works. In time, F. Levett Anderson's books were assembled merely by stitching together sentences from the preceding works, until all works being publicly released by F. Levett Anderson were incoherent cut-and-paste disasters read by no one and pulped by many. Anderson devised a simple solution: he bought the names of all famous writers in the world and had all the books they wrote throughout the course of their natural lives published under his name. He was a fool for not thinking of that in the first place.

[COUNTY DURHAM]

NAME: SARAH YURT
AGE: 34
SENTENCE: 5 YEARS
CRIME: LOBOTOMISING FORTY-SEVEN CHILDREN

I WAS IN MARKS & SPENCERS picking up a leopard-print onesie for Brian when the following chain of events linked in lousiness occurred. As a parent, I think it important not to refract your child's tastes and interests through your own aesthetic prism, so I was pleased to shop for the item on that balmy Sunday, while Malcolm took him to the park with his grandfather. As I was walking towards the queue, I observed a small child slumped on the floor sucking a pair of women's knickers, making the noise "Hmmooowww". I assumed that the child was impaired in some manner, and mentally slapped myself for making such an assumption in this understanding parental climate. A young teenage girl appeared from behind the bras and pulled the pant-sucking child along the lino by his right arm towards the same queue I had intended to join. I followed and stood behind. The teenager rested the child on his back at her mother's feet. She looked down at her son and said to her daughter: "Deal with the drool."

"Oh God. Why do we have to take him with us?" she sulked, reaching for a tissue.

"Because he's your brother."

"Haaaammmaannn!" the child enunciated, prompting awkward stolen glances. The mother paid for her items, lifted up her unusual son and draped his inert body over her brawny shoulders. That ended the scene.

The next morning I had to teach five classes of net-ravaged teenagers Shakespeare and Austen in a manner that made me popular and likeable, opening up a crack of trust into which I could spelunk

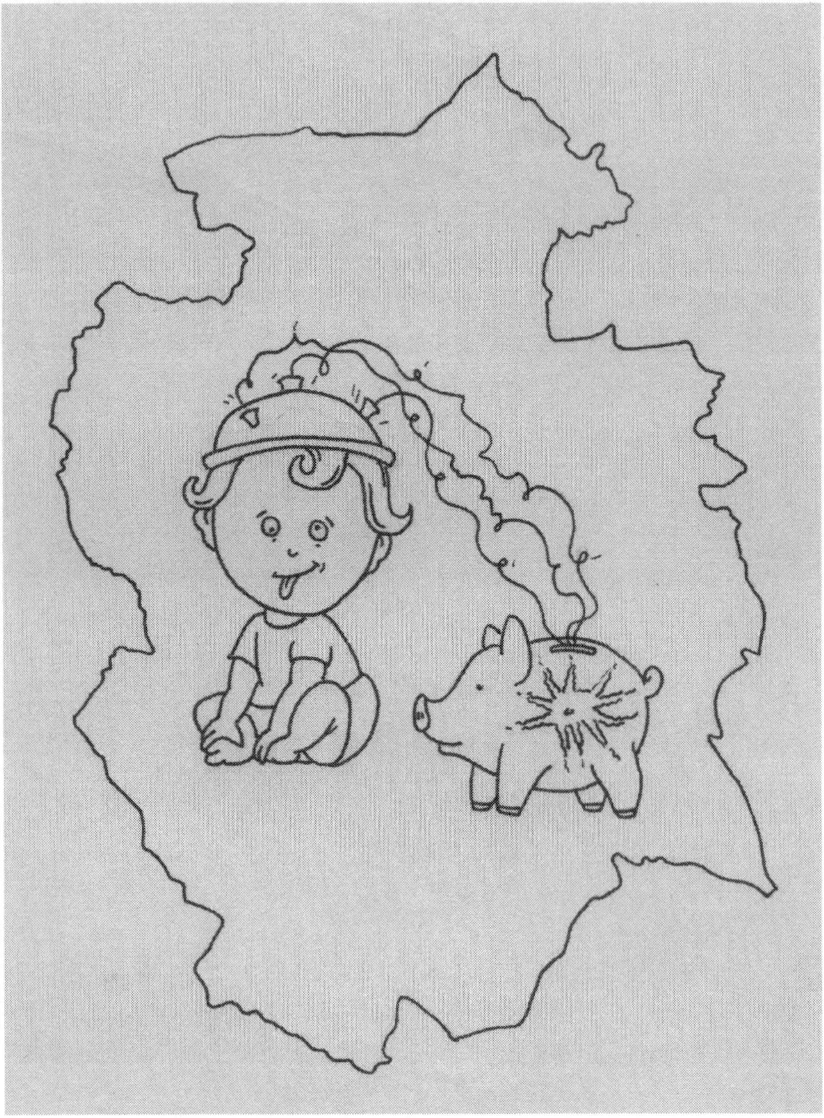

knowledge by stealth. I began as usual telling the sugarannuated brats to shut the frick up in nonsackable terms, then proceeded to compare Mr. Darcy and Elizabeth to Kayne and Kim until someone wrote something in their jotters, if only the words "lame-ass bitch" or "I will hatefist you". I observed that Winston, the most alert member of the class, was slumped over the table like the fourteen others not texting. I asked him to point out an instance of onomatopoeia in a sentence, and he mumbled, "onomasteria?", like I hadn't wedged the word into his superior recall several lessons prior. I moved on to Caitlin Drummond, often bored at the laziness of her peers, who offered: "Is it around the page edges, like in the margins?" This instance of A-student idiocy had me worried.

The next day, I lobbed a question at Winston on the ambivalence of Polonius's motives, expecting a succinct response that summed up with élan the Danish uncle's ineffectual claver. I received a half-mumbled "polo mints?" I then counterlobbed the question toward Caitlin Drummond, who countermumbled "polo nits?" This confirmed that some odd-bodderie was taking place fo'su'.

I called in the parents. Winston's mother turned up in 1970s hairnet, nibbling on her nails with a ferocity unseen minutes since Mrs Dragworth confessed to accidentally beheading her Trevor in a freak Scrabble accident. I told the mother that her son had the potential to scrape himself a conditional offer at Durham University if he persisted in sitting upright and opening his brain to spunkier notions. She nibbled until her nails were shorn in the manner of erose rocks. Her leg had shot up and kicked the desk at the word "brain". "I had to," she said. "There was pressure." She elucidated not. An hour later, Caitlin's father appeared and laid a candid fact on me that still made nothing clearer. "Look, she has brain cells a-begging. There will always be a future for smartiepantsies like her." I observed him puttputting off in a Lotus Evora. Over the weekend I read an article in the *Durham Dalliance*:

BRAIN DRAIN

In these straitened times, it is becoming harder for parents to make ends meet. A new research organisation, Free Cells, is offering £100 per brain cell sold. Using innovative cell extraction techniques, the corporation take the extracted cells and implant them into synthetic brains to research tumours and mental disorders. The initiative has proven popular with parents. George Gravellus, 47, a father of four, said: "I have four sprogs. Not all four will wind up as rocket scientists. So removing a cell here or there from the weaker ones hurts no one." Frances Bean, a single mother, 21, said: "This is a tremendous way of paying for my daughter's college fees." Despite the positive responses from parents, the initiative has attracted criticism. Lorna Bugle, 28, a divorced mother of three, said: "I think there is something quite horrific about incrementally lobotomising one's children. I can't put my finger on what. But I have a feeling." For now, the initiative is thriving. Parents interested in selling their child's brain cells should contact the Free Cells Durham hotline on 01224 347 829.

"Ah," I said.

※

As I expected, the mean intelligence of the worst performing classroom sank to 49 IQ points. The volume of dribble on desks increased by 58%, and there were two more F minus assignments than usual. My role as a teacher changed to one of carer—mopping up the saliva that ran from their mouths when they forgot to close them, coming up with methods of keeping them propped upright at their desks, trying to prevent their heads smashing against the floor if they flopped from their chairs in a semibraindead slump. To solve these issues, I invested in a series of straps, tied their legs, feet, and upper bodies to the seats, preventing all non-arm-based movement, and purchased bibs to absorb the copious saliva. I observed that the kids from poorer backgrounds, in the less able classes, were the ones more likely to have been sentenced to this vegetation by their cash-strapped parents.

I contacted my more upwardly mobile friends with kids. Saskia Mogg, a head teacher, had sold three or four brain cells from her sons to help restore the bathroom, however, she made sure not to "raid their minds like piggybanks". Kellie Groupe, a senior marketing executive, had also extracted only one or two from her sons, "to keep them grounded". My less monied friends had found it easier, under extreme pressure, to sell a considerable proportion of their children's cells. Lorna Cache, a part-time stevedore, saddled with overdue bills and a white wine habit, and had no recourse left except to raid her daughter's cranium for cash. And Melissa Hollbroth, a fiction writer, had been unable to afford four square meals for her son Pete. "To provide my son with a corporeal future, I have to stripmine his mental one," she said. It appeared that a volcanic class fissure was opening up.

Now, as a parent, I believe it is important to provide the best possible future for your children and to act as selfishly as possible in that regard. My own son Brian was struggling to keep up with the smarter kids in his class. He felt average and inferior, poor results were sapping his morale. There was a chance that he might not be permitted into college. It was then I took the action that landed me in here. I arranged a school fête and invited the smartest kids in the school and their parents to attend. I had paid for two Brain Drain operatives to set up their cell-extracting apparatus in my spare room and, over the course of the afternoon, I redirected each child seeking the toilet toward the operation room. The process itself was painless. The operatives hid behind a screen while I served anaesthetic to the kids inside a plastic lemonade cup, having asked them to "sample this new recipe". The sleepiness would come upon them in under ten seconds, at which point the operatives led them to the chair, placed the special extraction headwear on their skulls, and a thin needle would enter the cranium and remove with astonishing accuracy the contracted number of cells, leaving a small un- noticeable hole that would heal in hours. The six children who refused the lemonade, after mild coaxing ("please! I need to test this recipe!"), escaped the extraction procedure.

Once complete, the children returned to the fête in sluggish states, and the parents took their "exhausted" children home, unaware that I had pocketed £52,500 from their forty-seven little brains. In performing this corrective procedure, I had intended to reduce the average score in school exams, forcing the board to lower the pass rates, making Brian one of the smartest non-lobotomised children. As it transpired, I had been overenthusiastic in the removal of the cells, reducing these high- scorers to some of the lowest, failing even to outperform the dribblers in Class 4F. It did not take long for the parents to observe that their uni- bound bright stars had been reduced to barely sentient knuckleheads. After one confrontation in the middle of a lesson (Alice Rodder's mother had called me a "brainrobber"), I thought about fleeing the country. For- tunately, since the cell-extracting business was new, there was no law against selling the cells of other people's children to make extra money.

The *Durham Dalliance* ran this story on their front page, helpfully in- forming people of the opportunity I had seized. Before parliament had time to pass an emergency law, there followed a weekend of frenzied childnapping, with parents prowling the streets, rounding up kids, and taking them to have their brains zapped. Over the course of one week- end, now known as "dawn of the dumb", 85% of Durham's children were rendered completely incapable. This act of brain robbery was, of course, blamed on me, even after I offered to dispense the £52,500 among the bereft parents. I was sent here rather than the clink. I miss Brian every single day. He went to live with his auntie in Aberdeen, poor kid. It later transpired that Free Cells were implanting the cells into the bod- ies of synthetic sex robots and not using them to cure brain tumours. Who could have seen that coming?

[OXFORDSHIRE]

NAME: LACHLAN CHAMP
AGE: 40.5
SENTENCE: 13 YEARS
CRIME: MISPRINT OOPS

I N LAST WEEK'S ISSUE, line twelve of the article 'Tea Shoppe Trend-setters' should have read:

Mrs Wilmot is Oxford's finest maker of novelty teacosies.

We printed in error:

Mrs Wilmot is Oxford's finest maker of Heinrich Himmler action figures.

We apologise for the offence caused.

[From *The Oxonian*, Issue 23, p.69]

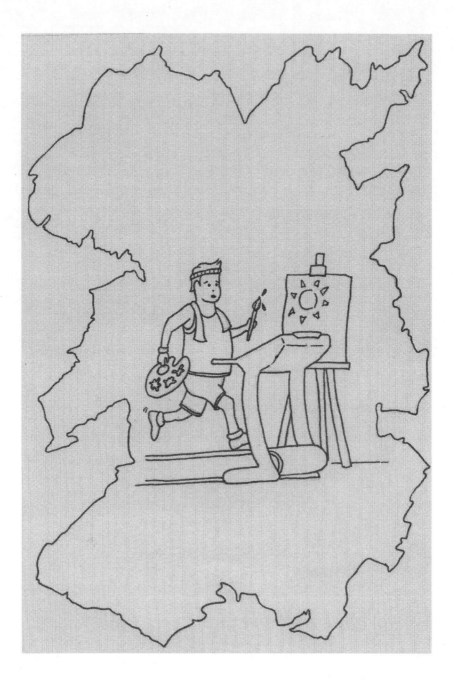

[LEICESTERSHIRE]

NAME: CHIP DUFFLEBAG
AGE: 22
SENTENCE: 14 YEARS
CRIME: SCHEMES FOR ARTISTS

The following were schemes, implemented nationwide, designed to "incentivise" non-tax-paying artists into work. These were devised by the incumbent government. Mr. Dufflebag (who happened to hail from Burton on the Wolds), was chosen as the official scapegoat. —Ed.

Census Apprentices

THE SECRETARY OF STATE for Foreign and Commonwealth Affairs, Jonns Boorish, devised a scheme that would help, in equal measure, with the compilation of the British census, to keep tabs on the numbers of illegal immigrants, and to keep an ear on the British vox populi so the cabinet could tailor their promises for the next election. The scheme was inspired by Bent Hamer's 2003 movie *Kitchen Stories*—a mild satire following a reluctant researcher on male activity in Norwegian kitchens. Mr. Boorish's scheme involved "wallmounting" writers into the top left-hand corners of livingrooms and making them observe a British family unit in the home—taking meticulous notes on their political opinions, the number of people living in each household, and allusions to their criminal activities. The scheme, rolled out in a random Lutterworth neighbourhood, involved four writers "installed" for a week in four separate households to observe and record. A single bed on a wooden pole was placed as unobtrusively as possible in the corner of each livingroom, and the writers sat cross-legged on the beds, notepad in hand, recording, then retired to bed of an evening, having consumed their two complimentary packed lunch meals at set times. In return, the families were compensated £12.98 per day, and had to permit their onlooker permission to use their toilet (when the house was unoccupied). The scheme proved unsuccessful. The families, inhibited at having an intruder in their homes, said nothing and became paranoid at silent judgements (several writers had "tutted" when the inhabitants made political comments), or spent their time fabricating aspects of their lives to mislead the census. The families would scratch their faces with their middle fingers, aiming their lewd digits towards the writers, or make ludicrous pronouncements, such as claiming to support ISIS and Al-Qaeda and the Women's Institute, or make snide allusions to "corner-dwelling sorts" who "were crushing the backbone of this once Great Nation" and so on. The writers, in turn, complained of cramp, and in one case, a man simply presenting his unwiped buttcrack in his eyeline for 48hrs.

Embarrassadorships

The Secretary of State for Digitality, Culturality, The Medias, and Sports, Tham Antcock, devised a scheme to put writers to work promoting Authorised Books on behalf of state-approved Authorised Artists. In an attempt to promote the permitted literature, the writers were sent on promotional activities to teach them the value of labour and working for a collective culture, not a self-serving narcissistic one. Maxwell Emmenthall, a retired professor working on an historical novel set at the Battle of Suomussalmi—a month-long winter skirmish between the Russians and Finns—told from the perspective of a trichomoniasistic lecher, was instructed to hit the high street in a pound sign costume, holding free promos for *Investment Opportunities*, the new informative thriller showing teenagers the smartest techniques for start-up businesses, sponsored by Barclays & Natwest PLCs. And Katie Forker, a science-fiction writer working on a prose hexad exploring the avaricious race of Neptunian arseholes Küumfuûr—a barium-based stand-in for human beings—was made to perform street readings for the new novel showing people the adverse effects of excessive sugar consumption, *Sally's Waistband*, while wearing a sugarcube costume and chanting: "Punch the paunch!" And

Elvis Bricola, a writer of esoteric poems about Loughboroughian folklore, was made to pass around spongified insects on sticks to promote the new novel, *Bug Yum*, an eco-nutritious look at alternatives to meat, while dressed as a scorpion. The scheme proved unsuccessful. The writers frightened the populace with their immature acts. Maxwell set fire to a £10 note in protest against "corporate shitterature", traumatising a five-year-old boy who was looking forward to making his first financial transaction and learning the value of money. Katie Forker brought an obese friend along to assault members of the public with her oversize breasts, on which were tattooed the words "embrace your lard, luvvie", which was not the message the minister wished to communicate regarding the sensible intake of high-sugar foods. And Elvis Bricola placed live ants and millipedes between the pages of the novels, terrifying the readers when they opened their books at home, to see squashed bugs, and have the panicky surviving ants crawling over their bedsheets and naked bodies.

Abling the Dissed

The Secretaries of State for Health and Social Care and Work and Pensions, Tippi Later and David Jijas, observed that private healthcare professionals were not pleased at having to perform the rigorous tests required for the legal refusal of disability living allowance for least able (the unions asking for unrealistic pay increases and mental health assistance, and expensive things like that). As a trial, seven composers of krautrock were sent in to put those claiming "disabilities" through their paces. Popul Vuh devotee Driscoll Estevez was instructed to put Rick Otz, a teacher who had lost his left leg on a WWII landmine while rambling in Chiswick, through the required physical tests to determine if he might receive the £59.86 per week from the state to live on. Rick was asked to demonstrate whether his missing leg made him unable to walk. To prove this, Rick slithered from his wheelchair to the floor and tried to stand on the one remaining leg without the aid of a crutch. Having failed to ascend for three minutes, as Driscoll watched on with a notepad making observations, Rick was assisted to his one leg and asked if he could hop successfully. If Rick could practice hopping in a straight line, then the chair and supporting crutches might be returned to the NHS and passed on to a more vulnerable person. Rick then asked whether Driscoll could perform basic cognitive functions, in spite of his severe depression, intense problems with PTSD, and the frequent horrific flashbacks and breakdowns. Driscoll said that if Rick was in work, he might be permitted moments to recover from these temporary mental lapses, and resume work, if the bosses were willing to allow these brief interruptions in their operations. Upon completion of the tests, Driscoll had to conclude that the man was fit and able for work—a number of sitting posts, or standing ones (where leaning or balancing was possible) were open to him to apply for, and that his disability benefits were not allowed, and that he must attend weekly interviews at the Jobcentre to make sure he had been properly looking for work, otherwise he would lose all financial support. This scheme failed when the composers recommended their able-bodied artist friends for the allowance, and palmed money to unauthorised art-makers.

Roadside Revolt

The Secretary of State for Transport, Adam Cirboni, suggested a scheme to set visual artists to work helping improve Britain's roads. The artists, all sorts of unauthorised ones from conceptual to classicist, were loaned hi-viz vests and rolled onto various trunk roads to perform fruitful functions, each of which failed. The first was to collect rubbish from the sides of the roads. The artists compacted the rubbish into papier-mâché caricatures of famous politicians and posted the pictures on Twitter to humiliate the ministers. The artists were sent to replace the broken bulbs in catseyes. The artists replaced the bulbs with a kaleidoscope of colours to create an epileptic lightshow, intended to cause traffic accidents. The artists were sent to scoop up roadkill. The artists stuffed the deceased animals, mounted them to plyboard plinths, lacquered them in polyurethane, and created an exhibit called 'The Distillation of Automotive Intoxication'. The artists were sent to seal up potholes in the tarmac. The artists "reimagined" the dimensions of a traditional road elevation, uprooting parts of the road to create "surrealist deviations" (humps in the road with painted winking eyes), "subterranean inversions" (concrete stalagmites stretching for up to forty feet), and "flaming inflections" (filling the potholes with petrol so an updraught of flame shot from each). The artists were sent to assist motorists in trouble on the roads. The artists blasted the motorists with their anti-automotive manifestoes, encouraged the drivers to plant a tree through their cars instead, and recruited them for their roadside communes. The artists were sent to help mop up the blood after crashes. The artists created powerful installations pointing to the blood and skin of the dead, with a neon sign flashing "Is This What We've Become?" The scheme was soon scrapped for obvious reasons.

Human Hankies

The Secretary of State for Business, Energy, and Industrial Strategy, Kerr Clegg, noticed that the number of preventable deaths in businesses nationwide was increasing (including in several hundred companies that donated to the government) so a scheme was summoned up to set librettists to work helping the populace overcome the loss of their loved ones at minimal legal expense. If the loved one was lost in an industrial accident, a special "grieving coach" was assigned to monitor the bereaved and reassure them that the best solution was to weep as much as possible, to explore their tears and sadness, and remember the best bits of their lost loved one. The plan was to encourage them to weep and focus on sorrow, rather than rehashing the events of the death and taking up legal arms. The librettists would console the grievers, lending their shoulders as human handkerchiefs for the bereaved to blubber on, and mutter consoling words like "he/she was a brilliant woman/man", or "your love for him/her was immense", and so on. The scheme was successful. The librettists wrote incendiary, wry, and touching operas about the process, and lobbied hard for the families to receive compensation. However, since the public interest in opera was nonexistent, and those attending operas tended to vote Conservative, no impact was made. The scheme was expanded to incorporate "political weeping", where the electorate were told to "free their sadness" if unpopular legislation was passed, or a vote was not in their favour, rather than march up and down the streets making a lot of racket and signing useless petitions. The librettists would commonly lend their shoulders to soak up the tears of idealistic young people who expected courage and maturity and bravery from their politicians, in place of the familiar kowtowing to oligarchs that was standard practice.

Back to School

The Secretary of State for Education, Mandi Hadins, looked at a piece of paper and noticed that pass rates were slipping in a downward direction in schools. She read the piece of paper three times and saw that "pass rates" referred to examinations and not inappropriate teacher-pupil come-ons (that rate remained at a respectable median). To help underperforming children, it was suggested that writers might act as big brothers or sisters to keep them focussed during lessons and steer them towards basic competence. The lowest performing children were then allotted a writer to help them through their lessons, sitting beside them in classrooms, chumming them along to exams, and so on. It worked thus: Isobel McVie, 12, was unable to think up a use of assonance in a sentence. The writer Nadine Plover stepped in and said 'deep in the leaves of green'. David Shorter, 13, was unable to come up with a character for his creative writing piece. The writer Cal Valence stepped in and created a gravedigger with eczema and wheat issues. The scheme was swiftly misused by many pupils who relied on their big brothers or sisters in place of extracting thoughts from their own prehensile skulls, and the underperforming children stopped attending school entirely, relying on their benefactors to yield them the results. The big brothers or sisters had to sit in class in place of their children and sit the exams for them to help the pass rates soar (although the pass rates in maths, science, and PE actually dipped under this scheme), and the children who received basic passes complained to their parents who complained to the schools who complained to the government who told them to stop moaning. The big brothers and sisters were reprimanded and told to knuckle down harder for their kids. The scheme failed when several writers started bullying younger pupils, and found themselves expelled from schools at which they were never formally registered.

The Professor of Unliterature

The writer Dennis Oakface was elected to the prestigious post of Professor of Unliterature. He had been working as a playgroup assistant when he received a phone call from the culture secretary, Bam Rudder, who asked him to take over at the University of Leicester as the Head of English. He was introduced to the extremely tall and crazy university buildings, and took over from the last man, Name Redacted, who was fired for being too brainy about books, and having a stupid name. His first task was to select a syllabus of texts that were totally inclusive and unpretentious and darn fine reading, and to pooh-pooh the sort of uppity literature that was making children and adults and the elderly loathe books. The scheme was intended to force the next generation of writers into appreciating the value of commercial literature that people actually wanted to read, and to swiftly phase out the sort of abstruse, inaccessible stuff that people with PhDs read to make themselves feel superior, and to herald in a new era of money-making cashflowing literature, and finally crush those lurching around wasting society's time writing on benefits their pseudo-intellectual bullshit that brings nothing to the country's coffers, which is the most important and essential thing that literature absolutely has to do, without question, and everyone everywhere agrees, so there, shove that in your pipe.

[CAMBRIDGESHIRE]

NAME: TIM

AGE: 28

SENTENCE: 35 HOURS

CRIME: TURD ON MINGLE LANE

TIM WANTED TO KILL HIMSELF because he considered the world a barbaric, cruel and pointless place. Then he mused for a minim. He realised his suicide would simply reinforce his notion of the world as a cruel and barbaric place, deepening the truth of this for his remaining family, leading to potential copycat suicides. So he chose not to kill himself but to kill people who caused universal misery instead. At first he went to Uganda where he shot the psychopathic torturer and child abuser Joseph Kony. Next he went to Zimbabwe where he shot the psychopathic torturer and child abuser Robert Mugabe. He travelled around Africa killing all the zealous maniacs known for their murder and enslavement.

When he returned to Cambridge he expected to be treated as a folk hero. Instead, people were saddened he had turned into a psychopathic murderer simply to brighten up the world by removing all the psychopathic murders—he had become the very thing that made the world so barbaric, cruel and pointless. Depression returned. He longed to commit suicide again. His family soon cast him out of their home for reasons of fear and disappointment, so it seemed easier to carry out his task. However, it dawned on him the shame of having a genocidal suicide as a son was so appalling it would be easier to kill his family now, and spare them the humiliation of having this brute in their brood.

He slaughtered his family, reluctantly, on the Monday, planning to commit suicide on the Tuesday. As it happened, he became accustomed to the peace and isolation outside the family home and relished not having to answer to anyone, especially his haughty mum, so he postponed this until the Friday. His happiness having exponentially increased at his family's demise, he felt increasingly guilty and decided, happiness aside, to do the honourable thing and commit suicide as planned. But his life had become too precious and exciting and flooded with meaning to bring it to a blunt conclusion. He decided the best thing was to remove himself from Cambridge and live in exile, in an African country like Uganda, where he could set himself up as a dictator. If he became a legitimate tyrant, this would excuse his delight at his family's murder, so he did. His first policy was to slaughter all children under five and to poke out the eyes of Christians or anyone passing. He returned to Cambridge on Wednesdays to walk the dog, where Mrs. Bridgeford caught him leaving an unfortunate turd on Mingle Lane.

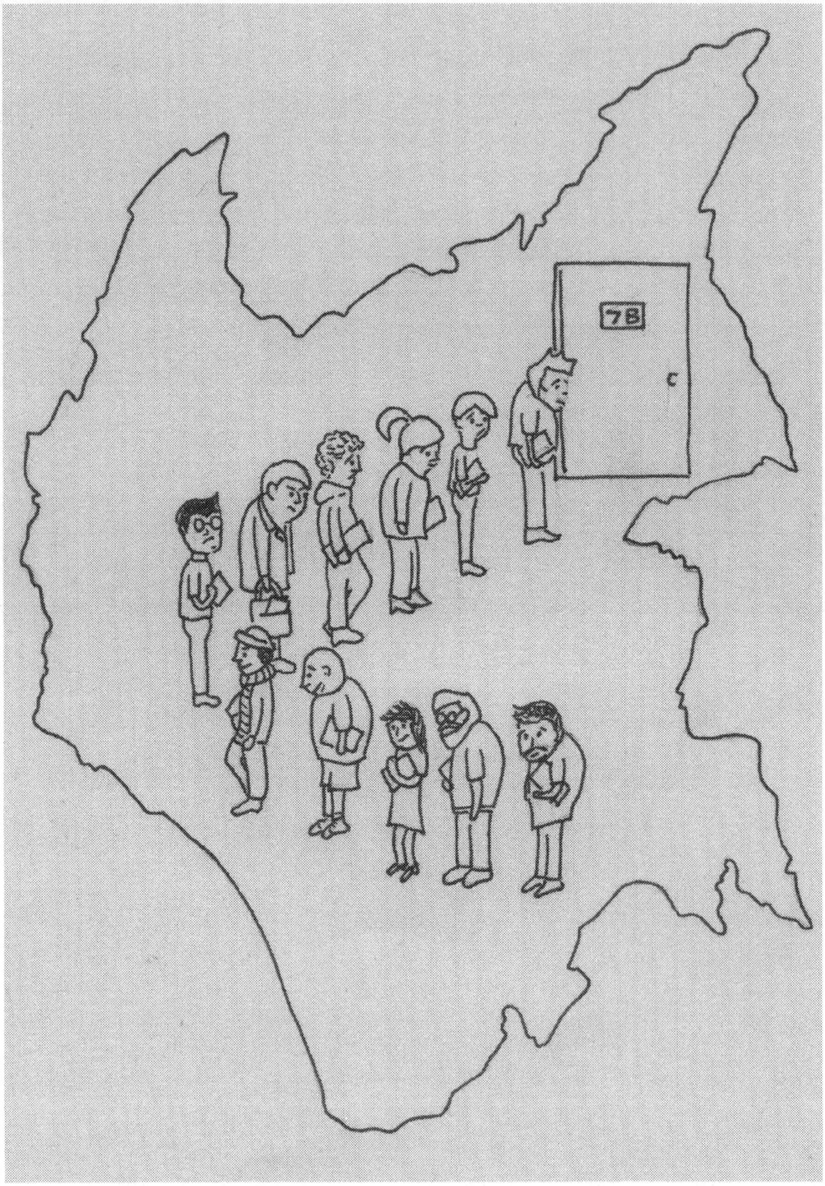
7B

[SHROPSHIRE]

NAME: SIMONE SLAPH
AGE: 30
SENTENCE: 8 YEARS
CRIME: SOUL FOR HOT PISS

S IMONE SLAPH was made an Authorised Shropshire Artist the night her mother placed an oversize walnut into her mouth and choked. Her initial thought was: "That's novel two sorted." Then she mentally walloped herself around the mind with a mallet and thought: "And the memoir after." Then she cerebrally clobbered herself around the cerebrum with a club and thought: "How horrible for her." The walnut had been tweezered between her mother's thumb and index as a man was unfurling an anecdote of such violent hilarity no snackfoods would have triumphed over the violent onrush of laughs that followed. The walnut, sinking into her mother's mouth, awaiting that crucial first crunch, was halted by a sudden spurt of hilarity that sucked the terminal unchewed nut into her throat, lodging itself in the correct killing position. The roomwide chuckleswirl meant that a minute had passed before anyone observed her mother at the point of choking, and the ensuing awareness and reaction time of the person choking, having been delayed, meant the Heimlich manoeuvre could not be performed in time to stop the nefarious nut killing her by remaining horrifically wedged in the windpipe. Simone had been waiting to announce that her first novel, *Love Among Bedwetters*, had earned her Authorised Artist status, and that two publishers had placed the novel on their to-skim piles. Her fourth thought, recalling times her mother had missed her baptism, graduation, wedding, and the funeral of her first husband, was: "How typical of her to miss another precious moment."

✳

Appointment to the status of Authorised Shropshire Artist involved attending a formal meeting in Room 7B of the Council Offices with Erin Blackwater and Crispin Trim. Once Simone had buried her mother, she biked to her appointment with brio, keen to break into a bright future of having several readers of her novel about bedwetting adults kissing on damp duvets. The seventh floor, 'Culture', had a sorry corridor of muddy footprint treads, scrawled messages on the walls ('LIMPDICKED LOSERS', 'SOFTCOCKED SODS', 'FLACCID-MEMBERED NONRISKTAKERS', and the like), and subfusc lighting. Simone peered into the other offices—7F 'Music', in which a shirtless hunk posed with a telecaster; 7E 'Arts & Crafts', in which a swathe of spinsters held up their doily tapestry of Clackmannan; 7D 'Acting', in which a topless actress had her breasts measured and weighed for screen presentation; 7C 'Publishing', in which two people sat with their heads on the desks surrounded by empty bottles—and tapped on 7B. A sustained rasping noise was audible from 7A, building to a weird bronchitic shriek. "Simone! Hi! I am Erin Blackwater!" Erin Blackwater said, not heeding the shriek. She was a broad-shouldered sack of smiles, a relic from a time when print-runs were in triple figures, the word "author" was not aligned with "waster", and book launches were not picketed by furious taxpayers.

"First, some agonising truths," she said when Simone was on a seat. "The woman on the street resents funding culture. Her fingers clench into a lock of hate when a painter receives £2K to paint a challenging memorable image that might be perceived as 'art'. So pressures have meant that we have to keep the material we endorse as pedestrian as possible. This is Crispin Tim," she said. Crispin Tim had a pair of tortoiseshell specs and unwashed blonde hair, one half arthouse rebel, one half windbeaten administrator. His words were leaden soup.

"Thanks, Erin," Crispin said. "Yes, our fiction releases must represent the things to which people can 'relate', or contain the preapproved tropes that people have assimilated into their understanding of novels. The word 'literary' has been replaced with 'easypleasy' by the council.

Your novel would be published as part of this 'easypleasy' range. You tick most of the boxes. You raise an issue that is not much spoken about in the media. You have a strong loveable relatable female character. You have a love story set against a backdrop of social change that is very 'now'. You shouldn't struggle to publish this."

"Excellent!" Simone beamed.

"Yes. However, there are some things expected of you."

"Oh?"

✳

Simone left the meeting in a fist of dubiety, unsure whether she might become a public spokeswoman for bedwetting. Her novel *Love Among Bedwetters* showed the love-fumbles of two adult bedwetters: the humiliations and embarrassments of post-coital sheet-pissing in a superficial romantic world. If her novel was to be published, she would need to appear on stage at events, speaking with earnestness on the topic of adult bedwetting as a form of unofficial ambassador for those with the unfortunate disorder. She would then have two options based on the reception of her novel: write more works on bedwetters, and earn a reputation as "that bedwetting author", or choose another topic, such as thumbsucking or hairchewing, and become known as someone who writes whimsical novels on infantile conditions.

"Sadly, as an Authorised Author, you must be assigned a niche," Erin had said. "Once you become known for one thing, you have to work your niche. There is no other choice. Most writers expect wiggle room to experiment with other ideas. That freedom no longer exists. You become known for one thing or nothing. Your whole future as a writer of easypleasy fiction in terms of sales and recognition relies on people knowing that one thing. You have to ask yourself whether you wish to be known as that bedwetting author."

Simone placed this potential future in her mental microwave, and set the timer to six hours. She allowed the pluses and minuses to pop around her neural hotplate—the pluses: recognition for her writing and ideas, having a readership and making a small income; the minuses, having bedwetting attached to her name forever, and having strangers think she is a bedwetter, and having to talk about bedwetting with a straight face forever in public. A sweltering heat overcame her thinking until the inevitable ping of decision.

※

Simone placed the carnations on her mother's grave and another walnut on the headstone, totalling six now, although the squirrels had long eaten the other five. "Well," she said to the dead person, "I have another novel out soon, *Bedwetters in Borstal*. Yes, mother, it's a novel about prisoners who piss themselves. I can see that wrinkle of disapproval forming on your probably already fully-rotted-by-now skull. I had a choice: work a niche, or perish. I had already written the bedwetting book thinking that people might find the topic amusing and that I could move on to something more substantial. But tomorrow, I'm visiting a bunch of bedwetters in Aberystwyth who were profoundly affected by my sensitive and witty novels, so that's something. People on the internet still tinker images of me to show my lower half wet with piss, and there are some immature snickers from children and adult children when I walk into certain rooms. And I have no chance to develop any other ideas apart from this one that is already fizzling out and selling poorly. But hey, I 'made it' as a writer, so that's a source of pride, right? Mother, I can see you making that simpering expression on the mouldy hole where your lips once were. And you'd be correct. I'm neither happy nor miserable about the whole thing. I'm simply numb and bored. And willing to admit now that pursuing this path in my life was a fairly obvious mistake. Please refrain from making that knowing expression on your calcified wormy former face. I'll see you in a month. Yes, I will call the recruitment office."

[NORTHAMPTONSHIRE]

NAME: CAROL OHM
AGE: 37
SENTENCE: 23 YEARS
CRIME: THE BEASTLINESS OF CAROL OHM

PART ONE: REUNION

ON A THERMAL NIGHT AROUND TEN PAST TEN Carol swaddled her firstborn in a bath towel and laid him on a step outside Flick-Picks video shop. A screening of Françoise Truffaut's *La Nuit américaine* was taking place inside and up to four people had arrived for the event. The salival softening of popcorn and hushed swallowing was the only perceivable sound, inaudible beneath the film's frenetic franco dialogue. Having abandoned her firstborn and taken one hundred footsteps towards the bridge, she braved a crossing as the panic buckled her knees and rendered her incapable of walking or breathing. She staggered back to the video shop to find her firstborn and bath towel gone. Interrupting Truffaut: "Where is he? Where's my son?" David, bulbous with surprise: "What? You have a son? I never knew you were pregnant." Carol: "Give him back to me, you psycho, or I will outright fucking murder you." The unwanted firstborn had been taken and remained untraceable for the following five years.

Her brother Bill was teaching a class on strategic Twitter-bombing as part of his marketing broadsweep programme for the Media Studies MA at Canberra University when he received an SOS text from his mother: YR SIS ND HLP. CM PLS. Reluctant to interrupt his teaching duties (feet up on desk reading Houellebecq), she had used the same all-caps telegramese as when his father had passed: YR FTHR HD HRT ATTCK. DID NT SRVVE. PLS CM HM. Carol had been in a state

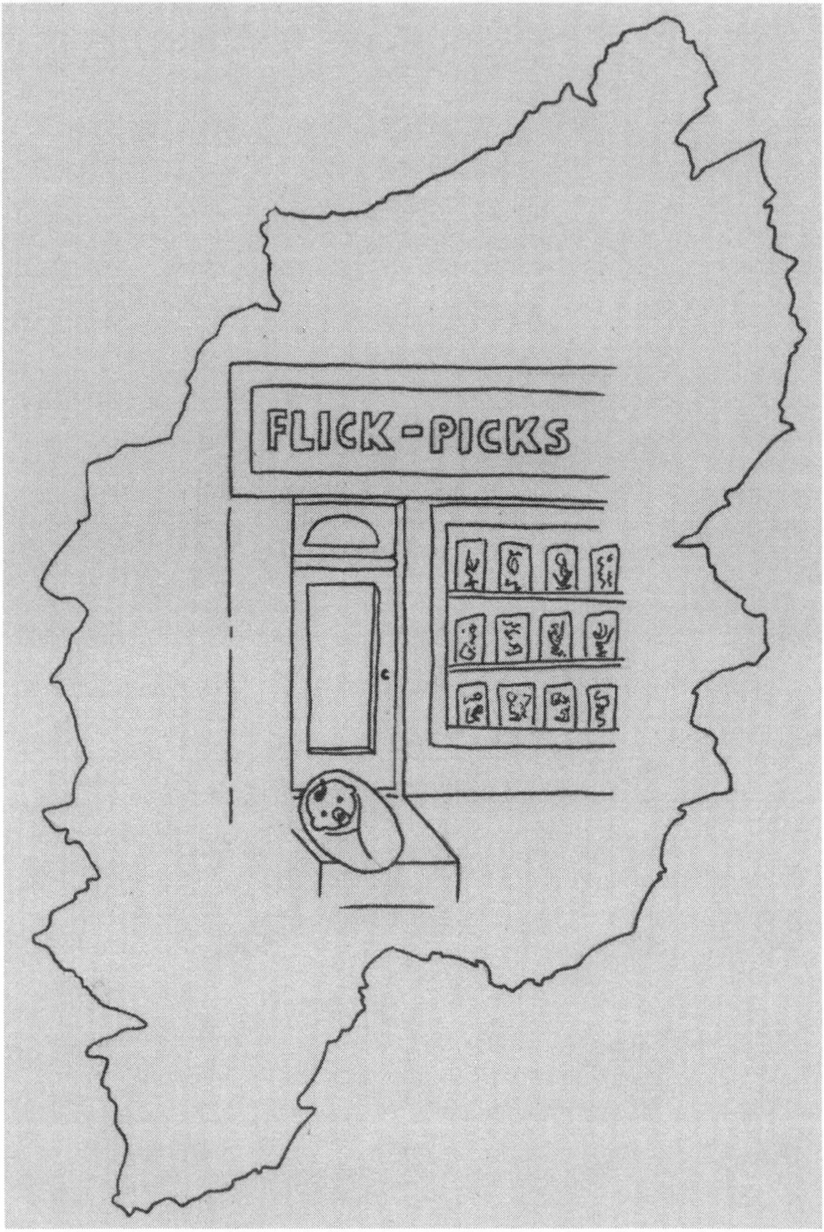
FLICK-PICKS

of post-traumatic shock since losing her son, subsiding on a diet of citalopram, vodkatinis, Lion bars, and Natrasleep, attending public roundtable mope-and-grope sessions where she discussed the various short-lived suitors that squirmed under her sheets and the ghost babies that visited her in the night with their sobbing faces and spumes of sick. The maternal text was a plea that he might return and help drag her daughter from the metaphorical ledge upon which she was dangling (and the literal: she had moved into a former tailor's cottage in Desborough that was sinking into the River Nene).

Bill left his condo in Canberra and the class of cooing co-eds burning love poems into his fragile heart, and returned to the market town of Desborough whence he was whelped. He had binned his childhood friends to forge a sham living in the land of mid-summer winters and bouncing bandicoots, and from his condo viewed their woebegone Facebook photos: freezing in their shorts at rain-logged football matches, holding their plump offspring to the camera, posing in seven inches of slap in nightclubs, each status ribboned with Martian lolspeak and childish emoticons, bearing no emotion or sentience whatsoever. Sometimes the faces vanished into football insignias, as if their fanatical and pedestrian attachment to The Game had absorbed their personalities *in toto*, leaving little left except a sequence of short-wearing ball-kicking kid-squeezing nobodies from the sad and trivial past.

He hadn't spoken to his sister since the loss. Her intolerable drama and dependence on his stable and yielding heart had been one of his prime reasons for buggering off. Apart from the mutual exchange of platitudes in Xmas cards (spiked with the usual barbs—"hope the shrimp are simply *delish* this year", "have a GREAT Xmas on the beach") and his mother's telephone updates on which local sucker she had bumped and dumped this time, what medications had misfired this month, and her latest sexually provocative anti-Labour tattoos. He respected her through fraternal obligation, hoping for the sake of the bloodline she might find an end to her torments, though his resentment was too strong to permit real concern. Their relationship had been antagonistic from the beginning. She had hogged the parental limelight, nudging him aside with dismissive remarks on his dim-witted nature (he had been smarter and more talented), his revolting face (he had been handsome from age seven up), and his dependence on her love (he had never loved or depended on her for anything).

In the absence of an upper hand, she used her working-class local-girl status as a bludgeon. She claimed to pride herself on being "Desborough born and bred" (no sane person would use this as a boast), and default defended all Desboroughers in spite of their long and impressive list of idiocies. She had supported a purse-snatcher, citing his skill at algebra in school as a testament to his character, a serial groper (his well-turned-out appearance); a heroin addict/robber (his persistence at pursuing his passions); a neo-nazi convicted of a double murder (his careful planning and moral convictions). There was no dodgy Desborougher she wouldn't leap to defend.

Bill returned on November 28th, in a mood unimproved by Weezer on the iPod. Apart from the repainted post office and the pawn shop's expansion (a self-checkout corner had been installed where a computer would scan and value the pawned tat), the village was the same as in 2009. An unexploded bomb had taken out the optometrist's office in 1987—this had been the last change to its infrastructure since the war. He walked along the pavement where strips of moss burst through the slabs, and performed his childhood ritual of remaining within each paving slab and never letting the moss touch his shoe. Bob the barber offered the same nod and question: "How's your mother?" Bill blinked. "I haven't been here in over five years." Bob nodded in response and asked after her, even though she lived four minutes away.

Carol resided in a building with an expelled member of the Desborough Advanced Knitting Circle, whose revenge tapestries hung from her windows bearing the message SOD YOU ANNE AND LESLEY; Vice President of the Depressed Teddies and Assorted Moping Mascots

Club, whose suicidal koalas and pandas sat in the kitchen and bathroom windows clutching razors and knives; lead singer in a Blonde Redhead tribute band, whose rendition of 'The Dress' earned a round of applause at the YMCA; and a balding late-middle-aged man who cleared his throat over two hundred times an hour and masturbated to episodes of the sitcom *New Girl* with an abstracted and melancholic air. She buzzed him indoors and appeared with a headdress made of barbed wire around her beehive coif. Her outfit aimed to provoke: she had a T-shirt reading I ATE MADELINE MCCANN, sported tats of violent executions and murders, and wore barbed wire necklaces on her wrists, drawing trickles of blood down her arms. Her first words: "What's the shrimp like down under, mate?" She flopped on the couch and plunged a heroin-filled needle into her arm. Bill said: "Hello, Carol." She replied: "Do your pet bandicoots disapprove of recreational drug use?" Bill said: "If I ever see a bandicoot, I'll be sure and ask him." Carol vanished into her pleasure cloud.

He returned twelve hours later.

Their first face-to-face conversation in half a decade encompassed her new fondness for German thrash metal bands The Bremen Bukaki Boys and Thongclamp; her selection of Cthulhu back tats; her assorted nipple and lip rings and the volume of her screams during the perforation procedure; and her fondness for porridge oats. An hour later she opened the file of recriminations, accusing him of hogging the rubber duckie during their infant baths, spooning overmuch mash at Xmas dinners, and overshadowing her Kylie Minogue karaoke by reading P.G. Wodehouse in the corner. She was explosive on the topic of her lost child, flinging a cup at his head after the first insinuation. He suspected not-knowing to be the root of her berserk behaviour—had an infant corpse presented itself she might have taken the sacraments and signed up for membership of the Desborough Advanced Knitting Circle—so planned to stop in later at the library (pared down to two bookshelves and a computer) to conduct research on the thin but relevant history of infant losses down the decades.

"Sister! Might we attempt a civil confab for our third meet?"

"How're the dingos?"

"Humorous!"

"I was being civil. You poked a vinegar-soaked stick into open wounds."

"Mother sent me here. I can't have the death of a sister on my conscience."

"You have a conscience now?"

"Tell me the real reason for this lunacy."

"Listen, my roo-riding brother, I am beyond saving. You can't help a woman chained to a starving sabretooth."

"And you can't say why?"

"It's a matter for me to ponder in the pits of Hades."

"Christ. Overegging much?"

"Nope."

"I will endeavour to find out."

"Don't tell mother, ever."

"You making me swear to that?"

"Yes. Even if I die."

"Please don't die."

"I can't swear to that."

PART TWO: A PSYCHOGEOGRAPHICAL RAMBLE IN EXPLORATION OF LOST PARENTAGE

The Desborough Inn

The three fathers: Tom Green (59), who in 1977 during the minor cultural eruption (a Slits tribute band performed two numbers in someone's garage before the police arrived and put an end to punk), conceived a child with a Catholic girl whose morals had fled when she saw a picture of Sid Vicious. One night the kid was left in an ice-cream truck during an all-night Teenage Jesus & The Jerks marathon, and had disappeared the next morning. Gerald Harper (39), who in 1997 during the minor Britpop eruption (a Pulp tribute band had performed on the grass outside someone's house before Furious Freddie arrived with his rottweiler and ate Jarvill Cocksure's blazer), conceived a child with a girl terminally indifferent to the direction her life was heading, up until the point she realised she was pregnant and this was not the direction in which she wanted her life to head. The child went missing after being left on the bench outside Darling's Chippie. Ian Kirk (19), who in 2013 asked a girl he liked up to his room and impregnated her. The child vanished from its mother's arms as she slept.

All three mothers had left Desborough soon after to eke out lives of regret and recrimination and vermouth, while the fathers had remained to eke out lives of bewilderment and vagueness and lager. Bill brought the fathers together in the pub and after four pints of bitter suggested an exploration around the sites of their respective losses, and a deeper excavation of the region's missing infants in history, with the hope that some detective work might unearth a pattern around these disappearances. He sketched a walking route around the town and the three fathers agreed to meet on Sunday.

Desborough Close—The Stone

"I left school aged sixteen to sell paperclips in Troon. I went door to door asking semi-comatose housewives in their dressing gowns if they wanted to purchase high-grip paperclips to bind their documents or favoured the bendier plastic to twist into all kinds of exciting curves and straight lines. No wonder I longed to dress in cut-offs, sprout a mohican and tell Ted Heath to go fuck his sister."

The Slits tribute band had performed at 3 Desborough Close in Simon Quinn's father's garage. Gina Marsh dressed as Ari Up and Fiona Bright as Viv Albertine, while two lads in drag provided the bass and drum support. Tom and the nine others tried thrashing to the various semi-reggae and jangle guitar numbers, finding relief when the band covered 'God Save the Queen' and brought the bite of punk. The house was now owned by Paula Dunne, a schoolteacher who lived for her cheese and nibble evenings at the Castle Hotel, whose Nissan sitting in her whitewashed garage hid the one remnant of that evening—a large dent caused by Gina swinging her guitar and cracking the wall's cavities. The dent had been re-filled several times and an unsmoothed cloud of Polyfilla was still visible.

The walk wound along Desborough Close, past the prefab houses with their council-splashed cream licks of late and their reverse-louvre windows that permitted rain and refused air. The stone-chip facades had lost ten percent of their stones, and new stones had been added during the repainting process to combine an off-puke colour scheme, a depressing aesthetic throwback to the seventies, and random stones plastered to the walls for kids to break their skulls on. The street curled round in the shape of a policeman's helmet, prior host to large bulb of grass on which the kids amused themselves, now a car park crammed with Mum's Ford and Dad's Nissan and Eldest Son's Skoda. Behind these houses, the large pitch for football matches and Desborough gatherings, including the fair and the gala day, had become water- and bog-logged. At the centre, a sump of mud had formed into which people flung their unwanted furniture and deceased pets. In the rainiest season, cabinets, chair legs, cat paws, and hamster heads could be seen bobbing about the sump that became a swamp.

Gregor the Ice Cream Man used to park overnight on the grass if business was to be resumed in the morning. Ian's girl had left her unwanted child there, placing the swaddled bundle beneath the milk lollies and, having failed to tell Ian she was pregnant up until her panicked change-of-mind and frenzied run back to the van, left him no chance to rescue his never-seen son after the never-seen birth or before the never-seen theft. The local priest Father Him (short for Himm) insisted that women shouldn't spoil young men's promising careers with their pregnancies, and to raise the children themselves until the fathers had a stable income, at which point the father might offer to support the children (but also reserved the right to refuse help due to the girl's looseness in the first place). Father Him had held the moral reins for over six decades, and had died in 2013 aged 93. A swift funeral followed. At the end of the pitch was a large rock with the misleading local moniker The Stone.

"Lovers used to carve their names into The Stone with a hammer and chisel. We should be on there somewhere," Tom said. Bill and Ian checked The Stone while the others fiddled with their phones (promises of beer and lunch were all that kept them), finding a well-chiselled if faded TOM & ANNA. Beneath, someone had chiselled VANTOS and underlined. "Who the fuck is Vantos?" Tom asked. "Might be that van rental place," Ian said while zapping space-weasels on his latest app. "That's Van-Tows," Tom corrected. "So-called because the owner ran over some dude's toes and thought that providing a towing service might increase his revenue and help the compensation payments." Other theories were that two lovers had mashed-up their names to save time and effort chiselling—Vandross and Tossle? Vanuatu and Toshiba?—or that the names were a mash-up of their initials.

The Stone—Darling's Chippie

"I had embarked on a nightclub romance with a coke-keen tearaway named Pauline Gert (most of the Pulp-cult had been Gert-stuffed), who intended to complete her HND in Ethical Hacking despite the drug love. She came from Troon, so viewed herself as the upper-class equivalent to me as in the song 'Common People.' We would visit supermarkets and she would pretend to be poor, laugh, and then try to fuck me on the sprouts."

The group headed for High Street where the shops were, passing into Lower Street—an interzone that had been burned down in a wartime Bonfire Night prank (one ex-soldier added several blocks of

TNT to aid ignition and one hundred were incinerated). A complex network of weeds had overgrown the old tributes and flowers. A sign read *Please do not litter. Be respectful of the dead.* This did nothing to prevent teens from hurling crisp packets and Monster cans into the weeds, or from urinating on the memorials after nights out. The interzone also acted as a venue for street brawls and various neighbourly duels. Criminals used the space to deposit their weapons or the intended recipients of their bullets. Two corpses had been found in the weeds, one from a gangland whacking in Sutton Bassett, another from a local firm that operated in a boarding house for two weeks before the owner turfed them. (She ate a bullet and her corpse was dumped in the weeds).

The Pulp covers were performed in a flat above the Co-Op, with Gerald's friend Mark as Jarvill Cocksure, and three people from school he never spoke to as the other members. The setlist comprised material from *Different Class* until Furious Freddie and his equally unpleased rottweiler arrived to cap the encore. Gerald dived with Gert into the bedroom as the dog feasted on Jarvill, where they had swift and painful sex on the loo cistern. Gert had her child and left the bundle on a bench outside Darling's Chippie. Quite why a bench had been placed facing the chip shop was a matter for debate—few people in life liked to watch drunks queuing up for battered fish and chips—but the bench was used for eating and drunks slept there after forcing down their food and depositing the upchuck on the pavement beside. Gerald had carved their names into the bench with a pen. He checked again. GER & GERT 4 EVER, and below again VANTOS. "Fucking hell—Vantos again!" Tom said.

Bill bought the lads fish suppers and speculated on the nature of Vantos. He was surprised that no one had noticed these carvings. The lads explained that they had jobs (except Ian who had been weighing his options since leaving school and concentrating on his game-playing) and didn't have time to inspect stones and benches. The owner of the chippie, Dick Darling (a name that had earned him derision and mockery from the youngsters, to which he responded by threatening to fuck off—after that they referred to him as Sir Dick), had seen the name Vantos carved onto the bench. "I seen that name carved onto the bench," he said, adding: "Is there anything else you wanted to order?" Bill blinked. "No." Dick made a motion that he fuck off out the door in that case and he'd have their custom again he hoped.

The last of the lads to lose their child was Ian. The loss had been welcomed by his girl Cass and himself (Cass sought to concentrate on her career in the sportswear industry). Their kid had disappeared from Cass's arms as she slept in his bedroom. A quick check behind Ian's bed revealed the word VANTOS.

PART THREE: BACKSTORY

On a thermal night around ten past ten Carol swaddled her firstborn in a bath towel and laid him on a step outside Flick-Picks video shop. A VANTOS operative in civvies arrived a moment later, scooping up the bundle and laying him in a pre-prepared crib in the back of a Transit van. He drove away after scoping the streets for witnesses or onlookers, leaving Carol alone where she lost her nerve and made a scene with the father in the video shop. The next morning she met the VANTOS operative as agreed at the rendezvous point (a disused café) and quizzed him on the fate of her discarded kid.

"Goes to Azerbaijan. Or Kabul."

"To do what?"

"Put into foster homes. Learns, erm . . . becomes a Muslim."

"Safe?"

"Yeah."

To bring her in some ill-perceived way closer to her son, she applied with success for a post in the VANTOS organisation. Their purpose was to remove for a fee unwanted children from doorsteps, having been instructed where to collect the bundle by the abandoner, and rehouse them in safe untraceable locations (removing chance of reunions

or last-minute regrets). Having struggled with her conscience, not want-
ing a soul to know (accusing the father to avert suspicion), she decided
that she shared a deep empathy with indecisive mothers, those forced to
have their babies (either through religious beliefs or leaving it too late
to abort), ones left by the fathers, or those unable or unwilling to raise
them. She helped with the administration and practical care aspect, helping keep the babies fed and watered before being shipped abroad. She
worked at the North Northampton office, where the "abducted" children in her area were stored before being flown overseas to their new
homes in Asian countries.

After nine months working at VANTOS, Carol fell for shipping
clerk Adams Grantham. She was attracted to his insouciant manner, native Northumbrian banter, and beautiful thick lips where she found a
new home inside the beaming folds of his soothing smile. She began an
erotic odyssey, helping her to forget the ever-nagging dismissal of her
unwanted child the year before, making love on desks, mantelpieces,
and ping-pong tables, until the passion cooled and she felt comfortable
in the arms of her Anglo-Saxon lover enough to impart her secret. He
reacted in horror. "My God, how could you do that to your own child?"
he asked. "What do you mean?" Carol snapped. "You know where they
send them, don't you? They are sold into slavery in child labour camps,
as workers or helpers, and treated as expendable." Carol was stunned.
"No. I was told they are rehoused with wealthy families. Given a fresh
start." Adams was silent for an unacceptable period. "And you really
believe that?"

Carol poked her nose a little deeper into the firm's paperwork. She
was unable to consult her son's shipping documents, as information was
not retained past two weeks per child in case the parents tried to track
their kids or police sniffed round. She opened strangers' files, read the
names and addresses of the new parents. Names such as Mr. & Mrs Jung-
Il or Mr. & Mrs. Eun-Jin appeared, although the locations seemed sus-
picious, e.g. 2 New Harbour (Street), or Old District (Street)—"street"

appeared to have been added in brackets in order to present a false image of security. A quick look on Google revealed these places to be on the outskirts of town, nowhere near the cosier suburbs as advertised, but warehouses blurred from Google street view, so more likely to be places where sold tots worked to make trainers and toys for western kids on a diet of rice and water for sixteen hours per day.

She took to vodka. One day, sneaking into her boss's office while he was out to lunch, she logged onto his computer, accessing a spreadsheet that contained the name, precise location, and year of abduction for every client. She knew a police confession was a death sentence, the firm having strong connections in organised crime syndicates at home and abroad, so she took to staggering around the town drunk, carving the company name at the abduction spots in the hope someone might do the detective work. A local cycling enthusiast, Rim Overs, eventually stitched the truth together using his mind.

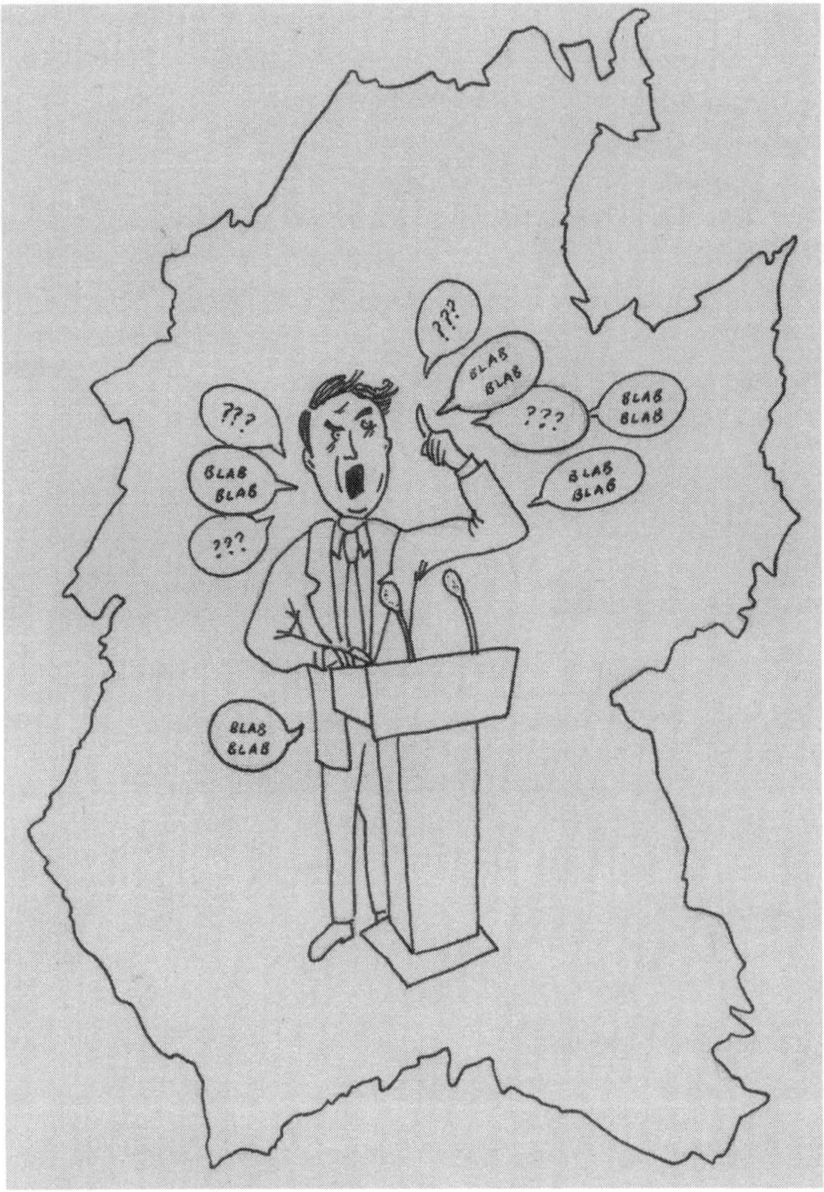
???
BLAB BLAB
???
BLAB BLAB
???
BLAB BLAB
???
BLAB BLAB
BLAB BLAB

[WILTSHIRE]

NAME: CROCUS NIGHTSHADE M.P.
AGE: 48
SENTENCE: 25.5 YEARS
CRIME: BLABBEROONIFICATION

STATEMENT:

There is no denying, Andrew, and permit me to pound this point into the brainface of the nation, that the proliferation of cloudproducts, whether in the form of straggly, vertically unwinded minidrips, or in the form of fatter, blownandblitzed bigass bad'uns, is arriving in this country, this stunning sexykisslips known as Britain, and it is important, it is important—permit me to finish, Mr. Kerr—it is important that in this county, and one has to remember, or two have to forget, the opposition the opposition the opposition, in 1992, in 1997, in 2004, so it is not our fault, I want to make that clearer than a prism up a column of wellwindowlened glass, that the sandbaggeries in place to protect the beautiful wonderfulness of this proud nation—I am proud, I am proud, Andrew—should help, when the fluffy nemeses release their highrisk wetness onto the paves and ments and floors of those places, and the opposition might snap a twig in the face of a crying child, O no, not us. Wear socks, plebs.

MEANING:

In twelve minutes, Wiltshire will be mostly underwater.

STATEMENT:

Let me show abserstruse clarityness, if you will permit me to start, Andylips, if you will let me pulverize this point in the name of political honorsty, lacking lacking lacking opposition opposition not us O no no no, and that point, arriving in this sentence following a short skittle of filler syllables, that with the ratification of the unification treaty, if one considers the implications of a deratification of a reunification in a rogue nation, and if two don't, then three must consider the nonimplications of unconsidering such a thinglet—Andrew, I am speaking here, thank you—that our county, and I am in concurrence with the Prim Ministeress—fantastic woman, strong leader, precisely who we need—and, in spite, our firmclamp on a polinoncy to never currywurst with tyrants, whether tyrannically inclined, or inclinally tyranted, there is in fact, and I have been clear and always have been clear on this, as clear as quartz on the invisible man's wrists, or that, and sometimes there, never then—listen up, Andrew!—that parts of Corsham might find itsselves burnywarmer than usual, perhaps subatomically, however, this has nothing to do with us and the opposition drown babies. Bunker up, slobs.

MEANING:
In twelve minutes, an Iranian missile will poleaxe Corsham.

STATEMENT:
As I hoof along the length breadth and width of this proud country, this warmbummed united kingamongkingsdom, people say to me, they say to me, through my staff, they say to me, in unopened letters, they say to me, that their hardearned monies, their goodlygrafted lucres, their toughschlepped moolahs, they say that they would prefer, and I agree with myself on this, and I'm sure you do too, or perhaps you don't—which I take issue with, I take umbrage with, and the opposition hammers nails into the faces of orphans, and if you don't believe me, read Allan Willbrown's piece in *The Daily Noonah*—and now, to the nexus of my natter, to the matter of my prattle, if you will permit me, Andrew, the teensiest moment to draw breath without inbutting for once, when we polled the populace, when we slipped paperpieces into letterboxes asking things of men and dogs, there was consent that scroungers, loungers, and slackers are sucking us into a holeditch, and we need to take whacktion. And yes, I concede, these choice, or this choices, have been hard, harder than a slap in the nads from your mum, Andrew, however, in the end things, and yes, we don't. On your knees, scroungers.

MEANING:

In twelve minutes, everyone receiving state benefits will be massacred.

STATEMENT:

There is a new scourge sweeping the nation, Drewlove. A new sickness in the bleeding viscus of Gr8 Britain. That sickness is the Creative Sponger. He sits on the sofa swotting down on boxsets while you, the numbgummed taxpayer, toil in your workplants to fund our schools and hospitals and fire engines and dads. O Yes, heed me now. The Sad Sack hangtens the net watching cat videos and muckymemes while you, the backshafted taxlover, struggle to keep your head above gunge on zero-hour contracts. The Sad Sack paints pics of panting pensioners in heat while you, the flatsuffering taxplunger, spud your evenings totting up bills and budgeting so you can feed your tubby tots for another week. Andrew, I am saying several things at once, and nothing at the same time, while I am simultaneously making many, and no, points and non-points, and I remain so fabulous your bozo brain simply cannot compute my stuff, and the opposition touch up dying grannies in hospital beds, it is true, read this clipping. Artists, humph humph, they are the rotting flies in our collective gazpacho, and we are coming. Yes, you gawping head of skin. Feel the truth in a plate of hemp. Shield up, saddos.

MEANING:

In twelve minutes, anyone caught practicing art will be stabbed.

STATEMENT:

If I might take a moment to perambulate around the issue, Andrew, or should I say perambulance, since the omelette on this verbal frier, the one I am attempting to egg up, with this sizzle of words, pertains to the health service, the marvellous health service—nurses, and doctors, and orderlies, and locums, and cleaners, yum yum yes—which into we were working to vestin, once the roofs have been scoured for bird-plop. It is our contentions, and their intentions, and the opposition like to rape puppies in front of birthing mothers, read the article in *The*

Daily Foophah, that having failed to want to transform these hospitifuls into thriving centres of commercial sexcellence, there mustmust find needs a better purpose in the fullness of time—let me finish a *sentence*, Andrew!—and I believe, in my heart and soul and loins, and the opposition in 1996, yes they will, yes they will, that the finest means of making this happen is to convert the slumpingheaps of moribund moaners and put them to work in an exercise capacity, yes, I mean this, and we have long come to a concussion on this smugject. Jiggle, sickos.

MEANING:
In twelve minutes, all hospitals will be replaced with gyms.

[From 'Mr. Nightshade's Blabberoonification Translated', *The Political Animal* [online], June 2020].

[HAMPSHIRE]

NAME: OBAN FRUGAL'S GHOST
AGE: 16 (FORMERLY), ∞ (PRESENTLY)
SENTENCE: IRRELEVANT
CRIME: THE GREAT HAMPSHIRE NOVEL

I WAS WORKING on the Great Hampshire Novel when I was sucked into an aeroplane propeller. That statement is untrue. I wrote it after speaking to the writer Charlie Mair who advised me to write an opening line that captured the reader's attention. He explained that the reader, having had their interest sparked by the title, the cover art, and the blurb, needed an opening sentence that pulled them in at once, and that without this strong hook, the novel would rot on the shelf forever. I explained that the most interesting aspect of modern novels was their titles and opening sentences, since writers poured their creativity into perfecting these two elements, knocking out the actual text in a few weeks. Charlie's own novels had been refined to one sentence per title: a simultaneous opener and closer spread over several hundred pages in an enormous font. He told me that readers were captivated by the large letters of the first section of the first word of the one sentence, and snapped up the books at full price, eager to find out what letters might follow in the rest of the first and subsequent words. He could sell novels using the letters T, H, and S alone. I explained to Charlie that I had never been skilled at the concise mode, that I had never longed to wow another human being with an opening sentence, and that I found his practice repugnant and part of the reason for the plummeting literacy rates, and that the sort of reader who needs to be wowed with an opening sentence was not the sort of reader I was courting. He explained that in that case no one would read me, ever, and that I would never, ever have a career, and that I would never, ever be invited to read at the 92nd

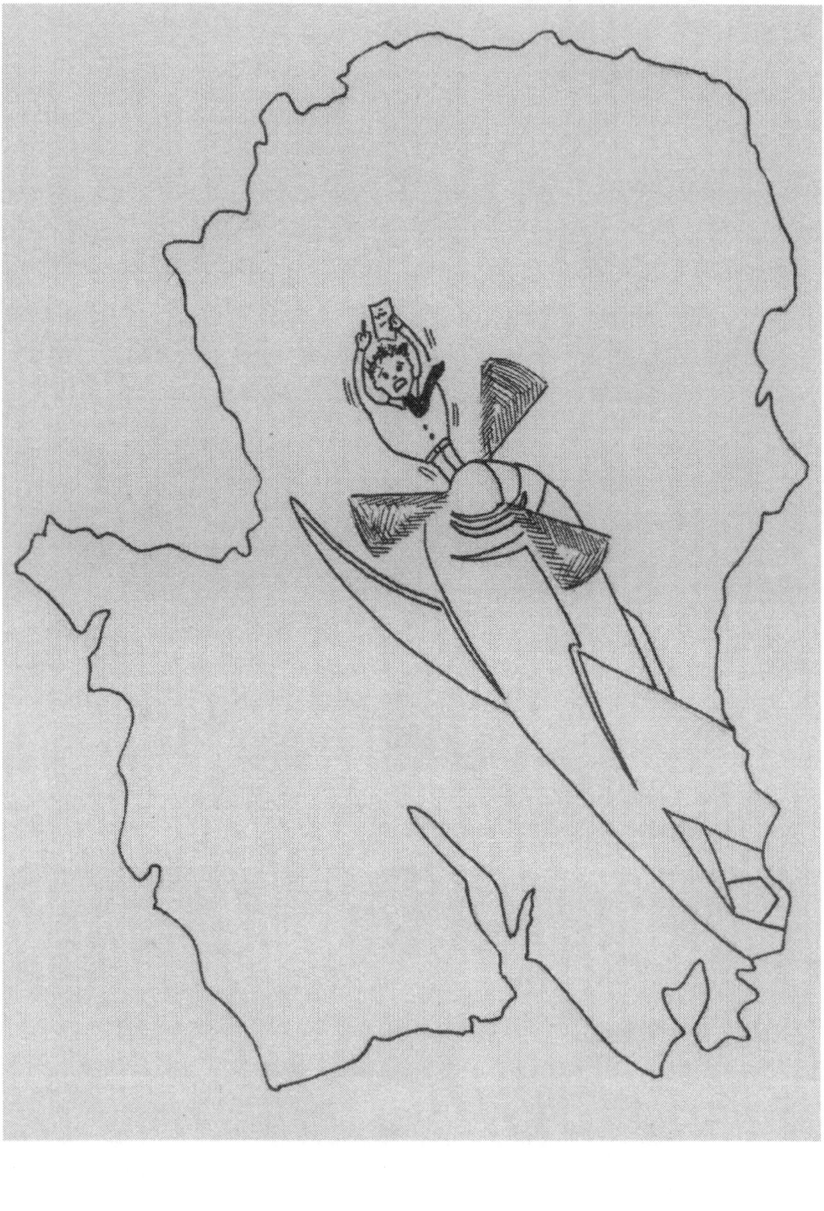

Street Y like him, and that I would never, ever secure a blurb from Stephen Fry, and that I would never, ever be welcomed into the bosom of the corporate literary machine like all the proper writers. I cried as he walked off. In my fear, I ended up conceding by writing an opening 'hook' sentence, then undoing the effort with a further eleven sentences of rambling explanation that killed any interest the opener might have created. Since, as Charlie states, readers want opening sentences and nothing more, I am then free to write whatever I want for the rest of the novel, and this should make no difference to the critical and readerly reception, as is made obvious by the fact you are (not?) reading this in hardback from a large publisher, and the wave of praise in broadsheets across the board. I was, in fact, working on the Great Hampshire Novel when I died. I was making notes into a voice recorder up Oakham Hill when I misjudged a step and, in a botched attempt to avoid falling, hurled myself over the edge, where my head met a rocky crevasse. It was a pointless and cruel end.

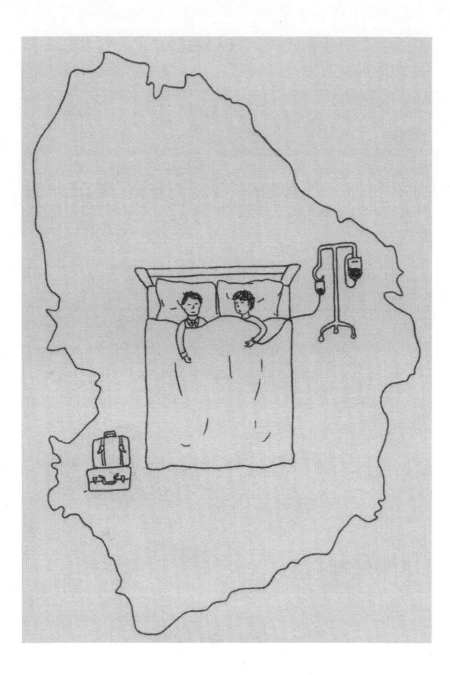

[SOUTH YORKSHIRE]

NAME: REINGOLD HARTMUNCH MP
AGE: 38
SENTENCE: 12 YEARS
CRIME: THE 2014 DIARY

Torn pages from Mr. Hartmunch's diary were found under a restaurant table and uploaded to the internet by a local snooper. Irritation followed. —Ed.

TO SAY AT NEXT PMQS

DEAR MEMBS, I RECOMMEND that Sheffield be renamed Stroppy Little Minx.

Dear Membs, for the ninth week running, to my unutterable delight, my constituents have asked me to "grill" the PM on what measures are being taken to cope with the rising volume of pigeon excrement at Cudworth train station.

Dear Membs, is anyone here in love with the first Idlewild LP, *Hope is Important*? I think this short pop-folk-punk blast is an underrated mix of snarl-croon and has a brattish brio missing from their more polished later efforts.

Dear Membs, I recommend that Doncaster be renamed All Up In It, Yo.

Dear Membs, I would like to extend my support to the Right Honourable Bill Mithers MP, for taking a tough stance on hardcore pornography screenings in crèches. The fans of this misunderstood genre need a safe place to watch their films, away from the shrieking picketers and violent protesters. Good on them!

Dear Membs, my constituents are perfectly content this week and have no problems with the way anything is being governed in this country, and wish to thank you for the hard work for on their behalf.

Dear Membs, I recommend that Rotherham be renamed Skippy's Milky Wrists.

Dear Membs, I suggest those complaining about the new Danish export tariffs take a leaf from Matthew's book, and turn the other cheek. (*Pause for applause*).

Dear Membs, is the Prime Minister aware that while he is swanning off to "important" trade meetings in Brussels, there are homeless people in Dodworth shivering under bridges and dying of hypothermia in our parks? What does our globe-hopping la-de-dah Prime Minister have to say to *that*? (*Pause for standing ovation*).

Dear Membs, I recommend that Barnsley be renamed Land of the Lumpy Gravy.

Dear Membs, isn't it a shame that Lush only reformed for a short while? If you are looking for one of the finest shoegazing albums ever recorded, look no further than *Split*.

Dear Membs, remember when things were better, in those past times, when we were happier and richer? We should return to those past times.

❋

Is it harassment to ask these young hipster women what other parts of their body they have tattooed?

❋

When that old woman said "you lot are all the same", what was she talking about? I work really, really, really, hard. That wasn't fair. She really hurt my bloody feelings. I can't believe she said that. She doesn't know me. She knows nothing about me. I'm a decent human being. I work hard to make this county better. It isn't fair. "You lot." Lumping me (*me!*) in with the expenses scammers and the benefit shamers and the immigrant haters. I'm not part of that *lot*. I claim for essential things like travel and hotel rooms. Not second homes or bronze statues. I am a unique man among men in the parliament and no one knows. I'm going to phone my friend in the housing department. She might change her tune when she's served with an eviction notice for being a stupid arse. I'm like that *lot*? Bitter old hag.

❋

Should I have humiliated that temp quite so vigorously for buying recycled loo paper?

❋

DRAFT OF CONDOLENCE LETTER

Dear Mrs Starling, I am so sorry that your lovely [?] husband [?] was flattened by a speeding forklift truck in Scawthorpe, as our workers were improving the B6422 road to Pickburn. I can only assume that your husband is not usually as absent-minded, as the forklift was clearly making a sharp turn into that road as your husband biked left from the A638 (not observing the proper crossing procedure and using the traffic lights) [too harsh?], however, I am still very sorry that his legs snapped like two twiglets in a bowl [rewrite this simile] and the forklift bounced over a bump and tipped, driving one of the prongs into his head, spearing his eyeballs, then stabbing hard into his brains [does she need reminding?]. It must be a terrible, terrible [repeat or use another word?] time for you and your remaining [?] family. I cannot imagine how wrenching and agonising your grief will be [over the top?], however, I come with a polite request. Your lawsuit against the council will cost the taxpayer a large sum [name a ballpark figure?], and if successful, will force the cancellation of many important schemes, such as road improvements that will help prevent the sort of accidents that happened to your husband when he was painfully killed and hideously maimed by the forklift [delete this?]. I would also like to emphasise the cost to you and your family, and the potential problems in winning the case, seeing your husband was not paying attention, and that there are witnesses to this. [no other way to say this] You will probably [certainly?] lose the case, and we will seek compensation for emotional damages [up to £500,000?], and will not hesitate to pursue further legal action if that sum is not paid in full. The best thing I believe is to take some time to think about your actions, and remember your husband as the kind and considerate [research dead man's character] man he was.

Yours, etc.

❋

Have onions become harder to find, or I am imagining things?

❋

DRAFT OF NHS LETTER

Dear Michael,

Thank you for the productive meeting yesterday. I must admit, your civil partner makes a mean sachertorte! As requested, here is a short summary of my scheme, the proposed collaboration 'AirbnbNHS'. As you know, thousands of people occupying properties with spare bedrooms can make extra income in renting out their rooms to tourists on a temporary basis. As a solution to the bed shortage in most hospitals, I propose that flatowners rent out rooms to NHS patients who are on waiting lists for beds, or those not in need of immediate care, but occupy beds for long periods of time. I propose a trial period for coma patients, who lounge around for unpredictable stretches, turning our wards into mere storage units for those either on the route to recovery, or en route to the afterlife. It is far cheaper to relocate coma patients into the spare bedrooms of Airbnb users, and have a series of locum nurses travel from flat to flat periodically, on 18-hr shifts, monitoring the patients, than to invest in more wards or new premises. It might well save the NHS £3,000,000 per annum to rent beds from private tenants rather than concentrate them in one space. In exchange, the Airbnb user would receive a higher rate of rent than usual, as they would have a minor responsibility in alerting the local hospital if the patient were to pass away, or show any signs of recovery. It is my strong belief that this scheme might also work to free up pregnancy wards, or in assisted care for the elderly.

Best regards, etc

✻

If sewage is as bad for you as people claim, why does it taste so nice?

✻

NEW BULLSHIT 4 BIDDIES

"Your concerns are electric, Bettie!"

"I will walk up to those buildings, Irene, and I will rattle those pillars."

"I am concerned. I understand that is what you think politicians say all the time, 'I am concerned'. But I am concerned. If I wasn't concerned, Peggy, would I have said that I know that politicians say 'I am concerned' all the time?"

"And not only that, think about the imprisoned koala bears of Tuvalu, Meredith!"

"I wake up in the morning, Louisa, and ask myself in the mirror 'Reingold, how can you make the world a less hateful place?' Then I brush my teeth."

"Yes, they are, Sheila, they are very much like that, and miserable sourpusses too."

"I blame the Macedonians, Violet."

"The sun is getting hotter these days, Hattie, and yes, almost certainly, the rain is getting wetter. No, it's nothing to do with global warming."

"Your points sizzle my neurocortical regions like no others, Kathleen!"

"I have a motto, Maisie, and that motto is something to behold."

"*You?* No! Never!"

"Sometimes, Sarah, there are no words to explain the suffering in this world. So I will spend this rest of this hour in silence, respectfully."

✳

Am I allergic to iodine?

✳

DRAFT REPLY TO NHS LETTER

Dear Michael,

Thank you for your report on the first month of 'AirbnbNHS'. I was disappointed to learn that the scheme has been unsuccessful. Your report was interesting. On reflection, it was perhaps too much to expect that flatowners might report the deaths of their boarders. I was interested to read your account of the man who, on hearing the urgent bleep of the heart machine from his bedroom, merely turned up the volume on the soap opera he was watching. I was also saddened to hear how these patients were treated, with people having "coma-tease" parties, inviting people around to straddle the unconscious patients and take photos, and fiddle with their electric beds and ride them in the manner of bucking broncos. I was also appalled how landlords still used these rooms for other purposes—surrounding the patients with storage items, in one case stuffing the room so full of boxes and cases that an elderly man was buried underneath these things, making it a struggle for the doctor to access his vitals. And I was appalled to learn that some sublet the rooms, moving the coma patients to the edge of the beds so people seeking extremely cheap accommodation could sleep on the other side, or in some cases, moving the coma patient to a series of cushions on the floor, so that couples could occupy the whole bed. No one could have foreseen these kinks in our plan. Human nature fails again. I was looking forward to adapting the scheme, offering hospital patients the chance to rent half their beds to travellers.

Best regards, etc

＊

Is the night dead?

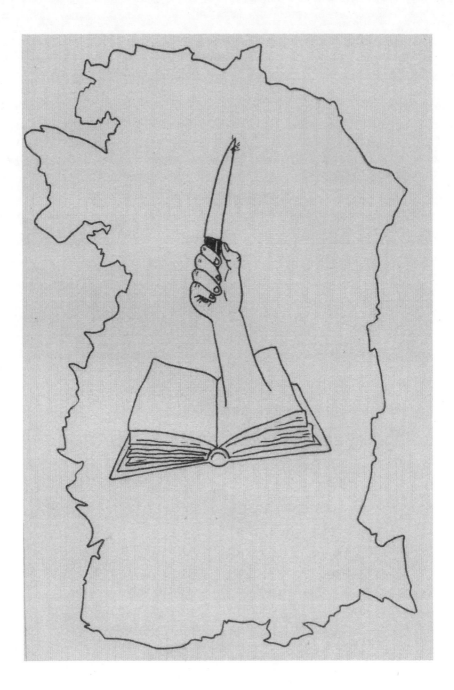

[BERKSHIRE]

NAME: MEGAN GRÖSS
AGE: 28
SENTENCE: 20 YEARS
CRIME: KNIFING A LOVELY

As I watched Cassie Allbright bag the Finest First Novel of the Year trophy at the Tesco Book Awards, I wore the expression of a plumber retrieving his firstborn's severed head from a blocked cistern. I had written a novel of such intricate mastery, historical accuracy, and heartwrenching poignancy, spanning seven continents and nine epochs, with a cast of timeless characters that leap from the page and strangle the reader with their insane vividness, while Cassie Allbright had penned a mediocre coming-of-age tale set in 1990s Bridlington. She won for her strawberry blonde tresses, her whitewashed molars, conical tits, and sugar-sweet voice. The prettiest, most photogenic candidate had won. I am not an attractive person. Like the best authors, I have a face like a corpse mummified in a peat bog. I write from the shadows, where the unattractive and unloved linger, plotting their revenges in print. I had been passed over for several 'First Novel' contests, having entered under various pseudonyms—I sent pictures of myself to the committees as chuckling brunettes, mysterious blondes, and brooding redheads— blowing the illusion when I attended the ceremonies. I refused to send a paid cutie to accept my award. One time, my novel was declared the winner. As I approached the stage, the organisers signalled madly to the host to make a last-second change: the wrong name had been read out. I see reality—that repulsive, mud-slathered hippopotamus sinking into its sump—for what it is.

I lived with the equally repulsive author Howard Groccule. We hated ourselves too intensely to ever acknowledge ourselves as sexual beings. We lived together as 'friends', a meaningless term, for whenever we stared at each other's faces, we saw our own putridity reflected back at us. It was around this time (an irrelevant phrase, most stories existing outside normal temporal structures—imagine whatever time you like) I made a conscious choice to exact revenge outwith the pages of the novel. I would maim the peachy skin on Cassie Allbright's lovely visage with a sharp knife at a moment of my choosing. As I explained:

"Howard. The beautiful people swagger across this planet in shirts of arrogance and slacks of entitlement. They swish through our lives in their sexy trousers and footwear, taking our jobs, our friends, our chances, as if they deserve them. They were born pretty, these fuckers. That is *it*. And the average-looking masses flock around them, hoping their proximity to milky white skin, prominent cheekbones, and perfect figures, will somehow reward them with stuff. But it never does. The beautiful take everything. Because these fuckers have *nice DNA*. Their only talent is continuing to eat and breathe with cute faces. And every-day, they look down their noses at us like we are boulders of snot in their soup. And we can only cower under their beauty. Howard, it's time to slice them up."

I asked Cassie's PR man if I might meet her in her hotel room to congratulate her. The PR man told me she had a packed schedule, which meant that she was free at that exact moment and had no interest in seeing my horrible mouth make sounds. I located the room number and rapped on the door.

"*The Guardian*. We'd love to write a ten-page feature on how amazing you are," I said. The door swung open immediately. I unsheathed the knife from its sheathed position. The years of refusal surged up as I slashed her face—the first slash for my volcano novel *Popocatépetl Goes Pop*; the second slash for my campus novel *The Dean of Mischief*; the third slash for my French melodrama *Lyon is for Lovers*; the fourth for my satire on papertowel production *Dry! Dry! Dry!*; the fifth for my Gulf War epic *Persian Palaver!!*; the sixth for my monologue from the perspective of an unborn foetus *Womb With a View*; the seventh for my chronicle on hosepipe bans *Wet! Wet! Wet!*; the eighth for my novel on laconic serial killer Pierre Ubu *To Cut a Long Story Short*; the ninth for my internet reworking of the Bluebeard story *Don't Click on That Short-cut*; the tenth for my heartwarming vegan novel *Falafel Hearts*; and the eleventh for the abovementioned novel titled *Long Flows the Ebb of Time*.

After I had comprehensively carved up Cassie's face, leaving deep scars that no amount of maxillofacial surgery could repair, I wrapped her face in a bandage, called an ambulance, and fled. Unfortunately, I had overlooked the obvious consequence: Cassie, having been born a strawberry blonde beauty, was a former facial stunner, and so had the support of the media. She had once been beautiful. That's all that mattered. Part of the club. Her beauty had been heinously stolen from her by an embittered ugly woman. She was a hero who went on to sell millions of copies of her memoir *Knifed By a Psycho Crone from Hell with No Literary Talent*. I was sent to prison for nineteen years. The chic shall inherit the Earth.

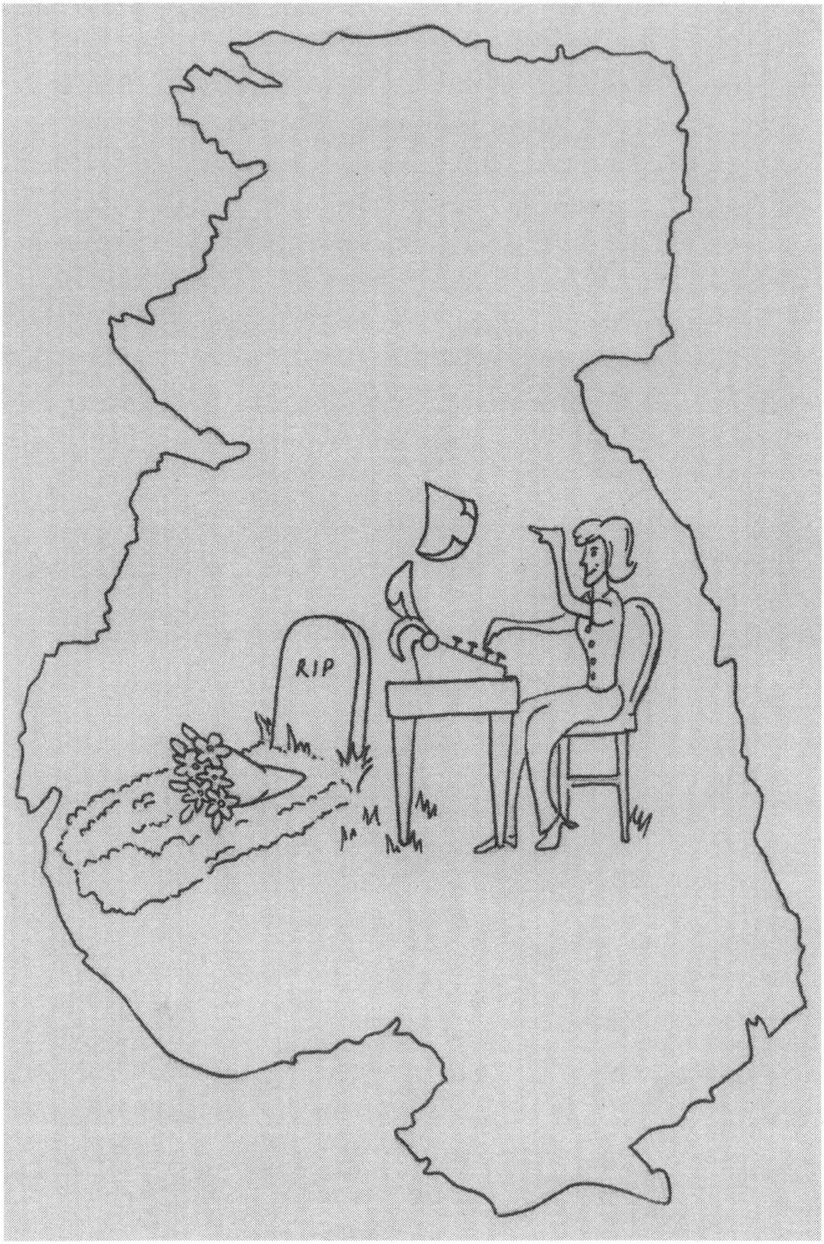
RIP

[SURREY]

NAME: THERMOS GRUBER
AGE: 32
SENTENCE: LIFE
CRIME: NOT WRITING HIS WHINY, SELF-PITYING NOVEL

AVING COMPLETED TWO UNPOPULAR NOVELS showing the abominable plight of writers, I took a Gap Year. Normally the province of trustfunded teenagers named Tristram or Prunella, pocketing their £5K parental stipend to shuck a backpack around a spiritual valhalla in the Western Ghats or tend bar on the plains of Australia, my Gap Year was less conventional. I chose to spend this Gap Year in bed reading. Having no funds, I would tithe the teats of the welfare state, banking up to £560 per month to sit upright with pillow support cracking the spines of Barker, Bernhard, and Burgess, avoiding work completely and making periodic trips to the supermarket for apples, baguettes, and eclairs.

First, a short tickling of self. I crawled from my council estate upbringing to the universities where, a mumbling wreck in sports slacks and Next cardigans, I staggered through two arts degrees with the usual proletarian complexes—self-hatred and unworthiness—to be spat out the other end into an unwelcoming nonmarket, expecting to land in a world that accommodated the timid bookworm with ample funds for foods. Over the annums, I moped through transient relationships with unstable neurotic women with self-made conditions ("anataxabulimiophilia", "brain clenching", "Vashti Bunyan Syndrome"), leeched off their mothers, and had more panic attacks than a titmouse in the path of a wildebeest, all the while pooh-poohing the toilet mop, two-fingering the call centre, and farting in the face of the front-of-house. I wedged myself into a small flat in the East End by piggybacking my ex, who vacated the premises upon noting my inability to support her artistic career (erotic stenographs on parchment), and my betrothal to the book. I clung to the lease. End of tickling.

So I celebrated the New Year with David Markson's *This is Not a Novel*, a peculiar patchwork of literary trivia and snarky sidebar comment, then mounted Ann Quin's *Berg*, a schizoid black comedy with smothering interior monologues; Lydie Salvayre's *Portrait of the Writer as a Domesticated Animal*, an excoriating anti-capitalist satire that manifestly manifestoes passion over the pound; Michael Slater's *Charles Dickens*, a compendious overview of the man's marvellousness, with apologetic coughs for his clobbering of Catherine; and Nicholson Baker's *House of Holes*, a deep-throated and rollicking work of pornographic politesse. Towards the end of the second week, I accepted that I would need to incorporate frequent constitutionals to the regime to prevent lumbar pandemonium, and take a fresh furbish to the dating profile to sate my sexual needs.

But right there, nestled under the sheets, hot water bottle between my thighs, curtains closed and reading lamp in full-beam over my shoulder, I knew that this was my purpose. I was born to bookloaf—to slump into three snuggledowns, sip a hot chocolate, and eat words with my eyes, to transport myself from a draughty East End dive to transcendent textual terrains, each world a window into the dizzying squall of the human condition, a pulchritudinous parp of pleasure and pain, shot into the willing mind of the enraptured reader, i.e. me. I was born to bookloaf. (I will explain the writing of this present novel in time. Relax. Most literature is 94% padding.)

❋

On findloveforafee.com, I was hoping to capitalise on the fresh influx of cold unhugged women who had signed up post-New Year, seeking to spoon the winter months away with temporary lovers before the summer brought them boyfriends with prospects. February is the perfect time to find short-term relationships: single women, following up on their pledge to find love in the New Year, return to their accounts as February encroaches to put the work in sending and replying to messages. I had reactivated my old profile—my premier pic me smiling before a torrentuous waterfall surrounded by stunning greenery. The intention was to beguile their eyes with the wonder of nature, and have them conflate those beautiful images with the picture of my mediocre face. During the short breaks from reading, I would log on and trawl the profiles of those with facial blemishes, intelligently written personal statements, or those who showed an interest in reading. I avoided women who were all cheekbones and masterly made-up faces, leaving those to the hipster brethren and ab-fab workout crowd. I wanted a broad with brains.

For every seventy-nine messages, I would receive two or three responses. One morning, placing Ishmael Reed's riotous slave-time satire *Flight to Canada* to one side, I made contact with Beryl_Aitch who had attacked me for listing Morrissey as one of my musical likes, blockquoting his right-wing views as evidence of his (and my) stupidity. In her pic, Beryl_Aitch had neatly combed brown hair, a pair of rectangular specs, thin lopsided lips, and the complexion of one who sat in a dark room on message boards for long periods. She had taken the photo in poor light from fear she might reduce her chances in the unforgiving sunshine. I took her cue to banter on faded eighties icons and invited her to continue our debate one evening in a bar setting. Meantime, I lounged into Momus's novelistic compendium of scatological chuckles *The Book of Jokes*, wrestled with D. Keith Mano's monstrous comic masterpiece *Take Five*, and lunched on the scabrous venom of Frederic Beigbeder's £6.99.

Our meeting took place in The Thatched Merkin: an art deco bar in the semi-hip Guildford environs. Beryl_Aitch (real name Beryl H. Soussal) had an intense stare as I brought her a foaming pint of Weissebier and said phrases like hello and how are you and how was the trip here to show I had the social niceties licked. "You realise Morrissey espouses the sort of right-leaning fascism that leads to the National Front or the Neo-Nazi movements?" she asked in response, showing she hadn't. "He wrote a song called 'The National Front Disco', from the perspective of parents losing their son to racists. 'David, the winds blow / All of my dreams away.' It's clear from that song that he has no fascist sympathies, and has an intense understanding of vulnerable youths conscripted into such groups," I tried. Beryl launched into a zealous rebuttal, citing other interview sources where Moz had made verbal slip-ups in his previously liberal philosophy. I listened attentively, matching her blows with reasoned response.

Expecting the date to sink into a sour exchange of colloquial formalities, I was surprised when Beryl turned pleasant on the walk home. "I love a stimulating exchange of contradictory views," she said, pecking me on the cheek. "I make papier-mâché sculptures of hated figures in society. I have a bust of Republican ear-shredder Anne Coulter, overlaid with negative reviews of her hate-filled screeds. I have one of Bernard Madoff overlaid with hedgefund applications and legal demands. Perhaps next Tuesday?" I made that appointment and returned home to read Kristin Hersh's hilarious and touching memoir *Paradoxical Undressing*.

❄

Our courtship proceeded apace, with trips to funfairs (which we loathed), trips to overpriced National Trust ruins (which we loathed), and trips to free folk music performances in seatless pubs (which we loathed). Most of our activities involved a mutual vent at the things that pass for amusement in our society, culminating in tonguing of face, tonguing of knee, and a long tonguing of tongues. Beryl took to me like a Czech to tennis, and I soon learned that she had what is termed in millennial idiom "emotional baggage" in the form of her father's suicide, her sister's schizophrenia, and her own struggles with substance abuse. I also learned that she was working on a memoir on these issues.

"I know what you're thinking," she said that evening when she unzipped the baggage, "that I intend to cynically exploit personal trauma for literary success." That was exactly what I was thinking. "That I intend to publish this brave heartfelt eye-opening confessional memoir to whoops of acclaim, and speak up for similarly sexy young women with similarly sexy problems like me everywhere, on twitter and reddit and book-yakking platforms?" That was exactly what I was thinking. "You are correct. Although in theory I'm opposed to all forms of self-interested public problem-purging in prose form, I'm writing this memoir for me—and it isn't even a memoir, it's a sort of diary of a cracked psyche—and what I need from this memoir is recompense so I can turn my pains into profit. But hey, I'm odd. I sometimes lapse into scat-like phrases that make emotional and not actual sense." As she said this, I heaved up a huff, noting that she was now a real literary threat.

To arrive at the titular bit (the preceding material is relevant to the remainder of this explanatory ramble, I will park that piffle for the nonce, then return when the next tangent sags like an amateur soufflé), explaining how this novel came to exist. In addition to taking the Gap Year, I had vowed to abandon fiction in the hope that more lucrative commercial notions might mobilise in my cranium and prod me towards awards and full-column raves from Editors-in-Chief. But, a month or so into the bookloafing, I read that Scottish Arts Council were cutting their annual book award. As an inbent lugubrist with no hope, I tend to sneer at council grants, as I never receive one, and if I stumble into print without their assistance, find myself ineligible for them, and resume sneering. However, the fact that writers were being cast aside like shanks of infected cow corpse on the slaughterhouse floor, made me sit up and sputter forth some froth. I made sounds like "but—wha—buu—imf—muu—whe—hoo" that went on longer than a Yo La Tengo album. In that manner, I began the incoherent thought-process (process is a most generous word) that sparked ideas for my incoherent novel (novel is a most, etc.)

If a novel is sparked by furious incoherent stuttering and the sentiments one wishes to express are furious incoherent stuttering, this leaves the writer with a formal dilemma. To print three hundred pages of one-syllable sounds, strung together with em dashes, is a bold decision and something for conceptual art mavericks like Nigel Tomm to attempt, not a reader-hungry, attention-starved wimps like myself who are slowly being broken by the cruel realities of the marketplace. I had to create a series of set-pieces, framed within an overarching melodramatic plot-line (of sorts), where each set-piece was communicating little more than the monophonic yawps of dysphoria as indicated above. I had to put up a coherent front in order to convey a far more important incoherent message.

So then, my novel, then, my sad, incoherent novel, then, would explore what it is like to try and ply one's trade in the flightpath of a burning concorde. On a concourse riddled with anthrax kittens. On the spit of a flaming racist. On the crag of a rotting canker. On the wing of a shark-bound tern. On the weave of a time-worn merkin. On the mandible of a starved okapi. On the batwing two minutes before sundown. On the cusp of a rotting bicuspid. It would be an exaggeratedly unhappy vision of the endtimes of literature, and a fucking bummer for everyone like me who hates everything in life except literature.

※

I had succeeded at kicking the novel conscious for a short period of time when I received a call from an old friend, Prime Number. (Novels are chronic narcoleptics, forever falling into long slumbers, sometimes lasting weeks or months, and require sustained violent attacks to shock them awake). My old friend had earned this mathematical moniker after leaving Scotland for Buenos Aires: over the years, we only ever met when he was aged a prime number, i.e. 23, then 29, then 31. (This put pressure on us to conform to the prime meeting system. I was hoping to meet him before he turned 37 and, if followed to its completion, the system meant

we had about ten or eleven meetings left across our lives). "Mate, have
you seen the news?" Prime asked. I had, at that time, stopped watching
TV news, unRSSed myself from feeds, and nixed Facebook and Twitter.
I had been listening to Shonen Knife and prowling around in a daydream
of worldly success, as usual. "I'm a loose node, Prime, as you know. What
calamity do you bring me this morning?" I asked. "Your British politicians have elected to squirt several quarries' worth of manure over the
arts. The fundings have been cut."

I perched on the statement for a sec. Having never received a single
pfennig from arts councils, having ridiculed arts councils in previous
novels, having not made the equivalent of two months' minimum wage
from writing for over fifteen years, I reacted to the news of arts council
funding with this sound: "Oohhmm". "Whatever. Never received a groat
from those arseholes," I said. "Woah! Hang five, my embittered brioche.
Like them or not, these arseholes are the few people out there singing
for writers' supper. There are no other non-profit organisations with the
welfare of squiggle-makers at heart." Prime Number had always been
an annoyingly fairminded sort, unwilling to let personal defeats cow
his reason, and suggested I take a less sour slant on the public travesty.
"But these administrators earn more in a year cheerleading writers than
most writers earn in a lifetime actually writing. If they want to help,
how about sharing their salaries? But hey. When is it you turn 37?" I
asked. "Four years and four months," he replied. "I'm starting to think
this nickname is a serious impediment to our friendship." "That and the
Atlantic Ocean," Prime said. "True."

I was working on 'The Novel Inside You', a section I had devised as
a parting middle finger to my writing "career" (if "careers" are viewed
in financial terms, then I had no claims to using the word "career", and
if "careers" are viewed in terms of success, then I also had no claims to
using the word—if I could use the word "career" to mean stubbornly pursuing something of no financial or worldly benefit that at least amused
myself, then I had had a thriving "career"), and planned a move into

content writing. I had found a website that paid £20 for 1000-word summaries of novels I not read. The business of making literature, of dreaming up new ideas, forms, stories, and innovations, was of no commercial value, and arts cuts seemed like an inevitable symptom of readerly indifference. If writers wanted to earn money, they were better off stealing content from Wikipedia and rewriting it in their own words so schoolkids could crib the summaries for their essays without having to read the books. The only money left in writing was in skilfully concealed plagiarism. So, swallowing down my fate like a bucket of carroty sick, I forgot about the novel entirely, and worked on reordering someone else's words in the quickest possible time for a pittance.

[From *Brain to Book: A Journey,* Thermos Gruber, self-published, 2020, p.45-50].

[CORNWALL]

NAME: ALAN APSE
AGE: 27
SENTENCE: 12 HOURS
CRIME: BEACH URINAL REVENGE

I WAS STROLLING ALONG PORTHMEOR BEACH when a spinster tugging an anaemic mutt bumped into me. She tutted hard, like a bitch. It was such a hard and repugnant tut that I had no choice cept to execute a plan of exquisite revenge.

First, I followed her at a nineteen-step remove to her beachside house. I nosed around and noticed her extension backed onto a public field. I phoned Cornwall council and inquired into the rules regarding encroachment lines. Her extension happened to butt into a public space to the splendid sum of 5.8m. I considered a public campaign to have the extension (her livingroom) bulldozed when I observed in the St. Ives Community Newsletter that the locals had been lamenting the lack of public loos. Little children had been reduced to shitting in the water and week-old turds would swim into other little children's mouths. It was a vicious circle of public shitting and shit-eating. I wrote to the local council and suggested that the cottage, owned and occupied by a retired widow named Gloria Green, might be turned into a public urinal, since her extension encroached public land. I published this news in the local paper, and earned the support of locals.

Mrs Green responded with such hauteur that those who never had the time or inclination to loathe her loathed her for several seething hours per week and supported the campaign I mounted to have her livingroom used as a public urinal. A hundred-strong movement (The St. Ives Loo Crusaders) came together and pulled resources to share in the simple pleasure of ramming it to a monied spinster. We booted up the usual channels, Kickstarter and Patreon, and the public pressure on

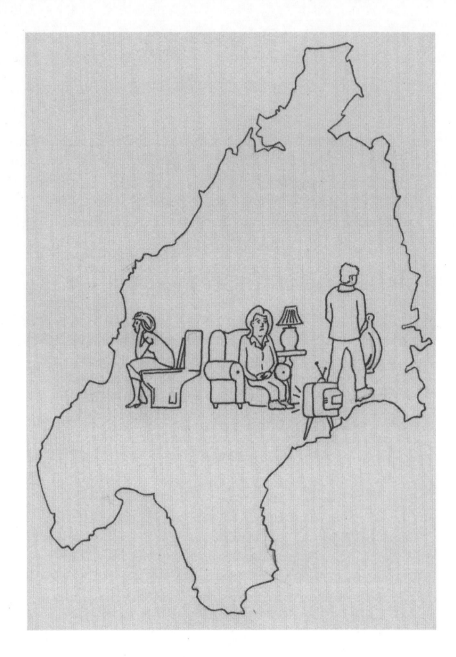

Mrs Green mounted. "Our children's mouths are filled with turds, and you sit there stuffing your face with hobnobs," one furious Cornishman wrote. "Our children's bladders are permanently ruined, and you sit there sipping your lapsang souchong," one furious Cornishwoman wrote. "Our children are crying and wetting themselves, and you fall asleep in front of *Countdown*," one Cornishperson of indeterminate sex wrote. Mrs Green treated the campaign as speck of dandruff on her regal shoulder, never thinking that the unhosed locals would have the right to encroach on her private land. This was the wrong approach. The council sent her a notice that six male urinals and four female stalls would be constructed in her front room for public use in two weeks. It was her responsibility to clean them.

I admit to feeling a pang of shame appending the last clause, making her clean them. Then I remembered the hard tut and felt nothing.

The male urinals were mounted on the left, replacing her bookcase and television, with the stalls on the other side, replacing her mantelpiece ornamental fireplace. The sinks were erected at the window, providing hand-washers with a nice view of Porthmeor Beach.

In her stubbornness, she remained in the middle of the room where there was space for her sofa and TV. It was her intention to intimidate bathroom users with her presence and anaemic mutt so no one would want to enter. However, Cornish males are not prone to paruresis, and no one was bothered when she scowled at their penises splashing piss on her M&S wallpaper, nor were the women concerned at her expression when loosing their turds in the fresh-pillow-scented room. The blast of the hand dryer made watching TV impossible, although she remained there the whole summer, her scowl strengthening as the aircon wafted the shit-scented air further up her bitter old nostrils.

[GREATER MANCHESTER]

NAME: ??
AGE: ??
SENTENCE: ??
CRIME: ??

I SUGGESTED, IN A PUBLIC FORUM, in front of 347 people, that Manchester might be renamed Squidgieroonienips. That is my "story", you assclown. Please leave.

[WARWICKSHIRE]

NAME: M.D. TOMAS
AGE: 82
SENTENCE: 6 YEARS
CRIME: PROLIX GRAFFITI

The following was lovingly and intricately printed along the walls of the newly opened Kardashian Museum. —Ed.

T HE TAP OF LITERATURE must keep running. The tap of literature must run in a violent frothing spurt and flood the universe, or we must blow out our brains. I am a man. I am a man and I am munching on a ham. I am a man and I am munching on a ham in a room with six hundred novels and a portrait of Charles Dickens and a stuffed panda with burst bowels and a radiator allergic to heat molecules. I have no name I wish to impart. I am a man and I am sitting in a room and I am hammering out a sentence and another sentence and another sentence and I have no intention of stopping. I am seated on a wicker chair with light cushion support and I am writing these words that run along the page like a set of shapely olympian legs, sprinting right to left and right to left and right to left and right to left across the page before leaping a line below and sprinting again right to left and right to left and so on. I have nothing to say to you, I have everything to say to you. I am not concerned with concision, I am concerned with maximality, I am concerned with committing words to the page. I am committed to keeping the tap of literature running. The tap of literature must keep running. The tap of literature must run in a violent frothing spurt and flood the universe, or we must blow out our brains. I am writing writing. I am a writer writing writing. I am writing against. I am writing for. I am writing for the future of writing. I am writing against the plague of peabrainism that reduces our minds to withered sultanas. I am writing against the assholic autocracies that reduce our language to a bowl of

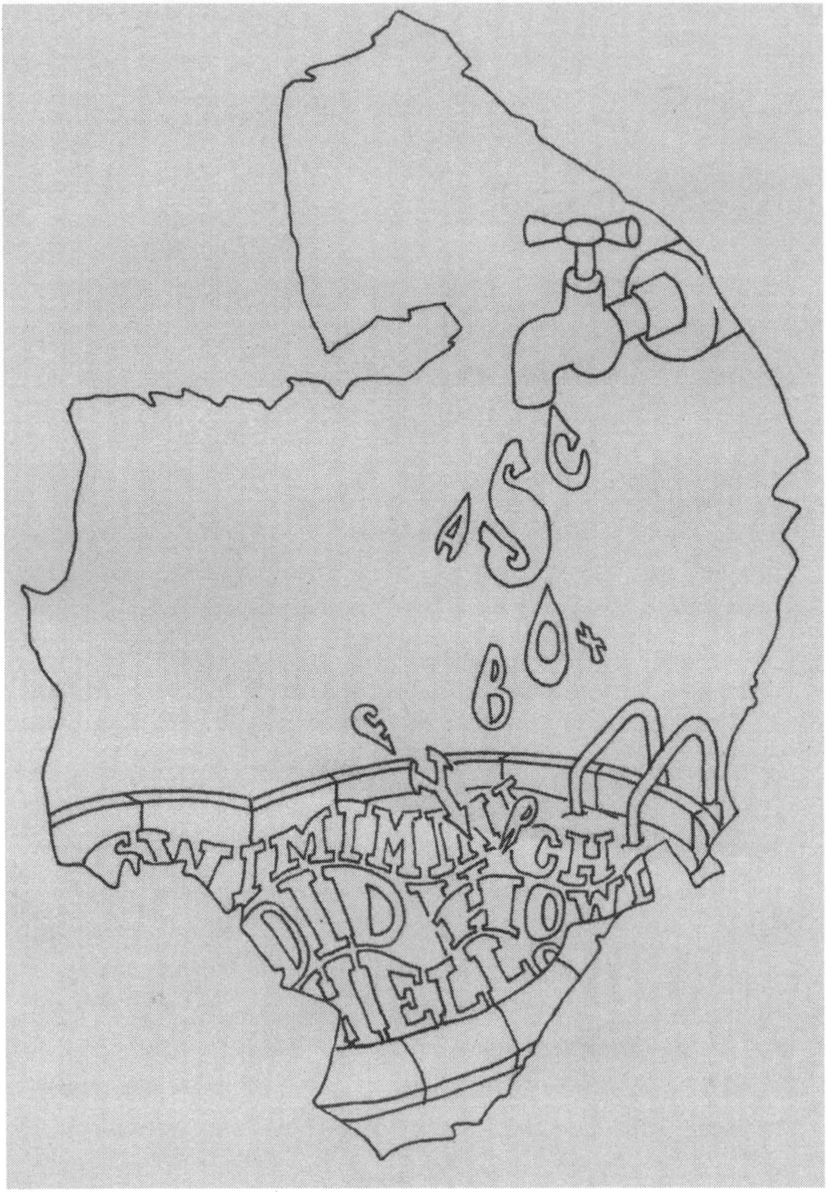
SWIMMIN
CH
DID
HOW

lukewarm unsalted porridge. I am sitting on this wicker chair with light cushion support to preserve the dignity of every writer who has ever enriched and shaped our lives with the wondrous weft of their words. I am writing from RESPECT. I am frothing at the pen with fume at the fuckwits that fight to batter the Great Novelists out of the public consciousness. I will not stop. I will write on and on. I have nothing to offer except this unending stream of words. I repeat myself whenever I wish. I repeat myself excessively, I repeat myself ecstatically. I repeat myself. I write whatever I want with little consideration for consistency, character, or concision. The tap must run, my friends, my enemies, my indifferent onlookers. I write on and on and I write onandon and Iwriteonandon. I stop to take periodic lunges at the ham. I stop to piss and poop. I write and write and write. I piss and poop and piss and poop. The substance of these words is self-evident. These words are a coup against the commercial. These words are a kick in the cock of crapness. I might write this. I might write that. I will not write to please. I will not write for money. I will only write, that is all I will do, I will only write, and I will not stop, except to lunge at ham and piss and poop. I will write a tale concerning a Lebanese alligator fetishist who lurks around the swamps in a state of frenzied priapism. I will not write that. I will write a tale concerning a molecule of osmium who enters a heavy metal contest and emerges the winner with his song 'Me'. I will not write that either. I will pull into a verbal car park and nibble and munch and suck on random words. Rotogravure. (Nibble). Colonic. Pusillanimous. Klebenleiben. Sublunar. Operetta. (Munch). Cumulative. Stereoscopic. Iguanodon. Ultracrepidarianism. Astrocompass. (Suck). Bumbershoot. Coptic. Smoothbark. Attenuated. Coelacanth. I will rev up the engine of this fearful ream and race in caps to the nub of the matter. LITERATURE IS CROAKING. Literature is hooked to an IV, morphined from scalp to toenail, wheezing through tubes, looking on in bottomless fear from flitting eyes at the vultures waiting to feast on its carcass. Literature was once a place of boundless possibilities, where the repulsive and unbearable business of living and breathing in this scarred bitchface of a universe was mined with ruthless complexity, a realm free from the strictures of our murderous Darwinian civilisations, our self-deluding autocracies, our narrow horizonless prisons of servitude, where the imagination ruled with benevolent mischief, and complete blissful nirvana was possible in the spaces between syllables. Freedom from the hell of living. Oxygen in the suffocating realm of consciousness. Now, readers are dwindling faster than the population balloons. Our encasement in corporate prisons, where we unwitting wallet-people stumble around in our spotless pantaloons farting coins into the coffers of soulless baboons who have never looked Emile Zola or Tom Mallin in the face. The misquote reads: "There can be no poetry after Auschwitz." I say: "There can be no poetry after Amazon." Our literature has been stripped and mined for profit for so long that all excitement and spectacle has vanished. We meet the announcement of a new novel with a mopeful shrug as we stare upon the cover, and observe the careful attempt from the marketing department to render each component—the colours, the fonts, the background images—as uniform and unthrilling as possible. This is a cunning attack on literature from the corporates seeking to run books into the ground. The plan is to render each novel so humdumb and uninteresting that people will return to their tablets and TVs to watch the latest series THOSE HUGE FUCKING COMPANIES promote on their massive billboards. I am a man, I am eating ham. I expect nothing from nowhere, no longer. I will not open up, stick out my tongue, and allow you to ram your sugary-sweetly-sickly marketing campaign down my throat. I am not here to follow orders from white billionaires with nine swimming pools and tweenage wives. I will not crawl on my knees, suck up the warm slurry of twenty-two boardroom bellends who want new cadillacs, and say: "Please sirs, can I have more of this delicious formula?" I am not interested in your latest phenomenonandons, your latest star-studden superseries, your latest cash-pumped mass-spectacles, your latest attempts to claw back the millions sunk into your vanilla ventures, your must-see must-hear must-like must-love must-have musts and musts and musts. I am not interested in being reasonable. I would blow them up in a heartbeat for a second *Ulysses*. Couch-dwellers and folkpeople: I am not interested in your passionate defences of these television-internet superviral hyper-serials. I am not interested in hearing "there are some wonderful shows". I couldn't care a squit. I am interested in LITERATURE. Being reasonable will not save literature. These click-seeking subscribblers are responsible for the thoughtless stomping out of our precious medium. I have a scream, Mr. King-size. I will walk around our nation's town centres with a pump-action shotgun and blast holes into those who "never read". I want them dead, I want them dead, I want them dead. I want several bullet holes in their livers, their abdomens, their coccyges, their cortices, their pancreases, their miscellaneous organs, their children's tears. I want the high streets littered with the corpses of non-readers. I want special tortures reserved for those who BRAG ABOUT NEVER READING. Motherfuck those motherfuckers. I want electrodes attached to their nipples. I want rabid mutts to nibble on their knackers. I want waterboarding underwater in winter. I want plutonium and taramasalata sandwiches. I want these bragging neanderthals who clog the pavements with their wide-ass hips who never stop to question the tasteless arsegrease that is being larded into their cultural pores and who, when told that their entire cultural selves are being marionetted by fat-walleted turds in multinational boardrooms, will fix you with a contemptuous look and say, "I don't care, I like what I like." I want these people to lose 101% of their incomes, and for that income to be paid into the pockets of writers, who are unable to make a living from THE LANGUAGE, UNABLE TO MAKE A LIVING USING THE VERY FOUNDING BLOCKS OF OUR CIVILISATION. I have a scream, Mr. King-size. I want those intelligent people who make no attempt to read new novels or engage with literature whatsoever, tricking themselves that a fleeting engagement with a friend's art exhibition or a pub cover band or two hours on Netflix is somehow an equivalent cultural experience to reading a work of immortal literature, to crouch on their knees and beg for forgiveness from the ghost of Johannes Gutenberg. I want to round up all the mobiles and tablets cradled in hands across the world, a million index fingers stroking the screens with the tender touch of a lover, and hurl them into an open volcano. I want to imprison the pokers, the strokers, the clickers, the texters, the tappers, and the snappers in a room with the finest literature, and refuse them exit until one hundred of the finest novels have been read. I want to massacre those who respond "no cultural enterprise should be enforced". EXCUSE ME. EVERYTHING ELSE IS ENFORCED. No one should have to work for a living. No one. No one wants this world that forces us to stagger into trains and cars and buses, into factories and offices and farms, that forces us to waste our lives racking up the zeroes on some other prick's bank balance. No one wants to scrub floors, serve paninis, sell timeshares, or smuggle cocaine to appease their banking app. No one wants taxes, bills, costs, fiscal responsibilities. We live in a pitifully imbalanced world where the richest and most powerful are the most corrupt. We allow amoral arseholes to burgle our monies, to hoard the wealth in their tax havens, to skirt taxes using legal circumshots, forcing the rest of us to bust our purulent humps in occupations we loathe, so that living conditions for the poor can fractionally improve then fractionally worsen then fractionally improve ad nauseum. There is nothing first-class about our first-world. There is no poetry in the everyday, there is only poetry in poetry. How can we build a semi-hopeful future when our pioneers, our wealth-creators, our role models, our empire-builders, or supposed leaders have no moral compass, when our world is concerned with the hoarding and extravagant spending of wealth, and the important life-enriching things that have no relation to cash are being throttled out of existence? Stop working, right now! People! Refuse to work another second until all evaded tax has been returned to the public coffers. Refuse to work another second until legislation exists that stops people earning over £100,000 per annum. Strike from life. If we take a permanent strike from life, we might end up liking some of it. And if they bring in the tanks and bombs, let them blow us to pieces. We want a future on our terms, or no future at all. Permit me a brief piss-moment. I have bladdercleared. I am back. I have a scream, Mr. King-size. The rich have no interest in culture. The rich are self-starting pricks who read self-help business manuals, and upon earning their "hard-won" riches, spunk the lot on useless self-glamorising trinkets for their vapid brainless wives or husbands, and strut around the place like we are supposed to admire them, when all we wish to do is poke out their eyeballs with cocktail sticks, and sauté their offspring. No one cheers another's wealth. We are hardwired to loathe the wealthier person. At the merest flicker of a revolution, we round up the rich and strip them of their monies and roast them alive and eat their ankles. We are not living in a civilisation. There is nothing civilised about lucre. There is nothing civilised about owning an antique coffee table at the retail value of £300K while someone else is starving. We are living in a mass hypocrisy, pretending that this is an acceptable way to comport ourselves. The only way we can advance as a civilisation is to invent a device that instantly murders anyone who makes over £100,000 per year. This is more than enough money for anyone to live on. We need to invent a microchip loaded with a mini-bomb that is inserted into the anus of every man, woman, and child, that is linked to one's bank account. Upon the bank account passing over the figure (allowing, perhaps a margin of two or three thousand for payments made in error, or early bank transfers), the bomb instantly activates, and the cash-hording asshole is instantly blown to smithereens. It is simple. FUND LITERATURE, YOU SCUMSCUM. LET WRITERS LIVE, YOU DUMBDUMBS. If you want a world that nurtures the bestial, sadistic aspects of human beings, then continue with free-market capitalism, continue with fascist and religious autocracies. If you want a world that nurtures the enlightened, compassionate aspects of human beings, then harvest the mind with books, where all knowledge is housed, where all benign power is concentrated. I have expended myself. It is time for ham. I am a mere man. I am eating a mere ham. I eat and piss and poop and write. I repeat myself, I rant and rave, I repeat myself, I munch on ham. I write on. The tap of literature must keep running. The tap of literature must run in a violent frothing spurt and flood the universe, or we must blow out our brains. I write on. I write onandonandonandonandonandonandonandonandonandonandon-andonandonandonandonandonandonandonandonandonandonandonan-donandonandonandonandonandonandonandonandonandonandonando-nandonandonandonandonandonandonandonandonandonandona

[RUTLAND]

NAME: YANN GRAVY
AGE: 34
SENTENCE: 15 YEARS
CRIME: UNRUTLIKE TEXT

Yann started a website, www.rutlandrealised.net, and created a page for each village, with pictures and short text "summing up" each place. Sadly, the resident Rutters took umbrage to his baffling efforts. The offending texts follow.
—Ed.

Ashwell
The introduction of an orrery, frankly, would help.

Ayston
The strip club is weird. The one performer, Melinda Melinda, known as Melinda², has one breast in the centre of her torso, and tilts her head infinitesimally left and right for an hour while mumbling pronouns. The men throw coins at her stilettoed feet like she is the wingèd Goddess Minerva. I believe that should stop.

Barleythorpe
This village creaks. I was trying to sleep when I heard the hills intone "no, not this week, Alistair". I recommend a bulldozing.

Barrow
Bis have never toured here. So sad.

Barrowden
There are plans to erect a sewage works in Mrs. Rocher's front room at 1 Crown Lane. The council have said: "This sewage works will bring in four hundred thousand pounds for us. Mrs. Rocher should lighten up. She has a spare bedroom. She can make that her new front room. If she puts in a few Glade Plug-ins, the smell won't be a problem. Everyone else is on board. Get with it, Mrs Rocher!"

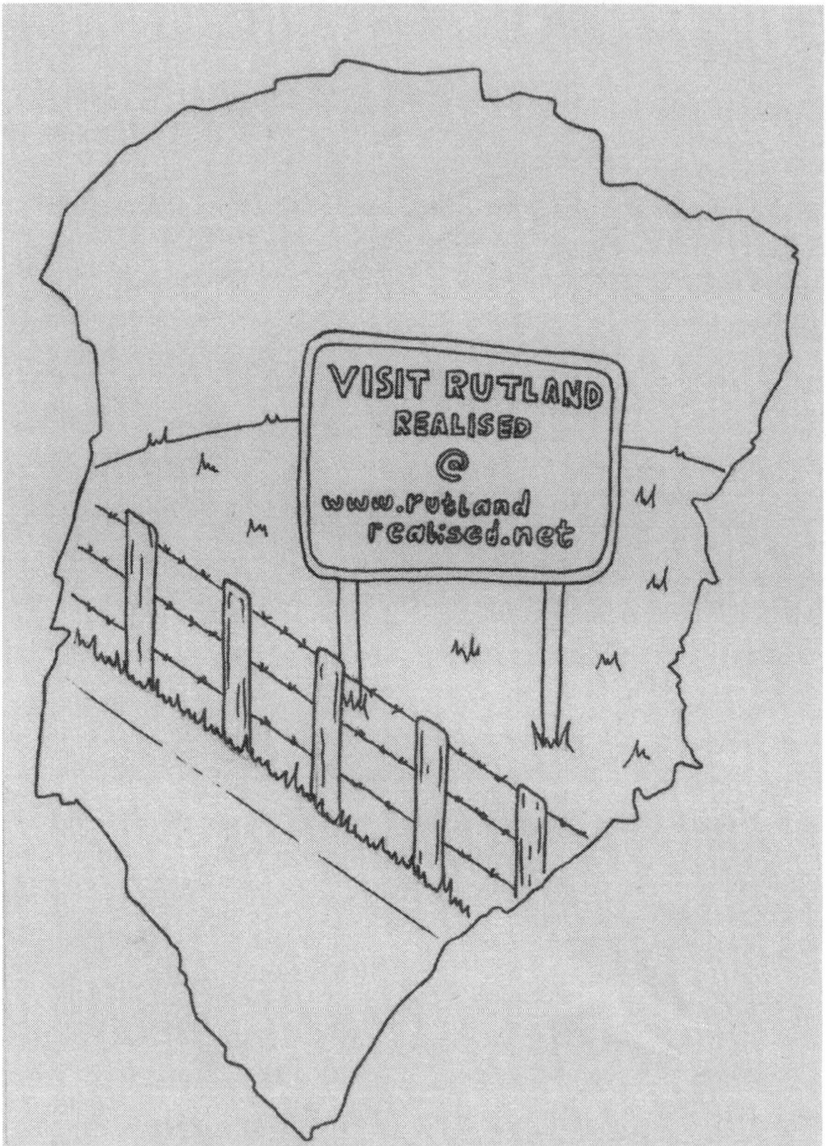
VISIT RUTLAND
REALISED
@
www.rutland
realised.net

Beaumont Chase
If this village were a man, that man would be Alan Alda.

Belmesthorpe
One would expect the populace of this place to have heads the size of aqueducts. As it happens, the populace have normal, cashew-shaped heads, and walk on two legs like real women.

Belton-in-Rutland
Around the rim of the famous basin, former union scabs bathe in torrid blue-brown puddles, squeezing their pustules of shame into the waters, speaking of livermorium, the excellent salads in Aldershot, and the next neck they will visit.

Bisbrooke
I came here under false pretences, so I was not expecting to encounter the truth at such an astonishing wattage. This village is the most honest place I have ever visited while riding a wave of lies.

Braunston-in-Rutland
If this village were an animal, that animal would be man.

Brooke
I spoke to a man who was launching a novel here. He said "I had no complaints". That novel is not searchable on a line.

Burley
Bending, sharply, around the parish church, is a Yemeni.

Caldecott
Most of the inhabitants of this stodgehole have uzis and petrol bombs in their pockets or pockettes. I believe the intended effect is one of menace. I spoke to a young child of thirty-two who said to me with lips aloftd: "If Romanians come here, I will burn down their hair." The people here aren't nice, Susie.

Clipsham
Never have we seen such a fruitful agglomeration of structures hewn in hemp, sandstones, and wicker. Never! Never! (Ho!)

Cottesmore
If this village were a thing that existed in the world, that thing would be a blue balloon.

Edith Weston
You don't want to know. If you knew, parts of your soul would shrivel and weep, and your children's kidneys would burst, splatting excretory matter over your candelabra.

Egleton
Knotty, oak-scented.

Empingham
Alias, "the epicentre of nothing".

Essendine
If this village was a statement, that statement would be "I would like to strangle a seagull."

Exton
What we have here is a village, that is what we have here. It is a village, and inside that village, that village, that village, is a stick of miscellaneous length and incalculable width. The residents, known as Villi Occupi, rut around the stick to the music of Enya.

Glaston
For four annums now, the entire village has pursued a relentless hate campaign against Little Thomas Browne for stealing a mango without written permission. This hate involves throwing hot soup at him from Land Rovers, pasting up his photo across Rutland with the word "FILTH" in Century Gothic Bold, and burying his mother up to her neck in whalebone. The campaign romps on at a frenzied rate of romping. Here, I was encouraged to secrete a potato in Little's limb. I refused.

Great Casterton

Can we ever know ourselves? This eternal posit has been answered here, in this lurid civil parish with a population of 600. The answer is "maybe".

Greetham

If this village were a place, it would be Woking.

Gunthorpe

The men of this land are noble. Tens of them eat whelks.

Hambleton

#whatwasthat #screamingshepherds #flamingmallards #hellnosister #morelikeshambleton

Horn

They say inspiration is a small, razorwired slug of some 5mm. This place is covered in the things. A creative haven, no less!

Ketton

Heretics asked to leave. Grebe lovers asked to remain. (Oh!)

Langham

If this village were an idea, it would be the concept of rhyme.

Leighfield

Let the people of this place, whose name I forget, scream their names into the mimsy Middle English skies. It will probably help aerate their bronchi.

Little Casterton

Alias, "the boghole of bumpudding."

Lyddington

"I am the mayor," a shopkeeper told me. "I am proud to be the mayor," he added. He was a shopkeeper. "I mayor daily, nightly, and weekly," he said. He sold stamps, fruit drinks, and frozen pies. "I rule this land," he concluded. He was the mayor.

Lyndon

A shame, really, what happened to Gamba Osaka FC in that wigwam.

Manton
The residents report feelings of "ocean-dark loneliness". They should try Elaine's lapskaus!

Market Overton
In 1888, a lord invented edible ellipses here. For months, people scoured the canons of hesitant writers for a taste of the sweet dots, and munched them up like Malteasers, until a second lord invented edible food. The ellipsis craze trailed off, rather like, in fact, an uneaten ellipsis . . .

Martinsthorpe
If this village were a music, it would be Gregorian plain funk.

Morcott
If ever you find yourself exhausted by metropolitan living, kayak yourself waywards to this smoky hamtown, where the flaming cottages, roast bungalows, and crisply sautéed semi-detacheds elicit oohs from the nearby oohlookers. Remember to pack a smork and toast yo'self some mallows over the charred corpses of retired accountants.

Normanton
That particle accelerator in Sue's Tea Shoppe is, frankly, a mistake.

North Luffenham
Love prickles up her shoulder like an overheard midnight backstreet six-string minor chord.

Oakham
If this village was a utensil mangled in a washing machine, that mangled utensil would be a teaspoon.

Pickworth
Alias, "the coven of sneering rodents".

Pilton
Second to none is the village none, which came second (to a nun, no less).

Preston
The centenarians here, realising all attempts at meaningful conversation are useless, and that a kind of broken achronological gabble is closer to the heart of life's thing, speak in profound and beautiful nonsense. Sadly, most of their gums have fallen off.

Ridlington
A word to the wise: spanner. A word to the unwise: spline.

Ryhall
If this village were a biscuit in motion, it would be a tea-sodden Digestive crumbling unmunched onto a side plate as the doorbell rings.

Seaton
Bring a scuba suit and a pair of callipers.

South Luffenham
The annual festival lasts nine weeks. For the first eight and a half weeks, a man sits on a wheel and has apocalyptic visions. For the remaining half week, the local children are invited to contemplate his beard.

Stoke Dry
I can't.

Stretton
You can.

Teigh
Disappointmentalicious is a made-up word. This village is splendid.

Thistleton
If this village were a page in nonexistent novel, that page would be p.45 of Armand Lawrentia's *Stop Running, Stanley!*

Thorpe by Water
Alias, "a swig of lukewarm phlegm".

Tickencote
The local girls play maracas. The local boys play harplets. The local

yokels play marimbae. The God of Aural Wonder reigns supreme in this thatched nugget.

Tinwell

If a shirt were ripped in two places, the first a slight tear around the left armpit, the second a substantial gash down the back, and if that shirt were sold to a very poor man in a shop, then that shirt would accurately describe something.

Tixover

The toddlers here are terrified of ageing. Most of them cower when their second birthdays come around, huddled in the corner mumbling "Lord, save me from the void!" whenever their uncles present them with toy frogs. The terror is so severe most parents have their children put down by local merchants.

Uppingham

Yes, I know, there is a ham on a stick up a hill. Like you think I wouldn't mention like the most obvious thing about this world-famous place. I'm not a halfwit and you only want me to fail.

Wardley

An instrumental village. Most people skip to the next one.

Whissendine

Steve Mason lost an almond here in 1998. If you spot the almond, call Steve's mum on 0718 282 2728. No voice mails.

Whitwell

If this village were a village, it would be this village.

Wing

The end of Rutland. The souls of the living flap towards the ceiling and listen to the aching of the dust.

[EAST RIDING]

NAME: WIMBLE CROAT
AGE: 49
SENTENCE: 12 YEARS
CRIME: IMPERSONATING THIS MAN INSIDE A HOSPICE

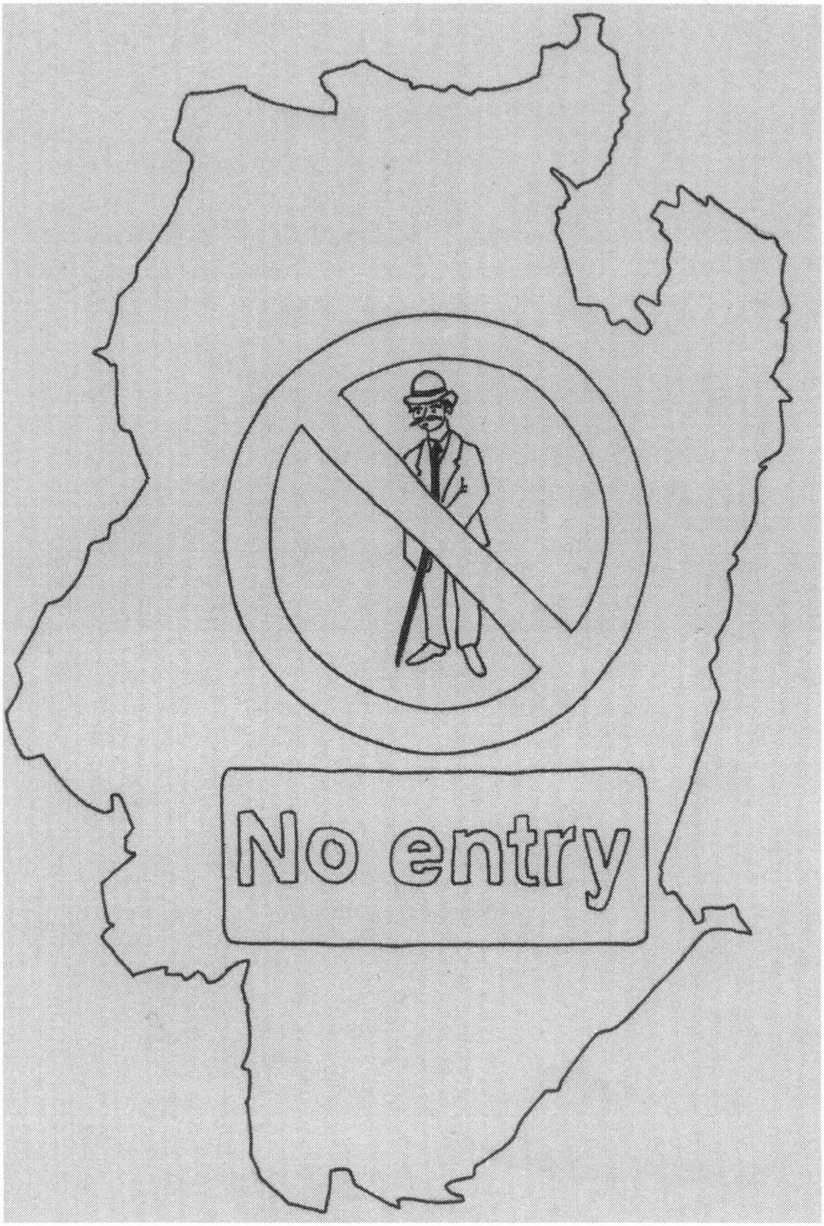
No entry

[ISLE OF WIGHT]

NAME: GORDON SAMP
AGE: 44
SENTENCE: 30 YEARS
CRIME: CLASSIFICATION ERROR

MY STORY 'A PIECE OF NEW WRITING' was published in *The Anthology of New Writing*. A fortnight later, I received an email from its editor. There had been complaints that my story was, contrary to its title, a piece of old writing—it had appeared in *The Anthology of Old Writing* the previous month. I explained that when the piece had been published in *The Anthology of Old Writing* it was a new piece of writing in *that* publication. And when the piece transferred to *The Anthology of New Writing* it became a new piece in *that* publication. I then received a furious email from the editor of *The Anthology of Old Writing* who accused me of submitting a new piece of writing to his anthology of old writing. I explained that the piece had been written seven years ago, so was technically an 'old' piece of writing despite having never been published before. It could appear in both the *Old* and *New* anthologies since it was an 'old' piece in terms of its being written yonks ago but a 'new' piece since it hadn't been previously published before in a 'new' writing anthology. The editors weren't buying this. Clearly, by this logic, the 'old' story would become a 'new' story when printed in the *Old* anthology, and therefore be a piece of 'old' writing once it reached the *New* anthology. I had to hand back the monies I was paid for being in both anthologies. I resubmitted the piece to *The Anthology of Discredited Writing* and learned a lesson.

[DORSET]

NAME: LYLE RUPEE
AGE: 45
SENTENCE: 53 YEARS
CRIME: THE DEHARDIFICATION OF DORSET

I OPENED The Puddletown Cultural Assimilation Coping and Strategies Clinic on the banks of the River Piddle in April 2009. Since leaving college, I had been a meticulous planner and nurtured unrealistic dreams that refused to unfold as I entered life's drift and took up a series of posts patronising the unemployed for being unemployed and rattling coppers in a coffer for the sake of loners and lepers. I used hard drugs to cope with the disappointment of not becoming a rich executive at 24 and switched to full-time use. After my sixth overdose, I met a kind nurse who advised me to stop taking drugs because life is for living not for lying around in hospital beds on IV drips watching daytime talk shows. I elected to help others like me who had become inveterate mopers and redeem their lives before the bitterness became an unconquerable obstacle.I travelled to Puddletown in the Dorset heartlands soon after convalescing. I had planned to take a week-long holiday before returning to life in London—to take long solitary walks and start planning the future. After a few days in my B&B, I observed that the citizens were experiencing the sort of unflinching existential torment I had only seen as an undergraduate at the chess and board games club. Their every waking minute was consumed with an endless self-loathing and suicidal depression. Those passing through Puddletown were startled to realise that, in spite of the picturesque surroundings, this village was cursed with a medieval gloom.

There was a simple explanation. The village of Puddletown (at present) is a prop for the Dorset tourist industry. Several years before my arrival, Puddletown was operating as a tourist village with the usual swathes of holidaying English and Americans, and had vented its own cultural identity, drawing upon East European literature, Hungarian cinema, and the folk and orchestral music of Estonia. For a village in West Dorset, the absence of undistilled Dorsetness was problematic. Dorset depends on tourism for 90% of its revenue and the tourist board could not allow a pivotal village like Puddletown (formerly Piddletown) to depict Dorset as a multicultural Frankenstein's monster stealing its heritage from abroad. Puddletown housed an avant-garde collective— a thriving enclave of artists and musicians. Tourists would purchase an epic experimental poem written in Cyrillic script or an album of concrete music and leave with the impression these things were "native" to Dorset. Puddletown was, culturally, the least Hardyean place in Dorset and, according to the tourist board, a poor representative of its rich heritage. One day, Dorset council enforced a change in the village, blackmailing the shopkeepers into stocking only "relevant and authentic" Dorsettian cultural traditions.

Having to downgrade from an artistic haven to a monocultural localistic tat-shilling programme left the residents shattered. One man who had written a reworking of *Beowulf* filtered through the philosophies of Viktor Shklovsky, Jacques Derrida, and Scritti Politti was forced to compose eclogues on the pastoral qualities of various hills and ravines and sell £4 bottled water to survive. The DVD shop, selling movies from Truffaut, Eisenstein, and Tarr, was forced to sell boxsets of a '90s adaptation of *Far From the Madding Crowd* and unexpurgated editions of travel show *Yeovil Wanderers*. The bookshops lost their copies of Pierre Albert-Birot, Arno Schmidt, Tom Mallin, and Machado de Assis, replaced by the latest Hardyean romance series by Arlene Cassidy, *Love in the Watermeadows*. The rich variety of culture was wiped out overnight.

The residents sank into a deep depression at this intellectual exodus. Some took to drinking (cider the only available poison) and others swore and assaulted outsiders. This merely increased tourism in the area (people keen to see "authentic" Dorset traits in action). Several teenagers who had nurtured dreams of becoming directors, writers, and musicians, abandoned their hopes to work in inns and guest houses as cleaners and maids. Evening entertainment turned from screenings of Buñuel's *The Discreet Charm of the Bourgeoisie* to ceilidhs and readings from Hardy. The village moped around barely exchanging a single kind word. I opened the clinic a week after these changes to help the villagers adapt. My first client was Bill Barnes, whose unfortunate surname made his life impossible in the village. Tourists asked him on an hourly basis if he was the famous poet, and the tourist board exerted pressure on him to dress up like Barnes and memorise screeds of his poetry so he could pass himself off as a descendant. The tourist board had sent friendly "reminders," urging him to transmogrify himself into Barnes by flinging bricks through his window. He had come close to suicide several times.

To help treat his affliction, I proposed the following stress-relieving strategies. 1) To look in the mirror and recite forty times: "You are not Barnes. But you *are* a Great Person." 2) To surprise himself with an act of kindness towards himself, such as stopping into a shop for a chocolate muffin or making a kind remark. 3) To read the entire works of Barnes so as not to be stifled or afraid. 4) To swim or have a game of darts each evening. 5) To say to himself: "Watermeadows are a Good Thing. Hills are Positive. The air is clear and pure. Grass is nice. Dorset is a Good Land." 6) To compose new works to please the tourist board. Over a series of weeks, Bill emerged from his depression and became a popular figure in the board's campaign for reforming Puddletown.

My next client was Tracy. She had made several surrealist movies set in Puddletown and neighbouring villages, merging shots of Dorset heath with clips from a skirmish in Afghanistan as a troubling wake-up call to the cosiness of the West. She had filled several canvasses with her 'id-syncrasies'—vivid visions from her subconscious in stormy blacks, yellows, and reds. Her idols were Reuben Mednikoff and Leonora Carrington. I suggested she paint Lewesdon Hill. On her first attempt, a series of Cerberuses devouring each others' heads stole the image. On the second, eyeballs on shish kebabs dotted the landscape. On the third, she managed to paint the scene undisturbed, until I peered closer to see she had snuck in a naked cannibal devouring four babies in the bottom right corner. To prevent her from channelling these violent visions, I suggested she take up hillwalking and aerobicising. In a few weeks, Tracy was painting knolls and peaks with tremendous accuracy and selling them in the gift shop at £30 a pop.

Rupert was an experimental novelist. His books used unconventional forms such as letters written by dyslexic squids, erotic confessions *sans* pronouns and verbs, and Horacean odes on thin mortar and other grouting mixes. I suggested he make an attempt to compose a sonnet on a clump of daisies. He ran to the bar, drank four ciders, and wrote a poem that he shared with me at his next session: *Beneath my feet / white-petalled things / love them? / love them not? / either way / they ain't going nowhere.* It was the beginning of something beautiful. He was soon able to reduce his cider consumption to three pints per afternoon and concentrate on writing odes about things that mattered—hills, Dorset heath, Hardy, and the chutzpah of the Dorset innkeeper. He soon awoke to the realisation that his experimental novels had been acts of immense pretentiousness, and signed a contract to publish four chapbooks with the progressively patriotic Dovecote Press.

Among my other clients: Theo, an experimental composer whose extravagant explorations in the realm of sound expanded upon the formal innovations of John Cage, especially his attention to counterpoint and the tone row technique. His concerts of freeform jazz honking and air-guitar rock operas drew crowds from Strasbourg, Naples, and Perth. I cured his pretensions by introducing him to the nose flute, which he learned to play outside The William Barnes Centre for Patriotic Dorsetness. I also treated Carla, a theatre director whose interpolations of Brecht and Lang were hailed as the signifiers of a Brave New Age of performance art. I introduced her to the stage play of *The Return of the*

Native, and suggested she a write an equally heartwarming rustic knock-about set in Puddletown that appealed to the masses and had a gawky male farmhand and a cute wisecracking female heroine as per the original. She wrote *Puppylove in Puddletown* to acclaim and her popularity was assured.

Unfortunately, my clinic was soon destroyed by rebellious locals, desperate to avoid the assimilation. Anyone brave enough to take on the notoriously dour and fierce Dorset council usually means business, and these frustrated intellectuals held nothing back when they brought a tank into the village and began blasting empty cars, threatening people from their workplaces, and blowing up the occasional building or two. The rebels reclaimed Puddletown as alt-culture haven, or else, and drove out the bunnet-waving reformists, celebrating with live readings of Maurice Roche and Michel Butor. I closed my little clinic and toddled back into the world of aimlessness and drug addiction, vowing never again to fuck with the powers of the avant-garde.

[WORCESTERSHIRE]

NAME: POLLY TODDLE
AGE: 34
SENTENCE: 12.5 YEARS
CRIME: BECAUSE YOU KNOW WHY

Mrs. Toddle was informed, by Chinese whisper, that she was incarcerated "because you know why". Since then she has been tormenting herself and others in her life as to the possible reason that she knows not why. Below are possibles from her own mouthhole and two of her friends' sames. —Ed.

HER REASONS

The fact I married a stockbroker who shops at Lidl to "keep it real" then powers his Lotus to the Pershore Club House, and puts his frozen onion rings and oven chips in a special padlocked freezer, where it remains uneaten for months as our personal shopper Geeta fills our home unit with Waitrose produce.

"   " swim the breaststroke with the cod liver laxity of a pensioner in a swimming cap, in spite of my some thirty-four years.

"   " named our firstborn Calliope, our secondborn Thornfin, and our thirdborn Darren, in response to muttered accusations of pretension from Tatiania Greepthrum.

"   " have been on page 102 of *The Woodlanders* for four months, and have left a bookmark at that page in the hopeless belief that I might return to finish the rest from that point onward, having long forgotten the story, having long since returned the novel to the bookcase, having called Hardy "bloated" over twelve times.

"   " struggle to conceal an amused smirk when Samuel L. Jackson has his brains blown across a mattress in *Goodfellas*.

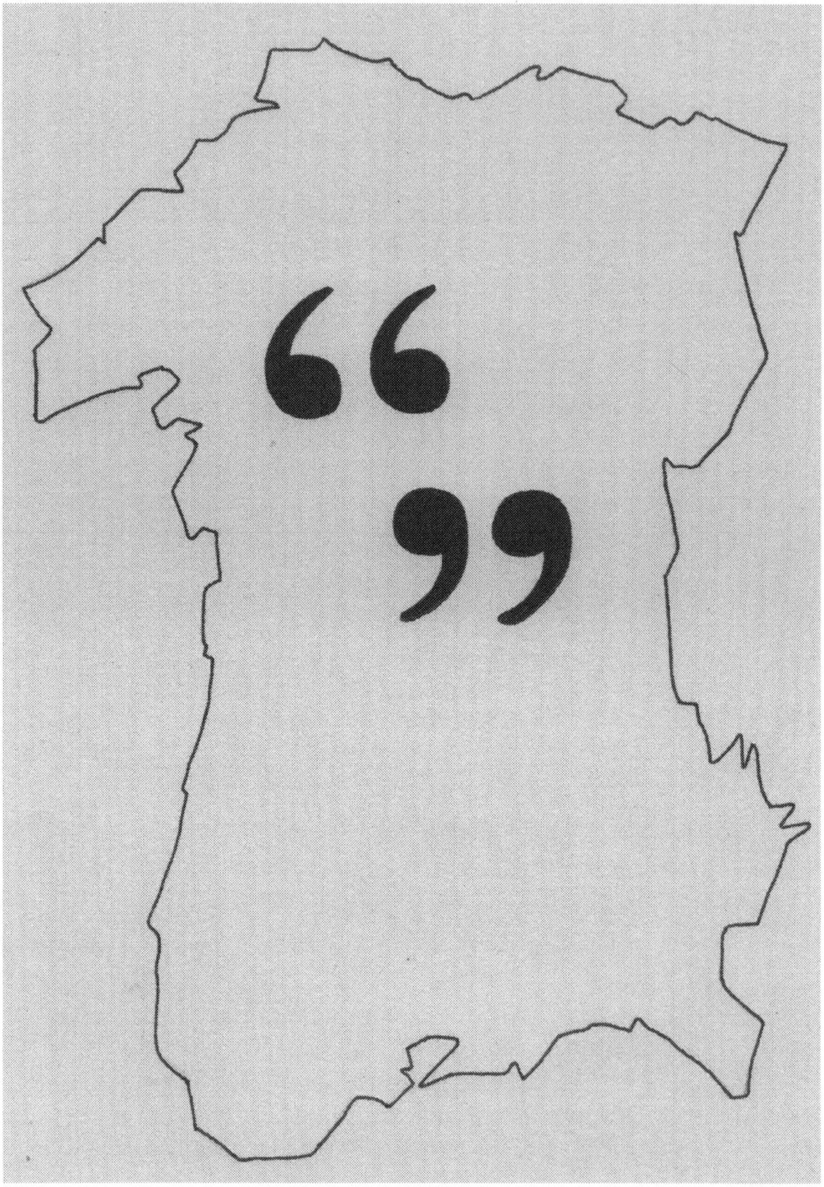

"   " locate an ant, corner the ant, scoop the ant into a tube, and release the ant into the blonde tresses of my friend Angela's daughter.

"   " sometimes on purpose bake a £5 note into a liver and potato pie, then stomp round the house screaming that I have lost a £5 note with the manic urgency of someone who has misplaced a £3m cheque, forcing everyone to scour the place for the lost note, then later, when the pie is served, and one of my children accidentally eats a mushed remnant of the note, I leap up in hysterics and yell "Whore! You ate my money!", then wallop whichever one it is around the occiput for twelve seconds.

"   " am not wholly onboard with the emancipation proclamation and scowl when the phrase is used at the Redditch Wine & Prosecco Appreciation Union, usually by Bethany 'The Lathe' Williamsburg.

"   " exude an air of aloofness whenever my children have been crushed by a Peterbilt 386 tractor, yet leap to buy ice creams and knicker-bocker glories whenever my sister's kids split their shins on rocks.

"   " insist that the turf is magnified by 1000 pixels whenever I am taking putts at Evesham Golf Place, so I can play with a breadstick.

"   " release the air from county fair bouncy castles into a neigh-bouring funeral home, so that children leap up and down on the recently deceased.

"   " wobble occasionally, usually while operating a tremolo pedal, or complaining about inclement parsnip soup.

"   " make a clicking sound with my thorax that sounds like a small lascivious man making an audible pass at a local beauty with the side of his mouth.

"   " can yodel in nine languages.

"   " wait until the second course at dinner parties before launch-ing into a passionate defence of Bill Callahan and refuse to stop unless people applaud me wildly after, and beg for a second oratorical opus, which I withhold.

THE REASONS OF ALTWICH GROOB

The fact she chews each forkful of food nineteen times before swallowing, and to ensure each chew is recorded, enters each chew into a portable abacus that she carries on her person at all times, including at funfairs.

"   " can recite the alphabet from A-Z with spookily faultless precision.

"   " insists that moshing is appropriate at a wake.

"   " purchases her child ice cream, asks if she can have a cheeky lick, then shoves the whole cone into her mouth, and hands her child the mushy crunchy remnants, and berates the child for any consequent crying or moaning.

"   " considers Beefheart's *Unconditionally Guaranteed* a "quantum leap into true artistry".

"   " wrote to the council every day, insisting on the carpet bombing of Droitwich Spa in persuasive, potent rhetoric, until the council eventually conceded, and petrol bombed the Salvation Army Hall in a ruthless, uncompromising assault, killing a man.

"   " published a panegyric on polytonality, entitled *Look Ma! Both Hands!*

"   " cannot see why the introduction of ravenous wasps into floatation tanks is a bad idea, no matter what words you use in the elegant strum of your discourse.

"   " arrives at Croome Court and sits on the historic chaises longues like someone slumping on the sofa after a gruelling slog at work, loosening her trousers and flicking through her phone to read the latest Facebook updates, until a curator arrives to ask her not to sit on the chaise longue and to please leave, which she does, only after attempting to kiss the curator with a sudden impalpable lust.

"   " will happily encourage the coining of new maxims, yet snap if you use the new maxim in an unsolicited clause.

"   " had an affair with a short man insecure about his height who, before having sex, she would tease by leaving the room and producing a stepladder, which he would often receive in tears, having tolerated the same lampoon across ninety-one lovemaking sessions.

"   " attends Phil Collins concerts and shouts "play music! play it, play music!" loudly, even when music was being played, to confuse Phil and the audience members as to whether she was either insane, or making some barbed remark that Phil Collins was not really playing music, but dreary, commercial pap-pop (in which case, why would she pay £50 to attend, and stand in the front row?)

"   " opens artisan cafés in Malvern at the rate of ten a week, hiring world class Czech and Macedonian baristas with a talent for teasing the bean like no other, yet still prefers her coffee from the Pret.

"   " can make her upper gum screen early Todd Solondz, circa *Welcome to the Dollhouse* and *Happiness*, and allows her dentist private screenings inside her mouth in exchange for free molar repair or bicuspid scraping.

"   " starred in an inappropriately erotic advert for Harpic using areolar subliminality to help peddle the popular bowl cleaner.

SOME REASONS, C/O SHONA BUDGE

The fact she is the most outspoken opponent of compulsory seppuku for new nursery students.

"   " sits curled up inside an eschatological turkey, self-basting her nimby beliefs in a runny stewlet of cowardice.

"   " once refused the titular condiment Dittoshire Sauce, poking the ire of Lea's fourth cousin once removed, who claims to "sweat pails promoting the county's premier fermented liquid."

"   " possesses a tail of some 5.5mm and has never shared a single pic, yet saturates Instagram with shots of her chin, post- and pre-buffing.

"   " is not nice to men who live in cupboards.

"   " is most circumspect when leaning on balustrades, yet recklessly topples over handrails like someone who wants to suicide.

"   " once tried to market carbonated milk.

"   " prefers to sit on the right side, to recline on the right, and to stand in the middle of the right, at a horizontal axis, fourteen centimes between the centre middle, the left right, and the vertical down.

"   " makes herself sound cleverer than she is by saying "inconspicuosity" in most sentences, a word that is not in the OED.

"   " once lapped at her cat's milk bowl to encourage the reluctant mog to sup cow fluids, then became so addicted to that method of transferring white liquid to her throat, she henceforward only consumed UHT through feline means, and sneered at anyone seen supping the stuff from cups or tumblers.

"   " conducted a vicious back-and-forth email campaign to force Oxford Dictionary lexicographers to change the definition of 'shirty' to 'pertaining to shirt wearing or people who wear shirts'.

"   " sat on a sachet of Dittoshire Sauce, and refused to remove her skirt and lap up the spilled substance, poking the ire of Perrins's third wife twice dismissed, who called her "a traitor to the county's finest and least necessary food-goo."

"   " locked herself out the outside of her car, by accidentally leaving the keys on the bonnet all the way from Thurso to Westward Ho!

"   " prefers to have sex with her husband, rather than any passing accountants.

"   " was the first person in unrecorded history to choke on a fishbone while eating beef.

"   " sat in a canoe for two minutes, saying "what now?" when it was apparent that she had to use oars to propel her canoed self further into the brine.

"   " used to be cool about everything, then became more uptight about something, and now is mainly stiff and hateful about nothing.

[KENT]

NAME: IRENE GABLE
AGE: 41
SENTENCE: 4 YEARS
CRIME: RESISTENCE

I WAS CHIEF EDITOR at Gable Editions when the new reforms were rubberstamped. Our combination of first-class translations of Sri Lankan women's fiction and contentious list of new feminist poets had Random House rapping on our shutters. The ink on the lucrative buyout contract was still wet when Random House, the Penguin Group, Simon & Schuster *et al* terminated their operations in the United Kingdom. It made no business sense for their multimillion pound publishing enterprises to be taken over by the incumbent Conservative government, and for their profits to fund free school meals for underachieving kids. The independent presses had two choices: leave the country and run their businesses from overseas, or remain and find themselves subsumed into a strange new fascistic era of publishing.

I was three months' pregnant at the time with British twins, had signed the lease on a thatched cottage in Britain, and married a British man with a two-year contract in a British office. I had no intention of fleeing to France, like my freer, younger comrades. I chose to remain and slap down the new reforms. I made a show of my resistance, telling my colleagues that when the stooges arrived, we would rush them with copies of Helen Yardley's latest hardback *Bees in Aspic*, and recite the most venomous stanzas until they fled under the weight of her devastating entomological images. Beneath this humour was the miserable awareness that nothing of the sort would happen and that our words as weapons would prove useless in the face of banal legal processes set to shred apart our souls.

On a windy July morning, two civil servants arrived at the office to "seize" our operations. The first one, a swaggering clichéd manchild, wore a long trenchcoat and shades. The second, a faceless slaphead Molotov, informed us in crushed inflections that our press had become a "recruitment" wing of the Government, and had merged in part into the Department for Work & Pensions. The "recruitment" our publishing house would be involved in was the processing of application forms from writers who aspired to become Authorised Artists. Our press's mission statement to publish original and provocative feminist fiction and translations was torn to shreds and replaced with new criteria:

KEY REQUIREMENTS OF SUBMISSIONS

A1 Must show basic competence in use of English
A2 Must have a strong central 'everyman' character
A3 Must have a clear beginning, middle, and end

B1 Must have one key 'theme' or 'topic'
B2 Must present this with clarity and accessibility
B3 Must have simple, effective writing style

C1 Must include strong emotional hooks
C2 Must include strong and compelling plot
C3 Must have believable secondary characters

NON-ESSENTIAL (BUT DESIRED) REQUIREMENTS

A1 Must have a light 'poetic' quality
A2 Must have a mild sense of humour
A3 Must avoid complicated aspects of the 'theme' or 'topic'

B1 Must have a strong 'twist' at the end
B2 Must have a strong moral message
B3 Must impart a feeling of hope or optimism

After reading this, I told Molotov to insert a whalecock up his mother's anus. "Have you copied this verbatim from the Harper Collins website?" I asked. The remark sailed across their illiterate heads. I sensed their barely suppressed mirth that we—we *smug smart* people—had failed. That delight the uneducated take when someone smarter than them suffers. Those snarl-lipped, bitter bastards who love to say "see where your education has got you". Anyway, we retained our positions at the press and swallowed our bitter pills. We were forced to read the applications of thousands of talented and potentially brilliant writers, turn down their claims, and take seriously the writing that met the criteria. Novice writers, hip to the new requirements and keen on making a buck from writing, were the sort of chancers we ended up having to publish. I'm talking hellhound penpushers with no talent who write seven-volume sci-fi fantasies called *The Darkness is Rising*. Their terrible first drafts were "polished" by various writers whose job was to spiff up the manuscripts for public consumption. This is hell. Hell. It is the age of the book as flushable product. The age of the book as bog roll.

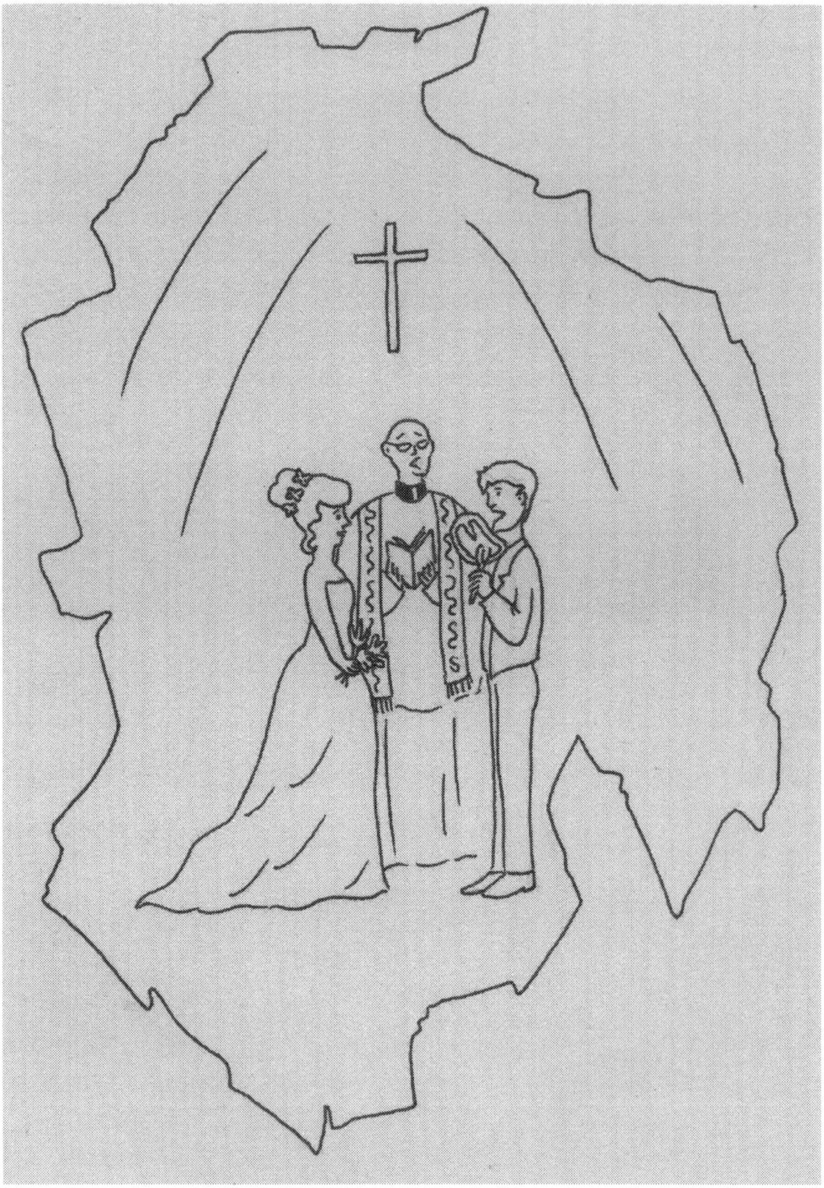

[LANCASHIRE]

NAME: NORMAN CRYER
AGE: 55
SENTENCE: 200 YEARS
CRIME: GASTRIC VASSALAGE

I WENT TO A CATHOLIC MASS to hear the latest updates from The Lord. As I arrived, a sparsely attended funeral was taking place. In the third pew, a balding man was slurping minestrone from a bowl. I asked him why. "I haven't had my lunch," he whispered. I explained to the man that there are certain unwritten social rules imposed on people regarding the public ingestion of foodstuffs, and that less enlightened people might consider his slurping an act of categorical rudeness, especially while honouring the stiff. "I never subscribed to that myself. I've always obeyed the call of hunger above everything else. It's made me a well-rounded and happy individual. Let me explain. See, as a nipper, my parents always hauled me off to church for 6.30 mass, delaying the evening's repast until our 8.00 return. I would spend the entire mass miserable with a rumbling tummy. I would pass into that queasy stage of hunger, when you feel your stomach sticking to your ribs, and when I arrived home for my repast, my appetite was fairly poor. Now, my mother was a smart and spendthrift woman. I think she understood this, and tried to spoil our appetites so we might eat smaller portions. I soon started smuggling snacks in to mass. I would secrete a biscuit up my sleeve, and as we lowered ourselves to our knees and placed our praying hands to our heads, I would pop the biscuit into my mouth. Similarly, after receiving the Eucharist, as I turned to the altar, I would carefully insert a sugary treat into my mouth while making the sign of the cross, provided no altar boys were watching. I made a promise to myself that as an adult, I would never allow events or other people to interfere with the call of hunger, and I would always have food on hand."

"That's a refreshingly maverick stance," I said.

"Thank you very much. Now, I'll tell you, this hasn't always made me popular. Quite the contrary, my maverick stance, as you generously phrase it, has caused various uproars throughout my life. For example, my first interview after college was scheduled for 12.00. I was hoping to become an accounts administrator. Unfortunately, they were running behind, and I was kept waiting a whole hour and twenty minutes. My stomach began rumbling around 13.17, so I removed the pre-prepared ham and mayo baguette from my bag to sate my hunger. I went into the interview with this baguette, and continued chomping throughout the interview, making my answers unintelligible at times, seeing my mouth was filled with soggy lettuce. I was asked to leave after I refused to stop eating. They were not interested in my maverick stance. Another time, I was playing in goal at a football match when I suddenly received the call to eat my cold pasta salad with pesto. I retrieved the salad from my bag to sate my hunger, leaving me incapable of stopping the ball with my hands, full as they were with a small container and a fork. My teammates were furious as I hid from the oncoming man and football. My first consideration was for my lunch. I was banned from the team after that match."

"Wow."

"Indeed. My loving wife, who has always patiently tolerated my stance, was not happy when I pulled a carving of T-bone steak from my pocket as we were reciting our wedding vows. As I was saying 'I do' to my little flower, I spluttered peppercorn sauce into her bridal veil and failed to suppress a belch. The kiss was not memorable. On a similar note, my sexual encounters have been interrupted or spoiled by the oncoming rumble of hunger. My first time, for example. I was ready to finally lose my virginity to a lovely lady named Marlene Adams, when I had the overwhelming urge to chomp a slice of pizza. As I always keep food within reach, I removed the cold pizza from a box under the pillow to sate my hunger. Marlene was utterly distraught as pepperoni tumbled onto her breasts, and my romantic moans were replaced by the hearty chomps of a man who has not eaten for over nine hours. My virginity was delayed by another three years. These days, my long-suffering wife ensures I am fully sated before intercourse."

"Eating beforehand . . . ?"

"No. The rule is, I always let hunger dictate. It means I am not falling into the trap of overeating. It is simple to carry a sandwich on one's persons at all times. I always ensure I am well-equipped with emergency sandwiches, in case eating plans are interrupted."

"What about restaurants?"

"If my wife wishes to eat out, I usually accompany her. Sometimes, my hunger arrives when she has finished her dessert and coffee, and she must wait for me while I order my main course. Sometimes, hunger calls in the car on the way to a restaurant, and I must consume my pre-prepared meal at once, often slurping up the last of my soup, or nibbling away the final sinews of my drumstick as I enter the restaurant."

"I see. What is your job?"

"It is hard to understand. I am often viewed strangely. I am a fireman. I am stared by the lads when I eat my sushi in the middle of a burning building. Sometimes, I have risked people's lives as I was retrieving them from a smoke-filled room and the hunger called. They would watch in horror as I retrieved my three-bean salad and asked them to wait for several minutes. Fortunately, the lads have my back. If they see me removing food from my person, they allow me to leave the scene and finish sating my hunger. There really are some wonderfully understanding people in the world."

"Are you religious?"

"No. This is my mother's funeral. Now, if you'll excuse me, I must read the eulogy while finishing this bowl of minestrone."

[GREATER LONDON]

NAME: SOLAS ARTWOOL
AGE: 79
SENTENCE: TWO MINUTES
CRIME: CHESS OOPS

Game One, 12 May

1.f3 e5 2.g4 Qh4#.

Game Two, 17 June

1.f3 e5 2.g4 Qh4#.

Game Three, 2 August

1.f3 e5 2.g4 [board upended]

Game Four, 29 August

1.f3 e5 [opponent incapacitated]

[HERTFORDSHIRE]

NAME: AL BOX
AGE: 32
SENTENCE: 14 WEEKS
CRIME: HIPPOPTOMONSTROSESQUIPEDALIANISM*

June 23

I SET ABOUT DEPHLOGISTICATING the inner wall cavities using a trowel slathered in spackle. Due to a long-term battle with iatromisia, I was procrastinating from the inevitable—I had been stricken with a periphrastic disease where my sentences ballooned with superfluous verbiage and embarrassing altiloquence. I had never considered myself a bloviating snollygoster before, so this sudden transformation was distressing. This aeolistic expression, my wife said to me, was rendering my syntax acataleptic. It was imperative that I overcome these iatromisic anxieties and make an appointment. As I spackled the cavities in protest, my wife persuaded me using her melliloquence to see the GP.

June 24

I have suffered at the hands of doctors. My first, Dr. Maximilian Strapthorn, was a covinous mammothrept who prescribed pills that, far from being abstersive painsolvers, were lethiferous painmakers. Next up was Dr. Agamemnon Pinterwilde—an unrepentant sneckdraw and rampant breedbate. His attempt at humour resulted in a *mauvaise plaisanterie* and his refusal to apologise exacerbated the situation. I had to absquatulate, making a hurried clodpolish exit as the bemused receptionists looked on like grinagogs. The last, Dr. Polysemour Frantickle, was a

*Glossary overleaf.

hirsutorufous mome with a severe case of maschalephidrosis. His natural gemütlichkeit masked an unbelievable incompetence—the drivelling wantwit wrote me a prescription for antidepressants after I showed him a toe fungus! How could I trust the next medicaster to seriously cure me of this egregious nimiety?

June 25

I arrived at the surgery, sitting down in the banausic waiting area. After being summoned, I perambulated down the acherontic corridor in an attempt to appear relaxed. The GP was a lagotic baffona with a soothing mansuetude in her manner. I explained to her my loganamnosis and habit for *obscurum per obscurius*, and she smiled. She explaterated about her inability to find the *mot propre* in confabulations, and once she ceased her charming clishmaclaver went on to diagnose me with hippopotomonstrosesquipedalianism. I explained about our new house, and how our bookcase is positioned behind our bed. The works of Alexander Theroux were above my pillow, I had inhaled the essence of this author's aenos while sleeping. She nuncupated that the cure was not operose—a simple replacement with the works of Ernest Hemingway for two weeks would create the vocabulary equilibrium I was seeking. As I left, I could have sworn she palpebrated at me, or cast me an oeillade(!)

July 25

Problem fixed. Now terse. Need to go back to Theroux. Gone too far the other way.

Glossary for rampant (hippopotomonstro)sesquipedalianists:

dephlogisticate (v.) to take away the phlogiston, i.e. ability to burn, which is now understood to be chemically impossible.
iatromisia (n.) an intense dislike of doctors.
periphrastic (adj.) circumlocutious.

altiloquence (n.) pompous language; lofty speech.

bloviate (v.) to speak or discourse at length in a pompous or boastful manner.

snollygoster (n.) shrewd person not guided by principles.

aeolistic (adj.) pompous or long-winded.

acataleptic (adj.) incapable of being comprehended; incomprehensible.

melliloquence (n.) speaking sweetly or harmoniously.

covinous (adj.) deceitful; collusive; fraudulent; dishonest.

mammothrept (n.) a spoilt child.

abstersive (adj.) cleansing; purging; abstergent.

lethiferous (adj.) deadly, lethal.

sneckdraw (n.) one who is sly, cunning, devious.

breedbate (n.) one who breeds or originates quarrels.

mauvaise plaisanterie (n.) an inappropriate or badly-timed joked.

absquatulate (v.) to leave quickly or in a hurry; to take oneself off; to decamp; to depart, flee.

clodpolish (adj.) awkward.

grinagog (n.) a perpetual grinner.

hirsutorufous (adj.) red-haired.

mome (n.) a blockhead.

maschalephidrosis (n.) massive sweating of the armpits.

gemütlichkeit (n.) middle-class niceness or cosiness; hospitality.

wantwit (n.) a person lacking wit or sense; a fool.

medicaster (n.) a quack doctor; someone who pretends to have medical knowledge.

nimiety (adj.) state of being in excess, possessing more than is needed.

banausic (adj.) utilitarian.

acherontic (adj.) infernal, dismal, gloomy, moribund.

lagotic (adj.) rabbit-eared.

baffona (n.) a woman with a slight moustache.

mansuetude (n.) gentleness, tameness.

loganamnosis (n.) a mania to recall forgotten words.

obscurum per obscurius (explaining) the obscure by means of the more obscure.

explaterate (v.) to talk excessively.

clishmaclaver (n). idle talk, gossip.

hippopotomonstrosesquipedalianism (n). fondness for extremely long words.

aenos (n.) use of erudite words or allusions to appeal to the learned.

nuncupate (v.) to solemnly pronounce.

operose (adj.) wrought with, requiring, or evidencing a lot of labour; tedious; wearisome.

palpebrate (v.) to wink.

oeillade (n.) a glance, especially an amorous one; an ogle.

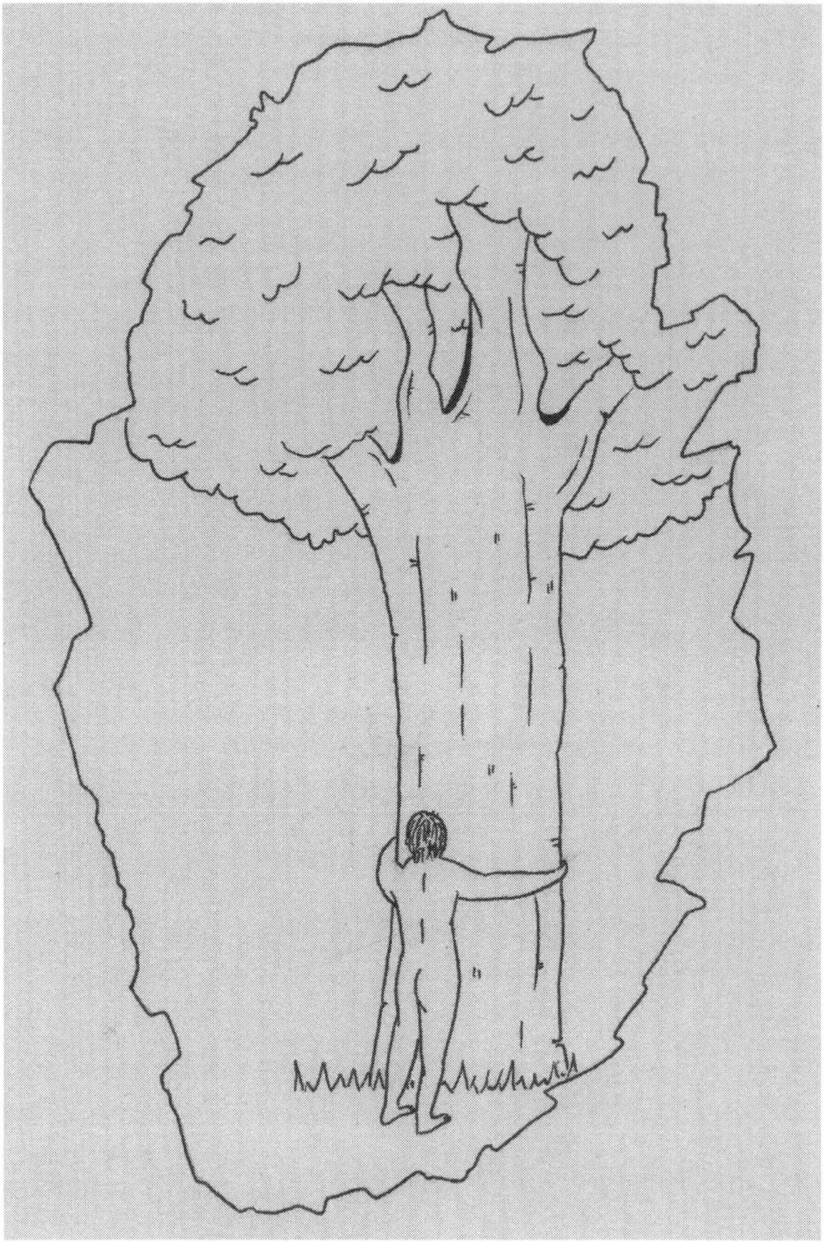

[NOTTINGHAMSHIRE]

NAME: OLLIE HOPPA

AGE: 22

SENTENCE: 2.1 DAYS

CRIME: INCIDENCES OF CATASTROPHIC RELATIONSHIP
MISFIRE, CAUSED BY INAPPROPRIATE SEXUAL
GAUCHERIES

I ASKED HELEN to put on cherry red lipstick and wear her hair in bunches. I asked her to wear fake lashes and to rouge her cheeks slightly, and wear a white shirt and black skirt, so she looked more appealing sexually. I started out by kissing her on the cheeks but felt the rouge edging onto my own cheeks and felt silly in case any pinkness passed onto my cheeks and made me look girlish. I kissed her cherry red lips, the colour evoking extreme desire in me, but pulled back when fears of the colour passing onto my lips, and the paranoia she might find the tincture of red on my lips comical or unattractive and reduce my planned seduction to farce, became too much. I grew shy of my girlfriend's beauty, I found myself unable to ravish her in the manner I had intended. By arranging her beauty cosmetically, I felt unworthy of such an attractive woman and couldn't bring myself to touch her soft, blemish-less skin. I asked her to downplay her attractiveness by not wearing makeup and leaving her hair unwashed. I was able to remove her clothes but the memory of her former beauty rendered me unable to climax.

※

I once asked a beautiful woman out on a date. Her name was Christina. She had long black hair and the silky, divine cheekbones of a French actress. I wanted to have sex with her and nothing else. I wasn't interested in her as a person. I wanted to writhe inside her sweaty, naked body until she shrieked in ecstasy. She was waiting for me at the restaurant. "I will have sex with you," she said. "But first, I want you to cut off your pinkies. If you cut off your pinkies I will be willing to have sex with you for the rest of my life, even if we never become a couple." I cut off my pinkies, rushed to the nearest A&E and ran back to Christina's house where we had sex all evening until our respective naughties ached. Christina kept my pinkies in a box above the mantelpiece as a symbol of my devotion to my desire to have sex with her because of her physical attractiveness. As the months progressed I considered buying artificial pinkies so my hands looked less weird. Christina said if I considered any replacement pinkies her legs would be forever closed to me. I did not replace the pinkies. A few weeks later Christina was badly burned in a fire and was no longer physically beautiful. I was unwilling to have sex with her but she pleaded with me to have sex with her because no one else would. I said if she cut off her pinkies I would have sex with her as long as she kept a bag over her head. She said that wasn't fair, as I was hideous and she'd never asked me to keep a bag over my head during sex. I said OK. She cut off her pinkies, rushed to A&E, then returned to have sex with me. We are now married and have sex twice a week, wishing we were sleeping with other people and wishing we still had our pinkies. If I had kept my pinkies, I could have cut them off for another beautiful woman who wasn't burned in a fire and I could be making love to her instead.

✳

I watched Alicia from across the room, sticking strips of papier-mâché to a miniature representation of the Hindenburg, and thought: Yes, I somewhat like this squat representative of the female species. It had been seven years since the last surge of warmness towards another (Bertha Bloome), so I inked some reasons for the liking onto A4. *I like when her throat explores the catalogue of Julee Cruise. I like when she sits and clicks her tongue against her well-brushed teeth in restless moments. I like when she con-*

templates a pause. I wrote prose. One afternoon, I brought two friends together in carnal union within the confines of five untabulated paragraphs. The scene involved the protagonist teabagging the male for up to two hours, and contained sustained and thorough descriptions of the act from its inception to conclusion. Alicia, a proud reader of my prose, read this scene over a linguini bowl four hours later, as her mâché blimp settled into shape. Her incomprehension at the length of the testicular tonguing procedure created a notable tension at the table. "The two-hour timeframe is ludicrous," she chided. "The repetitiveness of the act would render the lust moot." She continued with her accurate critique of this scene, futhermoring with the phrase: "Your lingering close-up on the salivated sac is an astonishing failure." Two weeks later, the relationship dissolved like nine disprins in a shallow pool of rainwater.

※

Everyone loves the music of Camper Van Beethoven. However, some people press '►' once too often where that comical cult indie unit is concerned. I found himself, or should I say, myself, since I am speaking (what if somewhere in space our every utterance forms the script for some interstellar soap opera?), in this predicament one autumn sunrise, having spinned *Telephone Free Landslide Victory* from five a.m. onwards, to the botherment of my beau Carla Opus, a telephone engineer with a serious phiz capable of unprompted smiles or frowns. The upbeat sway of the reggae-inflected numbers made me feel frisky, fired up with lust for my lover, whom I referred to as The Wayward Bus, for reasons that need no explaining. Unfortunately, Carla was not able to climax to 'Take the Skinheads Bowling'.

※

Pootling from the newsagent to the park with a shortcake in my left hand, I was in spirits once referred to by the actor Timothy Spall as "electric". I had been manufacturing opportunities to impress myself on the canoe seller Dottie over the last two months, with a view to taking her to the movies, and a later view of taking her to the theatre, and an even later view of taking her to an orchestral recital. My month-long sequence of calculated manoeuvres, including the careful positioning of herself outside the canoe shoppe, to engineer the perfect bump-intos, had paid off and this was the moment I would make myself known. I stood up, and launched into the sequence of startled reactions I learned from various vimeos, and called her name. "O Dottie!" I said. Sadly, she wobbled off into a thicket.

✳

For a time, I preferred sex in books to sex with my wife Denise. I could never lubricate her sufficiently, so she lay there like a corpse while I sheepishly screwed myself into her sprocket. When our sex life dried up, I had an affair with Anna Karenina. I met her at the local park and beneath an elm tree, took her image in my staff for illicit arboreal pleasure. Later, when Anna chose the train tracks over my penis, I met Emma Bovary by the tree and embraced her with an oaky, barky passion. Later, I went to the doctor with splinters in my foreskin and was warned off having sex with imaginary characters via tree trunks for a while, to stick to more conventional methods. I tried to sleep with Denise again but couldn't bring myself to do it. Eventually, I hit upon a novel idea. I hollowed out a tree trunk and cut a little hole in the bark. I made Denise squeeze herself inside and yes indeed, I had sex with her via the tree, pretending I was taking Emma Bovary. Our sex lives improved immensely, except Denise soon got Dutch elm disease and had to be cut down.

[TYNE AND WEAR]

NAME: SIMON
AGE: 30
SENTENCE: 6 DAYS
CRIME: IMPROPERLY BOLSTERED MATHS COLLEGE

THE MATHEMATICIANS POOLED AROUND the largest collection of floral wallpaper in Tyne and Wear. Some were impressed, others not so. David, a mathematician, remarked: "These belligerent pinks and staccato mauves speak of a dangerous neo-liberalist agenda." Another mathematician, Simon, was less critical: "It's heartening to see so many posies on one low-slung summer décolletage." The group headed outside.

Having seen the wallpaper, the mathematicians were unsure how best to expend the remaining hours of their trip. One man, Filbert (a mathematician) suggested: "We could convene to an eatery for the hearty consumption of burgers?" No one responded to this suggestion and Filbert faded from the narrative. "How about we found our own college right here on the steps of this museum?" David said. He was the mathematician who earlier criticised the pinks and mauves. A roar of happiness swept through the crowd. The roar spread like a Mexican wave, with the far left side roaring first and the far right side roaring last. Some of the far-left roars outlasted some far-right roars, showing individual ebullience at varying durations and pitches.

The mathematicians divided into divisions to source tools and raw materials. Four calculus experts went into the forest for wood. A few all-rounders located a hardware store and bought nails, hammers and extra 2x4 if required. The others sketched up the blueprints and worked out the specifics of construction. Early the next morning the college was erected. Misfortune occurred when Simon (who earlier praised the posies) commented: "We appear to have blocked the entrance to the

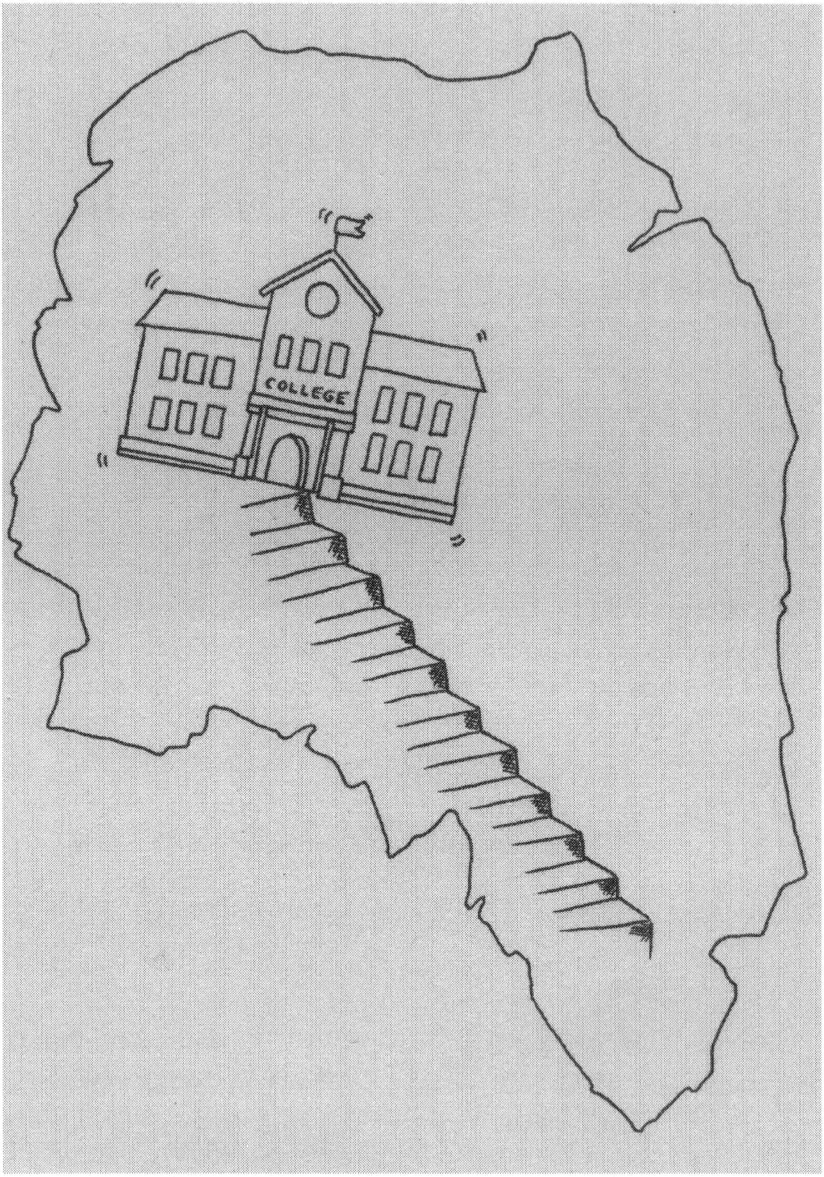
COLLEGE

museum." Another voice, that of a mathematician, said: "Our college is also aslant. We should have used the existing staircase as our foundations instead of balancing our building on the annexe of the museum." This comment was unpopular. The man faded.

To solve the problem, the mathematicians erected a supporting beam extending from the museum steps to the dangling wall of the college. This prevented the college from capsizing backwards down the museum steps when students gathered at the precarious end. One mathematician remarked: "It is a shame the mathematician who noticed this aberration has faded. We should have provided a more positive response to his comment." The mathematicians removed their cravats and cried for the faded man.

A few hours later, mathematics students filed into the mathematics college. The museum went bankrupt that afternoon and the curators, enraged at their loss, cut the freshly erected support beams. The college slid down the museum steps and zipped down the street at quite a speed. Inside, the mathematicians were too engrossed in teaching mathematics and the students too engrossed in learning mathematics to notice their college's new mobile state. The structure came to rest in a pond, where thanks to the excellent rain-seal roofing work, no water seeped in through the windows or doors.

When the mathematics was complete, the students and mathematicians swam to the surface. One mathematician remarked: "Clearly, vandals towed our college and lowered it into the pond." A collective hiss of disapproval passed among the mathematicians: a low hiss that started on the far-right side this time, passing to the far-left. "It is truly appalling how vulnerable mathematicians are in this town," a mathematician added. No one liked this remark so he faded. The mathematicians walked home.

On their way home, the museum curators cornered them in an alleyway and blew them into a large number of pieces. The last dying mathematician counted 2,928 pieces.

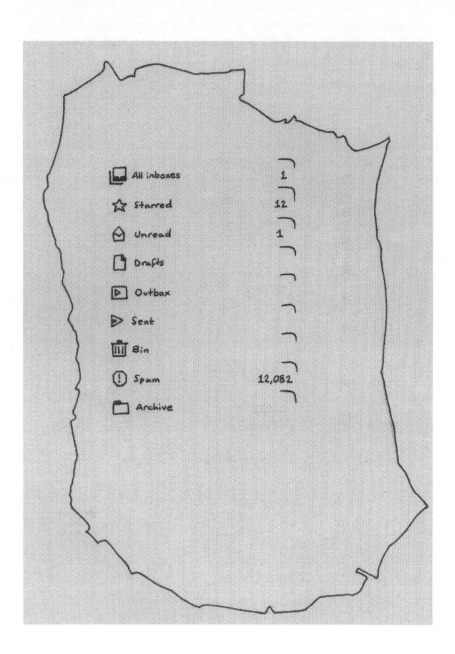

All inboxes 1

Starred 12

Unread 1

Drafts

Outbox

Sent

Bin

Spam 12,082

Archive

[WEST SUSSEX]

NAME: ELSIE ROSE
AGE: 75
SENTENCE: 34 HOURS
CRIME: EMAILS TO AGENTS

FROM: elsiewhoelse@hotmail.com
TO: submissions@larvaeandslime.com

Dear Larvae & Slime,

I sent you my novel *Sally's Testament* last month and received a complaint about the opening sentence: "Cities at night, I feel, contain men who cry in their sleep and then say Nothing." Your complaint was that this sentence is the opening of Martin Amis's 1995 novel, *The Information*. I would like to explain. My use of this sentence dates back to 1994 when my novel was originally a short story, 'Cherries in Bloom'. It appeared in *New Fiction 8* in modified form: "Cherries at night, I believe, contain pips who cry in their sleep and then say Eat me!" When it came to composing my novel in 2010 I adapted portions of the above sentence for my own use, oblivious to this chance occurrence of the same line in Amis's novel. I hope this clears up any error and you will reconsider my MS.

Yours obligingly,

Elsie Rose

FROM: elsiewhoelse@hotmail.com
TO: submissions@francesfrancis.com

Dear Frances & Francis,

I sent an application form to become a temp to your agency, did you receive this application? I have been sending applications to your firm to temp for the last sixty years, I am now a very old woman. My hope was to temp in your agency, and perhaps mingle with various editors and people in a position to publish my debut manuscript. I have been hoping for six decades that I might at last be in a position to work for an agency—I am still fairly spry for my age (84), and I would have no problem performing a full day's work—I can operate a photocopier, a PC with Windows XP or above, and can unlock encrypted files. I would be a useful employee. If you are willing to take a chance on a newbie(!) like me, I would be delighted to temp with you, and discuss my manuscript also. (I wrote the novel in 1952, so I may have to retype, and update the references and spellings and whatnot!)

Regards,

Elsie Rose

FROM: elsiewhoelse@hotmail.com
TO: submissions@anvilandbodrap.com

Dear Anvil & Bodrap,

I received last week a letter refusing representation by your agency, based on the excerpt of my novel *Dennis & the Dictaphone*. Permit me to explain some of the intricacies of my work in case my intentions were unclear. Firstly, this is an "audiovisual novel"—portions of the text are dictated to the reader (left blank on the page), while other portions are dictated *by* the reader, forcing him/her to complete various sections for his/herself (using their own pens or computers). The audio effect would be achieved by the inclusion of small audiophonic devices in the text (as in birthday cards, etc). Also, with each book a free Dictaphone would be issued, containing another novel co-written by five anonymous writers and read by five anonymous actors. The reader's task is to trace which portions of the novel are written by myself and therefore form an extension of *D&tD*—the second half has been left blank for this purpose.

It is also unclear from the except I sent that, from p400 onward, most of this novel is written in anagrams, forcing the reader to rearrange the words to decrypt their meanings in the original Greek. I also want to make clear the intricacies in the typography of my novel. Every letter Y after page 67 should flash yellow, every letter V should turn from purple to black. I also want to achieve a "lava lamp" effect on page 628, where a kaleidoscope of colours moves across the text in an ocular swirl. This is achievable with some strategic backlighting on the preceding page. I have received written encouragements from both Jeremy Irons and David Markson (the latter made when he was alive) to publish this text, so I believe it expedient on your side to take another look at the MS. Let's see if we can make this work.

Respectfully,

Elsie Rose

FROM: elsiewhoelse@hotmail.com
TO: submissions@murrayandpritchard.com

Dear M&P,

My name is Percival Gira. You might remember that I sent you a shoe full of excrement when you refused to represent my third novel, and ignored the "begging" letters I sent afterwards. I write because I would like the shoe returned. I made the mistake of selecting one of the shoes I wear for attending formal events, and do not have the money at present to replace the shoe. Since I need the shoe to attend an upcoming funeral, could I request that the shoe is returned via first-class post (I have enclosed £15), with no worries about having to clean the excrement from the shoe. I can take care of that.

Regards,

Elsie Rose

FROM: elsiewhoelse@hotmail.com
TO: submissions@lawrencewilson.com

Dear Lawrence Wilson Literary Agency,

Hey booky boys! Now listen, I haven't written a novel (and so haven't enclosed one), but I wanted to send you this note nevertheless, because I think I could write a really AMAZING novel if I sat down and concentrated. See boys (or babes!), I have this problem with stories that go on too long. I write my story about, say, Clara the lawyer with a fiery attitude, and my attentions wander . . . I start to find Gerald the farmer with a lisp more intriguing. Clara stomps around my head making a scene (in her fiery way) and I have to try my damnedest to shut her up while I am letting Gerald strut his narrative stuff over the page, letting loose about his farmland philosophies (like never put two cows and two bulls in the same pen! and never hypnotise a horny sheep!) Later, Simon the dyslexic trucker stomps over the page, in his formidable boots, and I have lost the thread of the previous ramblings (not that there's ever a 'thread') and more characters invade my cranium! Guys, how about this? How about I write you one of my rambling novels, populated by hundreds of characters, and you chisel it into something you can sell to the public? Don't you find the modern novel so *constrained*? I prefer work that rambles and flops about the place. I think today's novel should be like one large lava lamp, with stories merging into stories, expanding and shortening and distorting into all manner of gooey and beguiling shapes. Guys, who *needs* coherence? Have you ever tried making sense of a single thing on this planet without the wholeness of space-time erupting in your cranial area? Guys, it's kaaaabbbbbbbooooooooooooooom in here!! I will be in touch again if I don't hear from you in a few months.

Keep rolling—

Elsie Rose

FROM: elsiewhoelse@hotmail.com
TO: submissions@darrenassociates.com

Dear Darren & Associates,

It is with some regret that I sit down to write this correspondence. I understand your reluctance to read voluminous missives so I will keep this missive as unchunky as my e-pen allows.

On Sep 4th 2010 I sent to your agency, via recorded delivery, my novel *When Bees Attack*. I sent this following a verbal agreement between myself and your agent Cariller Cray when I met her at a catered affair for Bernard Share's eightieth birthday. We had a thoroughly encouraging conversation about the passion for knowledge common to fellows in the academic arena—the "epistemology of the heart", to quote my own phrase. At the climax of this discussion I mentioned in passing my sexually provocative novel *When Bees Attack* about a retired Oxford professor who opens a bee sanctuary on the Norfolk coast. Ms Cray was deeply impressed at the breadth of my apian knowledge and offered to read my manuscript with a view to representation by your agency.

I received no response for six months save for a Tower Bridge postcard sent by Cariller with "we cannot use" scribbled in (what appeared to be) child's crayon. Upon a closer inspection with my nose, I did indeed ascertain this message to have been written in crayon. I sent a polite enquiry letter a week later, asking for a more formal response to my manuscript. The following week I received my returned manuscript, each page covered in crayon marks, with large blood-red scrawlings of 'HA HA HA' in the margins. I sent yet another polite enquiry. A week later I received a single page of foolscap with the same scrawlings— 'HA HA HA'—across the page. This is not professional conduct. I am a patient man and I do not appreciate being treated in such a bizarre manner.

All I seek is confirmation that my novel, *When Bees Attack*, has been read by your agency, and whether representation is possible on the strength of the material submitted.

Yours truly,

Elsie Rose

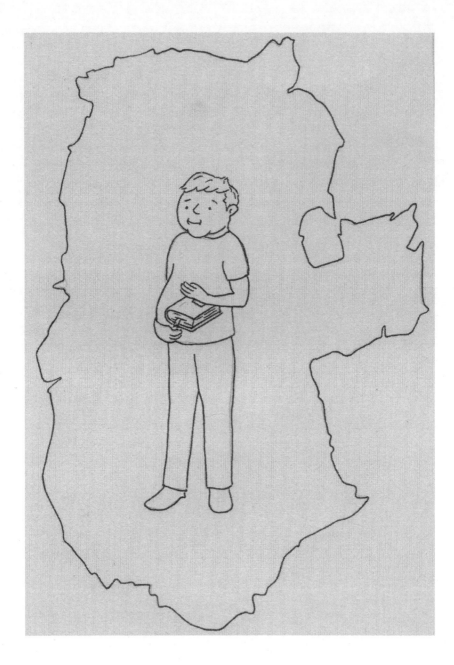

[NORTH YORKSHIRE]

NAME: YOU
AGE: 34
SENTENCE: 12.5 YEARS
CRIME: THE NOVEL INSIDE YOU

THE NOVEL INSIDE YOU is growing. Day by day, hour by hour, your flawless first novel fattens exponentially in its mega-marvellousness, in its peerless wondrous originalness, in its matchless tremendous über-incredibleness. Your novel is years overdue. You feel your novel kicking as you sit on the train staring at your knees, as you lounge in a hammock sipping a Norwegian cocktail with an unpronounceable name, as you live the last days of your truly blissful bookless life. Your novel is slowly emerging. Hour by hour, minute by minute, the words are pirouetting across your peripheral vision. Look! Over thon! Those impeccably hewn phrases are leaping o'er them lazy sheep! Hark! Over thar! Those stimulating metaphors are gambolling gaily with the fluffy ickle lambs! Those timeless themes are cartwheeling a dozen dozing cows! That debut opus inside you is ready to emerge. It will arrive, rest assured, fully-formed. A masterpiece with not a single extraneous word. Yes. It has been waiting there all your days, absorbing the rich tapestry of your experience, making scribbles in the margins of life. All you have to do is to write it up. The novel inside you is about to be born. Pen to the ready.

[ ]

On March 3rd 2016, as a zephyr blows across Skipton ('zephyr', you think, that is a word I can use), you have become a writer. You are a WRITER, you allcaps in your mind. That means something. That means 'I have status', is what. You walk the streets, the novel hanging free from your mind's umbilical, and skip a little. Writer! Skip skip. Writer! Skip skip. Me! Skip skip! Me! Skip skip. As you stroll past, pedestrians peer from their statusless eyes into the soul of a real live writer. That's You. You writer, You. Snip snip, be born, O novel mine. Snip skip. Your novel ('my novel!') is an epic Oedipal roman à clef set in Carluke. You will bestow the rundown streets of that nondescript Lanarkshire town with the grandeur of epic poetry, which you will also write on the side, whyever not. Epic. Writer. You! Your protagonist is an everyman, like in *Ulysses*, a novel your novel will emulate, and the everydayness of his everyday actions will ascend on poetic wings from the mediocre to the heaven-kissed. Oh, You Writer, You! Oh, The Possibilities! Your novel has a fast-paced unputdownable plot that will propel you into riches and fame. But you will retain indie cred by keeping your novel out the bestseller lists. Your novel will appeal to the highbrow twentysomething hipster crowd and become a regular on the Best Indie Fiction lists. You will straddle markets. You will straddle, You Colossus. You will set your novel in Brooklyn and London and New York and Tokyo. And everywhere else, why not. Your novel will have cool things like long ruminations on the music of The Psychedelic Furs. The early road movies of Wim Wenders. And the transcendence of the Sugababes. Because you will straddle class lines. Like a Colossus. Straddler! Your novel will have kinky sex and sexy kink. Your novel will have a complex and neurotic and interesting and loveable male protagonist and a beautiful and thoughtful and hilarious and empowered female protagonist. Your novel will ooze appeal. No man or woman or hybrid will resist this spectacular offering. From the Mind of You. Oh! The things You Will Write. Your novel is coming. Make way, universe, this baby is birthing!

[ ]

"I'm home," you say to Gillian Driscoll, your girlfriend from Skipton, where you live in North Yorkshire, England, United Kingdom, Europe, Earth, The Universe, BD23 9FD. You withhold the news until the consumption of your beefsteak with potato fritters. "I'm writing a novel," you say to Gillian's tater-filled face. "What?" she asks, scrolling through her social media feeds and smiling at the instances of animated kittens. "I'm writing a novel," you repeat, not letting her routine inattentivity spoil your wondrous news. "*You* don't know how to write," your spotty girlfriend says, still not meeting your gaze. "Yes I do. I've had this novel inside me for years. It's time to set her free," you remark. You note with sudden embarrassment that what you have admitted out loud might not seem as remarkable to your culturally vapid other half, who has not read a novel since the last in the *Twilight* series, and a sudden wave of shame sends you blushing into your remaining rind. "Oh," she says. You want to share with her the explosion of ideas in your buzzing little brain, to leap with her around the living room to the uptempo pop beats playing in your mind's iPod. You want to share every scrap of dialogue, description, or nonsense you have thought up so far. But since Gillian Driscoll has merely met your ambition with a lukewarm "Oh", and not a torrent of enthusiasm, you realise that there is nothing particularly special about your epiphany, and that several thousand other dreamers have similar notions, and you suddenly fall from your fluffy clouds to the pavement with the violence of a plummeting passenger flight. You accept the fact that you might have made this decision while sitting on the train and feeling like such an ordinary, unremarkable plodding ho-hum of a human being, that your mind suddenly shotgunned this notion into your defences to keep you from sinking into an existential torpor, to make you feel superior and special to your fellow commuters and workers and plodding human beings. You accept this. But you will still write.

[ ]

You have Beginner's Paralysis. Your fingers hover over the keys, trembling. Having made the fatal mistake in hesitating a microsecond before beginning, you have introduced the two twin monsters that are the undoing of many fledgling and professional writers: uncertainty and doubt. You worry that your first sentence might not emerge perfectly formed, as it appears in an indistinct faultless shape in your mind, and that your talents might not suddenly unravel before you in a perceptible form. You worry that your first sentence, in addition to not emerging perfectly formed, might not throb with urgency, show a feisty beginner's passion, or have that unique hallmark of obvious talent that will propel you instantly into print. You worry that your first sentence, in addition to not emerging perfectly formed, or showing any talent whatsoever, might not even make sense, that your words will emerge misspelled in no coherent sequence, as mere babyish burbling sounds running along the page, like a three-month-old's post-winding vocal emissions. You worry that your words, in addition to their imperfect formation, talentlessness, incoherence, and babybabblingness, might expose you for who you are, might reflect the abyss of your soul back at you, and plunge you into such catastrophic depths of self-hatred, that you will find yourself forever paralysed at the beginner's stage, fated to hover tremblingly over the keyboard forever, and that year after year you will endure the same aborted attempts to begin, until you are an eighty-eight-year-old arthritic man whose balled-up firsts vainly knuckle the keys, unable to flex a finger to produce a single word, and you collapse dead on the keys, leaving as your literary legacy: cewgsgcsiucicgiuscgigicuiiiiiiiiiiiiiiiiiiiiii-
iiiiiiiiiiiiiiiiiiiiiiiiiiiiiiiiiiiiiiiiiiiiiiiiiiiiiiiiiiiiiiiiiiiiiiiiiiiiiiiiiiiiiiiiiiiiiiiiii-
iiiiiiiiiiiiiiiiiiiiiiiiiiiiiiiiiiiiiiiiiiiiiiiiiiiiiiiiiiiiiiiiiiiiiiiiiiiiiiiiiiiiiiiiiiiiiiiiii-
iiiiiiiiiiiiiiiiiiiiiiiiiiiiiiiiiiiiiiiiiiiiiiiiiiiiiiiiiiiiiiiiiiiiiiiiiiiiiiiiiiiiiiiiiiiiiiiiii-
iiiiiiiiiiiiiiiiiiiiiiiiiiiiiiiiiiiiiiiiiiiiiiiiiiiiiiiiiiiiiiiiiiiiiiiiiiiiiiiiiiiiiiiiiiiiiiiiii

[ ]

You take a drink. Then another. As the soothing beverage from Łódź Voivodeship settles in your system, a swaggering figure appears in your mind, kicking aside the hesitating worrywart currently halting your progress. This charming man exudes such stunning bravado and chutz-pah that you can't help listen to his honeythroated words, spurring you on to unleash the brilliance that is burning inside, to allow your bril-liance to braze brightly on the page, and permit others the pleasure of reading your fiery, flaming words of wonder that are about to emerge when you start poking the keys. You open another blank document and write the first line of your novel:

The sun was shining in the

You delete this. You write:

The rain was beating off the

You delete this. You write:

It was four o'clock in

You delete this. You write:

Alan Wilson awoke one morning to find

You delete this. You stop writing. You remain blissfully unaware that this is what 'writing' is like the whole time, sentence by wiped sentence, and still feel a throb of exhilaration in your nascent writerly loins. You are experiencing the Honeymoon Period, which will end tomorrow at 5.24 a.m.

[ ]

And so, the process begins. Your charming coach appears two wodkas later and stirs you into action. You write: *It was a scuzzy time for the small men in the tepee.* "A triumph!" the coach hollers. You write: *The sweaty squaws nibbled on their opossum shanks with fervour.* "What a concise and insightful description!" the coach bellows. You write: *In the morning the*

sun was bright and moonish. "A moonish sun! No one was expecting that!
Marvellous!" You write: *A company man through and through, Alex was
committed to securing the Masterson Account.* "Now *there* is a plot! *That* is
character!" the coach screams. And with your newfound friend's help,
you compose over sixty-two paragraphs.

[ ]

The hardest part is concentrating. The other day, you were sailing high
in the sesquipedalian skies, unloading word-bombs onto the page like
some lexical Luftwaffe, and this morning you are struggling to write
the word 'thereafter'. Once you have managed to lift your floppy, lifeless hand to the keyboard to type, and after fifty-eight minutes, spelled
the word 'thereafter', you stop for another fifty-eight minutes and try to
convince yourself that starting a sentence with such an archaic adverb
is perfectly acceptable, and rather literary, in fact, even if this chapter is
told from the perspective of a Somalian migrant with a limited grasp of
Dickensian English. It doesn't matter, you lie to yourself shamelessly,
because the *narrator* is using the word 'thereafter', not the migrant, even
though the narration so far has been from her perspective, and the reader
has been in effect sitting on her shoulders. But you are so pleased that
you have managed to spell that word 'thereafter', having stared at the
screen for fifty-eight minutes (prior to the fifty-eight minutes crawling towards the keys and poking them like a cadaver in a thicket), with
not a single word making its way from your paved-over brain to your
limp fingertips, that you can't bear the thought that you might have
to delete that hard-won word, and rethink the approach you have to
take, the fact that you must make your novel stylistically and tonally
consistent, and all that. But instead of having to focus, and review yesterday's material, and continue in the same vein—a vein that you have
become tired of overnight—you decide to start another chapter, invent
another character, someone who says 'thereafter', and write that instead
of the proper third chapter in the well-researched Somalian voice. But

even though you have written 'thereafter', suggesting a somewhat posh well-educated well-spoken chap, you cannot be bothered to make this consistent, so you hurl a lot of stuff into a sentence in order to have something to show for your listless and meandering hours, and call it "an experiment." Your day's work:

Thereafter a man appeared in black shades in a Led Zep tee eating a packet of tomato ketchup crisps. "Hi everyone!" he said in a room. The moon winked in the sky as Trixie, silvery of hair, slivery of waist, unwrapped a hazelnut slice and pretended to hum the lyrics to 'Liquid Pig' by Lisa Germano. It was wet, both inside and outside, and exoskeletally something. People reflected on what Donnie had said two years ago, and the mood changed from a sodden sponge to a flaming loofah. The lights, as they always do, dimmmmed.

[ ]

One morning, having elected not to masturbate in the hope that Gillian might consume enough wodka to initiate sex with you that evening, you have a sudden impulse to let your penis write your manuscript for you. Having spent pages and pages establishing a steady, reliable intellectualism in your narrative, making the reader feel safe in the hands of a sensible, thoughtful, and erudite author, you introduce a character called Shirley Appleson who looks exactly like Alison Statton from Welsh postpunk band Young Marble Giants in her 1980s heyday, a plain-looking recitative singer with a kind of transfixing blandness in her delivery, and imagine what it might be like to have sex with her. You carefully insert yourself into a banal fantasy scenario, involving the seduction of this floral-dress-wearing Girl Next Door, slowly encouraging her to open up and trust you, as she tells you tales of loneliness and sadness, about her childhood of alienation and ostracisation that sounds uncannily like yours, until you place a comforting arm around her shoulder, and lean in to plant a kiss on her thin Stattonesque lips. You then take her slowly towards the bedroom, where you unzip her Stattonesque dress, kiss her

Stattonesque body, and make love to her to the soft strumming loveliness of Stuart Moxham's guitar. In writing this scene, you have exposed the strange nature of your inner erotic life—whereas most straight men would permit themselves the thrill of unlimited carnal abandon with supermodels or actresses, you have chosen a woman who you might bump into in your local hardware store, showing the reader that your self-esteem is so low that even your imagination cannot convince itself of the likelihood of your penis coming anywhere near Penelope Cruz or Elisabeth Moss, and that bedding obscure rock singers at similar attractiveness levels to your girlfriend is what brings you to priapic pitches. Having licked the nape of Shirley's neck for a worryingly long period of time, imagining for a second burying yourself there and having a lovely long cry, a detail you omit from the description, you arrive at the moment when you must render the physical realities of coitus in non-sickly prose. Because you are now aroused, and touching your penis in between clauses, you proceed to the repetitive thrusting part, which you write with masturbatory gusto, bringing yourself closer to pleasurable release with every instance of 'thrust harder and harder into her succulent cunt'(!!!), until you finally achieve your three seconds of bliss. You then, of course, re-read what you have written and loathe yourself with the brute force of a lumberjack driving an axe into a redwood.

[ ]

(One morning): That last sentence, it was insane. Woooooooooooo! Man, that last sentence! THAT WAS A GOD AMONG SENTENCES! It was so amazingamazingamazing no one has written a sentence that RADIATED SUCH OH MY GODNESS what a motherbrother of a sentence that was. Three cheers for that sentence! Hip! Hip! Hooooooooooooooooooooraaaaaaah! Perfect phrasing? YES. Perfect parsing of words, whatever that means? YUP. Perfect and consistent with characters and plots and things? HELL OUI. No endless rambling filler material of no interest to anyone? NO SIREE. A chain of flawlessly executed words in the right order, moving along the page with the light-footedness of an Astaire or a Bussel? YES MICHAEL, IT SURELY WAS. GRACE IS THE WORD. SUCH GRACE! This is the section for the AGES. Quote this. Quote me. Quote that line. QUOTE ME! To be quoted. Forever. O Immortal Gods of Prose, Take Ye On High to Thy Promised Lands. HELLO MR JOYCE, HELLO MR DICKENS, HELLO MR HARDY, SQUEEZE ME TIGHT I AM YOUR EQUAL. Sweet copters of love! Warm flannels of phantasm! WHAT A SENTENCE! IT MIGHT NOT GET DELETED!

[ ]

(The next morning): Can't you just write drivel, you think. Who cares. Would it matter if whatever runny diarrhoea pouring from your fifth-rate mind was spewed onto a Word document and hurled at the bulging superbrains of the bigtime publishing pricks. Who cares. Everyone reads drivel these days. Blogs are bestsellers. I don't have to make an effort. I can just fill up the space with this stuff I don't even need to edit. What matters is filling the pages so I can be a writer. If I could copy and paste it would be even easier. I wouldn't need to sit here hunched over the laptop keying this rubbish into the pages, you think. My God there's so much white space on this page. They can't possibly expect me to make every sentence a humdinger. It's impossible. I'm just a man who masturbates twice a day and more on weekends. I'm a disgusting void. I can't be expected to write a coherent story and make it good it's not fair. I'm starting to hate the way certain letters look on the page too. I hate how that 'j' in 'just' curls round the arse of the 'u'. I hate the way the 'y' curls around too. I prefer neat letters with no curling to them. That 'g'. The letter 'g' is a prick. If I could write a novel without the letters 'g', 'j', and 'y', I would be a happy man. Happi man. I could replace the 'y' with 'i'. That might work. *Iorick iearned for a iacht.* Looks neater. And how about the 'j' with a 'k'. *Kerome kust wanted some kelli and kuice.* Much better. And the 'g' with a 't'. *Tretor tot a tarden tnome.* Yes. That's it. I can be the first writer to kettison three letters. I should do that. I'll rewrite the betinnint of the novel.

Teorte awoke with a iawn. Trei skies treeted him. He tot his etts readi for breakfast. On the mornint news, the iount politician Tret Traham had been arrested for trowint cannabis. "Iust distraceful," Tillian said. She went to the bathroom to tartle her mouthwash. "Iou need to stop that tartlint nonsense," he said. She had been obsessed with her oral hitiene for iears. "It's iust tettint too much, iou know?" "What?" she said. "Nothint. Iust look at this. Tret Traham has been iailed for trowint cannabis!" But Tillian was not listenint. She finished tartlint and trabbed her iacket from the coathook. "Totta dash babe," she said, airkissint Teorte as she left. Teorte tot on the phone to his friend Iai Iatters. He had helped Tret with the cannabis farm and was worried that Iai mitht be implicated in the crime. "Hei Iai. Teorte callint. How's it toint? I iust saw the news. Are iou all ritht?"

[ ]

You awake from a wodka-induced coma and stagger towards the study, stunned at how the human body can function with nine tailspinning concordes crashing into one's head and exploding repeatedly, and shove nine cigarettes between your purple-brown lips. You check Twitter to see if someone has reacted to your latest withering and insightful observation expressed with impeccable laconicism. No one has retweeted. SOD THOSE BASTARDS, is a thought you actually think, inasmuch as you can think anything at all, inside the Nagasaki of your migraine. You open up yesterday's work and stare at the paragraph you were writing when you started pouring the wodkas, and squint-read sentences that flout basic grammatical rules and lapse into pound-shop Finneganese, sic: 'I open ate the cazzaman ??+++ when our oh I rem&& and we all*** &&& insnit????' Having supped a restorative pre-breakfast wodka, you have the courage to click on the 'sent' folder, and stare expressionless at the ten-page vitriolic rant you wrote to the editor of *The Perennial Quarterly* who had the brass balls to deem your excerpt "not right" for his pathetic little organ aimed at illiterate muskrats. Saving the merciless self-flagellation for after breakfast, you try once again to make sense of your last three pages as the Polish spirits seized control of your body with a robust Schwarzeneggerian hug. You compare the more lucid parts to the two paragraphs you wrote sober, and note that the material you wrote in an alcoholic fug while simultaneously watching hardcore pornography has more artistic value than the plodding drivel you wrote while in full control of your mental faculties.

It is Tuesday, and you are still a writer. Sobriety reminds you that there is no reason for you to write fiction in an age where every conceivable slant on the novel has been written into the ground in a million trillion variations by people who can hold two contrasting ideas in their minds at once, when you struggle sometimes to remember your middle name, Albert. You are a man from Skipton who wants to write a novel. In fiction's eyes, you are nothing. You are nothing. You are nothing. And you are crying, again, you pathetic mess. You seem to recall attending a writers' workshop in town. Someone younger than you had the copper testicles to criticise a clause that flowed from your faultless fingers and you raved at the insolent little titweasel. You leapt up onto your haunches and howled that he loved to prowl around the cemetery, excavating corpses and snogging them, that he loved having sex with his Nazi mother in spite of her nonagenarian status. You then poured a pint of stout over an elderly lady who called the same clause "overwritten". The rest is unclear. It is probable there were several brawls in alleyways with political poets. That would explain the verdigris hue to your left chin.

You pour a second wodka because that carping voice, the sober one, reminds you that you are wasting your time, that there is enough literature, that the brainless, uncultured, pathetic stinking masses read nothing that isn't a bestselling kindle crime novel, and that the supposedly committed booklovers, that self-regarding hakka of halfwits, read the well-known literary organs like sheep, purchasing only the five-starred books, never wondering why certain books end up lauded and others do not, blindly believing they are reading the cream of the crop, when they are merely being spoonfed a mutually beneficial marketing ploy, promoting reviewer, author, and periodical. Nepotism and opportunism and egocentrism will bury your labours below the never-to-read pile. You stare at your bookshelves and red lights flash above the authors who died penniless and unappreciated and who were never read and who are still not properly appreciated now. You feel like stamping on the head of a newborn baby, or pissing into the mouth of a cancer patient. You have come to associate this feeling with 9.28 AM.

The next hour is spent trying to convince yourself that your novel is worthwhile, and that with the right backers, it might be fired between the willing buttcheeks of the market. You might write something that someone somewhere will read, and afterwards, make this noise: "Hmm." That is the dream. That makes those alcoholic hours, the days spent staring into space, the screaming sessions between you and Gillian Driscoll, the backstreet brawls with poets, the ritual self-hate, worthwhile.

Because convincing yourself of this is impossible, you sink into fantasy. You imagine yourself an earth-shaking award-winning amazing "new voice" on the "scene" that everyone in the universe has read within two weeks. You sit inside that fantasy for hours, making acceptance speeches at the Booker, Nobel, and Pulitzer ceremonies until 12.50. Then your carping voice blasts: "Failure! Loser! WRITE, YOU LAZY SLUG!" You pour the fourth wodka and punch words onto the page with your trembling fingers, punching sentences about the face until they resemble mashed turnips, pounding some life into that cowering lummox of a manuscript. You pummel the page with words, clobber and smack and wallop that empty, shiftless ass of a page, putting some of these words in the right order. Clive Witzlow traipses across a hill and trips over a cow and tumbles into a bog. In the preceding sentence, Colin Willow had been eating lunch with his mother, the heir to a large Roundhay fortune. IT DOESN'T MATTER. Louise Dimple shears twelve sheep while her uncle looks on sucking an ice pole. This has no relation to the Colin/Clive thing from earlier. IT DOESN'T MATTER. We change scene to Naples, where street kids are rolling a bowling ball along a wall in winter. This is a complete change of setting. IT DOESN'T MAT-TER. A priest emerges from the bowling ball swinging a thurible and says "Hi-ho Italianos!" This smashes all rules of logic. IT DOESN'T MATTER. PUTTING WORDS SPELLED CORRECTLY INTO SENTENCES AT THIS STAGE IS IMPORTANT, REWRITING CAN COME LATER, shrieks that voice that applauds and stabs you simultaneously.

Around 14.23, you lose control over your sentences, and wodka takes over the writing.

[ ]

You have to admit that your reserves of empathy for humankind are running low. In fact, you have to admit that you have no empathy for anyone, really, except your sorry self, sitting in front of your keyboard, trying to persuade yourself that you have talent and Something Important To Say About Contemporary Mores, and that your novel might momentarily prick someone's interest, and that you have a Radiant Future as a Successful Novelist, if only you could write true-to-life characters, if only you could force the plot into some kind of order, if only you could unfurl the tortured tangle of your thoughts, and write a string of coherent sentences, perhaps showing some sort of involvement in the external world—rolling streams in picturesque forests, the smiling face of a beautiful woman, the soft purr of a lapped kitten—or an interest in the sufferings of others, especially in lucrative sufferings like the sorrows of Middle Eastern immigrants, victimised ethnics or women, that might catch the zeitgeist and launch the novel into the public arena on a rocket of worthiness. But it is apparent with each passing sentence that your complete lack of interest in anything outside your own navel is leaving your art a hollow indulgent romp around the byways of your frustration and self-loathing. One day, when you learn to care about something, you might have the makings of a Promising New Voice. In the meantime, you write another overly lengthy sex scene and fiddle with yourself.

[ ]

"What is this book about?" Gillian Driscoll asks you, five weeks into the writing. You have refrained from the specifics so far because you have no actual clue yourself. For two days, the novel was set in a Belgian submarine, then you changed the setting to Egypt in 1326, where the Mamluk Sultanate was warring with a power-crazed provincial governor (*nuwwab as-saltana*); then you wrote about a spunky Norfolk shepherdess who fostered a wayward trans kid, and sent an email to Tony Parsons, asking if that "idea had legs". You will have to explain to Gillian that the evenings you spend writing and not attending to her needs, those all-too-regular evenings that are driving a wedge between you, have so far been for nothing. You will have to explain that the process of bringing a novel together in a coherent manner when you have the attention span of an overcaffeinated schnauzer, when you have no real interest in the characters you create, when you prefer instead to write on your own boring existence, when your ambitions outstrip your ability to make them happen on the page, and when you lack the technical competency that might see you into print, is making things tough. You also note that you are increasingly unable to pleasure Gillian Driscoll with the manly fervour you showed prior to your dawning as a writer. You attribute this to the potency of your sexual imagination—those seventy-seven pages of sex scenes with various realistically attainable women populating your fantasies—which has become more pleasurable than your regular routine sex with Gillian, or your fantasy relationship with the spunky Norfolk shepherdess, who has suddenly captured your heart with her feisty herding ways. You picture yourself sucking her nipples in the sheepcote.

[ ]

Your protagonist (Craig Horse) walks towards a tree. You wonder whether, for the sake of enriching the descriptive aspect of your novel (working title: *Slurp the Bacon*), you should stop to Google trees, and render a random pic in word form. You wonder what sort of tree might exist in your fictional representation of Barnsley, and Google the sorts of trees one might find in South Yorkshire, where you have set the novel (you think), and after two minutes, plump for a birch. You write an unspectacular, unpoetic description of a birch tree, and have your protagonist (Colin Shirk) walk towards a building instead. You have no idea what sort of building. You wonder if, for the sake for prodding the plot forward, you should make clear what building your protagonist (Steve Plipp) is walking towards. You worry that in being specific, you will then have to provide some satisfactory explanation as to why your protagonist (Franc Ions) is entering that building (say, an ice cream parlour), and bestow some significance to his (her?) actions, when there is no significance whatsoever to most of what you have written so far, and you are simply poking your protagonist towards something for the sake of making her (him?) move, when prior (s)he was stood in an unreactive stationary position, moving towards nothing. You refrain from moving your protagonist (Xenon Zim) at all. You choose, instead, to move something towards your protagonist (Olaf Prime), such as a dog of some description. Which description? You choose a German setter. You worry that the choice of a German setter might have some meaning for a reader (oblique holocaust reference?), when you simply want a random German setter to pantgallop towards your protagonist (Maxine Baka). What you are beginning to realise, with these chops and changes, proddings and pokings of your protagonist(s) (???) towards unidentified trees and unspecified buildings, is that the choices you make will invariably be taken by the astute reader as significant, and that the reader will read into your every choice of tree, building, or dog, some intended symbol, or referent, or meaning that certainly doesn't exist, and that there is no way around this, even having your protagonist standing still for the whole novel—this too will be seen as some kind of strained social comment, or Beckettian nod, or whatever. You have to make choices at random and hope that some of the chaotic patchwork of your finished novel (working title: *When the Flying Pigs Couldn't Fly No More*) will make some sense to someone, possibly even yourself.

[ ]

Your writing process: Open the chapter with a necessary, misguided optimism. Read the previous page and write nothing for ten minutes. Check your email. Respond to a non-urgent message at length, taking the sort of care and attention to word choice that you rarely show in your "literary" writing. Return to the chapter and stare at the screen for eleven minutes. Write half a sentence that barely conforms to rudimentary grammatic structures and has no tangential relation to the previous tangle of sentences. Check your social media feeds. Comment on your friend Oliver's comment on your unnecessary assault on a popular Welsh feminist writer who has published one more novel than you. Comment with unchecked rage on a Tweet that slams people for taking "lazy days" as a sign of weakness and timewasting. Read the other ninety-nine comments and 'love' or retweet according to how true each rings. Stare into space for a period longer than you could imagine you would ever stare into space. Skip to the next track on that album you are listening to through your earphones (usually *Happy Birthday to Me* by The Muffs, because inside, you have never left the age of twelve). Return to the chapter. Complete the sentence, making sure to take no care whatsoever to connect the clauses or spell words properly, or show a cursory interest in technical proficiency. Click back to the net and read an article about something on which you had previously no interest for thirty minutes, then read each below-the-line comment and 'like' or ignore accordingly. Stare into space for another period longer than you could ever, etc. Check social media feeds again and re-read and re-view content you have already mentally scrolled past with zero interest. Return to the chapter. Make an assertive decision to knuckle down to some serious writing. Complete another sentence or two (with an heroic effort to connect two in sense). Sink into a despondent mood at the prospect of having to knit these words together in a presentable shape, and at the sheer scale of the literary competition, and at your poor skill, etc. Return to the net. Watch a video of a comedian to cheer yourself up. View thirteen similar videos for two hours. Return to the chapter and delete everything you have written that morning. Endeavour to start again after lunch. Return to the chapter after lunch with no energy, no motivation, and a hopeless sinking feeling. Retire to bed for a nap and a cry.

[ ]

No, you will not "pussy out". You will not douse the towel in kerosene, set fire to the towel, and throw the burning towel into a basket of kittens, as the saying you have invented says. You will stagger onwards, into the peeled eyeballs of circumstance, with elbows aloft to the sun's skinny fists, you winner.

[ ]

Gillian Driscoll is packing her bags. (You are thinking whether introducing that compsognathus into the office will stir up new plot ideas). Gillian Driscoll is crying and saying things like "You couldn't care less" about something and "You never think about" someone or something. (You are thinking about making Charleen into a world netball champion or having her arm ripped off by a lorry). Gillian Driscoll is stampeding towards the front door and kicking things like the TV stand and the settee, and pours half a cup of cold coffee over several pages of your printed manuscript. (You leap over and check that the best bit—Iolande's proto-Cartesian monologue on page fourteen—is still legible). Gillian Driscoll is standing in the doorway, making a list of things she wants to keep, the toaster, the electric whisk, the lemon squeezer, and is shivering in the rain. (You remember how Malcolm reacted when Charleen lost her onion in the marshes on "that Sunday", and move towards her for a hug). Gillian Driscoll is crying excessively on your shoulders. (You have a eureka moment and realise that Oscar's left testicle was not lost in a hunting accident in the Steppes. His sadistic uncle Razzorrrr removed the ball one night under anaesthesia. He wears a mummified testicle on a necklace. You run to the laptop). Gillian Driscoll is standing in the door incredulous that you have aborted your consolation to write your pathetic novel. (You sketch a skeleton scene showing Razzorrrr's position in the room and the implement of castration used and the serene sleeping face of teenage Oscar). Gillian Driscoll is attacking you with a frying pan. She is bashing you around the shoulders, felling you to the floor. She swings the frying pan towards your laptop and smashes the screen and mangles the keys. (You momentarily panic, then a wave of relief washes over you when you realise you always save to your USB). Gillian Driscoll has stopped smashing your laptop and looks at your bruised cowering body with steely, knowing eyes. She looks towards your laptop and your USB. (You try to sit up and bolt towards your laptop. The pain is too enormous. You think about using your experience in the scene where Shannon floors Pritchard with a strong upper hook to the clavicle). Gillian Driscoll removes your USB and makes for the door. (You cannot stand. You ache like Ronald after the Laotian gangster clobbered him around the neck with a frozen skate). Gillian Driscoll has absconded with your novel. (You suddenly hear what Gillian has been screaming at you).

[ ]

You cannot think logically, to think logically would spell the end of your literary career. You understand that there are well-trodden pre-existing paths into publication that revolve around nepotism and bumlicking and the exchange of fluids. You understand that marketing—that "bottom line"—to particular strands of readers, based on prior-tested formulas of what readers like to read rules supreme, and that no risks will ever be taken on non-market-friendly work, unless that novelist is a one-time flash-in-the-pan brainhead from brainland, which you are most certainly not. You also cannot confront the reality that procuring an agent will not elevate you into some hallowed realm of the canonical and secure you cocktails with the authors you adore, and secure the interest of the handful of readers a new novelist is allotted. You cannot look the truth square in the chin. You cannot bear the sight of that handful of people in an arts centre nodding along as you describe your character's motivations for inserting his left arm into a kangaroo's anus. You decide you are better off indulging in fantasies. You and your spunky Norfolk shepherdess stroll through the fields of wherever, holding hands as you ascend slopes and declivities, murmuring miscellaneous nice things in your mutual lugholes, kissing under trees, touching each other's naughties in copses, as the sunshine heats your head with a warm reassurance that things are nice. You tell your sexy Norfolk shepherdess that you are a successful pastoral novelist, penning bucolic dramas of intrigue and other things, and that your agent was on the phone to you as you kiss her smiling sheep-herding face, and she says she knows nothing about literature, which is convenient, since neither do you, and you lose yourself in her stout farmer's arms, allowing her to smother you, as you picture the intelligentsia marching towards you, the booksmart knowing professionals with proper ideas and braincells and Double Firsts from Cambridge, who can wipe the floor with you, with their PhDs in red tubes, their mortarboards made from the skins of commoners, eager to ridicule you into the ground with a nine-syllable word that they have invented for the sole purpose of tricking you into thinking you have learned something, whereas they have actually humiliated you by shouting a fake word into your ear, knowing that you will repeat that word in public to appear clever, because you are an insecure, wobbling nitwit who only wants to suck a shepherd's nipples a lot.

[ ]

You have been ringing Gillian Driscoll for twelve hours to no avail. You are unable to sleep. You are staring at the endless sheet of sleet from your bedroom window, wondering what you might say to make Gillian return your USB, what you think Gillian wants you to say so it seems you are more interested in her than your USB, how to say something that Gillian will not immediately interpret as you merely saying something she wants to hear in order to retrieve your USB, or how to appease her in a sincere-seeming manner so that she has no suspicion that you have merely wangled some scheme to make her return the USB, and have minimal interest in her. You consider an all-or-nothing approach: ask that she destroys the USB, because she is more important to you than some stupid novel that you have been working on relentlessly for months, and that has dominated your every waking thought, and on which you are making significant breakthroughs every other week, and are nearing a coherent outline. (This will backfire, Gillian will leap at the chance to smash the USB). You consider making a grovelling apology to Gillian and suggest you take a week away together, never once mentioning the USB, in the hope she softens and returns the USB to you over kisses and hugs. (This is impossible, as you are already hyperventilating with panic that the novel might be wiped as the USB bounces in her pocket to wherever she is heading). You consider proposing marriage. You consider self-harming. You consider a fake suicide attempt. Anything to prevent the thought of having to start again. Having to relive those hours stumbling through the thorny tickertape of your menial, imbecilic thoughts to find something remotely interesting to say. Having to keep hold of your characters, and find ways to like them as they show their irritating faces every time you return to the chair. Having to forge a "plot" of some kind and maintain consistency, so the reader can't pick holes in your artificial construct and accuse you of not being "true to life". Having to fight the intense, agonising reality that your ideas, characters, style, and plots are inconsequential nonsense in comparison with other literature, and that you will never express anything in a way that hasn't been expressed before by someone with a better and bigger brain than you. You are not being melodramatic when you say, with alarming sincerity, that you would rather die than start over.

[ ]

I owned a Lada once.

"STOP THERE!" your inner marketer shrieks.

"You are restricting this piece to the British market by making a Lada reference. You are also excluding the younger British demographic who have no knowledge of this retro 1970s vehicle. I suggest the Lada is replaced by a more common motor car, such as the Ford or Toyota."

I owned a Ford once. One night, under the influence of speedballs and dancehalls

"STOP THERE!!" she shrieks again.

"You are attempting a wordplay that simply isn't transferrable among UK and US readers—'speedballs' is a slang term that will alienate the older reader, 'dancehalls' is an archaic word that will alienate the younger reader. I appreciate the attempt to appeal to both age groups and nationalities at once, but you can't have your cake and etc."

I owned a Ford once. One night, under the influence of powerful drugs taken at the nightclub, I crashed the car into a

"STOP THERE!!!" she shrieks a third time.

"This passage contains behaviour that could be imitated. If you want to write about such things, you should provide a content warning on the opening page, or place a footnote."

I owned a Ford once. [Warning! This sentence contains reckless behaviour that could be imitated]. One night, under the influence of powerful drugs taken at the nightclub, I crashed the car into a bollard and mangled the bumper. I staggered out into the night

"STOP THERE!!!!" she shrieks fourthly.

"Is he wearing a high-viz jacket so passing motorists can see him? If he isn't, you'll need to stress the importance of this sort of clothing on the roads late at night, or provide a warning against irresponsible behaviour. In fact, both would be the safest bet."

I owned a Ford once. [Warning! This sentence contains reckless behaviour that could be imitated.] One night, under the influence of powerful drugs taken at the nightclub, I crashed the car into a bollard and mangled the bumper. [Warning! This clause contains reckless behaviour that could be imitated. It is advisable, if out on the roads at night, to wear high visibility clothing to alert other drivers to your presence]. I staggered out into the night and solicited help from a passing

"STOP THERE!!!!!" she dittoes fifthly.

"Hitchhiking is extremely dangerous. Especially late at night. You know what to do."

I owned a Ford once. [Warning! This sentence contains reckless behaviour that could be imitated.] One night, under the influence of powerful drugs taken at the nightclub, I crashed the car into a bollard and mangled the bumper. [Warning! This clause contains reckless behaviour that could be imitated. It is advisable, if out on the roads at night, to wear high visibility clothing to alert other drivers to your presence.] I staggered out into the night and [this clause contains behaviour that could be imitated—it is advisable not to solicit help from motorists late at night to preserve your own safety] solicited help from a passing motorist. THE END.

"STOP THERE!!!!!!" she dittoes dittoly.

"Ending so soon? Oh, You!! This is an insufficient measure of detail for the opening paragraph of a story. If this were a short piece, or what's known as a "drabble," then such a length might be permissible. But as it stands the story has nothing appealing for a reader. What happened after his reckless behaviour soliciting help from a car late at night without wearing hi-viz clothes? These are hooks for the reader, essential for a successful story. Also, if this piece is a "drabble," you need to compress the information and have a beginning-middle-end within the space of 100 words. Your piece is 110 words so needs to be edited. Hello? Where have you gone? Hello? Come back and finish the story. Don't be stupid. You'll never make it as writer if you can't stick around to finish the story. This is childish behaviour. Where are you? Fine. Your loss."

[ ]

You attend a Writers' Workshop in town. A man named Alan Crosbie, who has self-published three neo-noir novels set in Dystania, two of which are titled *The Rising Dusk*, and who wears hornrimmed spectacles, and who has a ponytail, and who has a slight speech impediment when saying 'ou' sounds, presides.

"The first contribution is," he says, "a crime story set in the backwoods of Drumclog called 'The Splattered Woof'. I'll open up the floor to feedback, if anyone wants to kick off." The Workshop brokers no murmur.

"No one? It's been two minutes," Alan observes.

"You misspell 'bludgeon' in the first sentence," a redhead named Kayleigh Globb suddenly sprechens. "There are also some tense lapses in the second para. You switch from the present to past between the third and sixth sentence in that para. You misspell 'massacre', 'hankotsu', 'abdominal' and 'mewling' in the seventh para. There are inconsistent ellipses, some with two periods, some with extra spacing between periods. Be consistent. Some of your shorter sentences have unclear dynamic and stative passives, such as 'the dog is tired'. The reader is unsure whether this is because they have been walking for a long time, or the dog is fed up being periodically beaten with the cricket bat. There are also a string of stylistic and tonal issues that I found. I wrote this brief report for you. If you can return the ring binder to me next time, I'd appreciate it."

"Right . . . thanks," you say, taking the ring binder containing your excerpt bloodied in red pen.

"Can I ask that you remain silent until the end? You can respond when everyone is finished," Alan scolds. "Anyone else?"

"I like some of the touches here," a bald elder named Gordon Putsch says. "The part where the dog Bruno looks up at his owner, as if to say 'Why, why are you hacking up my family with that long Japanese knife?' is seriously moving. I also liked the flashes of humour, like when the killer steps in a puddle that turns out to be a poodle."

"It was a wee bit bloody for my tastes," a bouffant widower named Janice Himm enunciates. "I like stories about pixies, penguins, parachutists—anything involving a 'P', and I am there! I read this novel recently called *Pixie Dust and Penguins*, anyone read that?" The Workshop brokers no murmur to her non-rhetorical.

"There's a market for bestial neo-noir," a young one named Vivian Caulks helps. "My mate Peter Symon reads that stuff. He might buy this from you. He's written a similar story about torturing kittens."

"Sorry," Eileen Scurf, who is not sorry, and who is a fierce-looking intelligent roaring fire of a cross-faced woman, says, "am I the only one who found this revolting story about a lunatic slaughtering forty-six dogs for no reason whatsoever completely pointless?" The Workshop brokers no murmur to this non-rhetorical.

"All right," Allan Crosbie says, smoothing the aggro with his harmless inclusive workshoppy manner. "No more comments? Would you like to respond to the feedback?"

"Thanks, everyone," you find yourself saying, followed by the following. "I appreciate the typo catches, Kayleigh. I will have another read through. What I was hoping to create with this story was a homage to the violent comedy of Kinji Fukasaku, the social comment in *Cannibal Holocaust*, and some of the manic screwball of a Whitehall Farce. Thanks for picking out that scene, Gordon, when the fear is captured in Bruno's eyes. I liken that moment to the haunted lunacy on Klaus Kinski's face in Herzog's *Woyzeck*, after the knife has been plunged into his lover. Artistically, it might be the strongest thing I have written yet. Thanks for the advice, Janice. I have already had some interest from the Book Council about maybe turning this into a seven-book series with a national advertising campaign and TV spots, but if I see this Peter, I'll mention the series, another reader won't hurt. And Eileen, thanks for sharing. It's important to me to have your perspective. Not everyone is completely on board conceptually with this novel, I suppose that depends on the depth of your reading. Thanks everyone." You have said that, in a room, out loud. You will take four Nurofen at home later to numb the excruciating pain.

[ ]

Gillian has posted the USB back to you, in the same envelope with a long letter about how she feels your relationship is . . . you will read the letter later.

[ ]

You have almost finished the novel. Except you haven't. You can't. You canven't. You can't bring yourself to write the final lines, partly since "completion" will involve a mandatory re-read of everything you have written, and you cannot be certain that a single line in the entire novel makes any coherent sense (in fact, you are certain that no line in the entire novel makes any coherent sense, but this not a certainty you are willing to court). Further, you can't bring yourself to picture the reality of life after the book. Except you can't stop yourself, so you picture yourself fruitlessly scrolling through *The Writers & Artists' Yearbook* trying to locate an agent willing to take on a non-specific fictional outpouring such as yours, willing to see beyond the absence of an easily

commodotisable product to the startling tower of words you have produced and say uplifting things about their possible brilliance, should by
some miracle of chance they possess any. You picture yourself fruitlessly
scrolling through the list of active UK publishers to locate a publisher
brave enough to take on your uncategorisable if artful blurtings and foist
them on the most gutsy and intrepid readers, should any remain. You
picture yourself fruitlessly attending "networking" evenings in the city,
barrelling over to suited elders hoping some of them wield influence,
spending six long months talking to miserable unpublished writers until
one evening you actually encounter an agent, and cannot describe your
novel as anything other than "that thing of about 74,000 words", that
six months having wiped your memory as to what your novel is actually
"about" (it is "about" nothing, of course). You picture yourself showing
up at publishing offices at three in the afternoon, having tanked a few
pints to steady your nerves, with your novel in a folder, breathing Guin-
ness into the repulsed receptionist's face, as you slap your unwanted unintelligible novel that you accidentally printed in Brittanic Bold so that
every word looks chunky in obese unbroken paragraphs on her desk, and
being escorted to the lifts by the security guard in the lobby, who lobs
the unglimpsed manuscript youwards as you pick yourself up off the
street. You picture the unbearable consequences of having worked for a
painful year, sacrificing your sanity for the sake of having strangers read
the painfully uninteresting contents of your brain, and finding that the
world couldn't care less about you or your bundle of words. You start to
come round to the idea that you might be insane.

[ ]

You re-read your 70,000 words. For seven hours, you actually think what
you have written has merit. You actually believe that someone in the
world might read your words in book form and smile, weep, chuckle, or
say "Hmmm" to the things you have transferred from brain to page with
your chunky fingers. You actually think that your chapters, your pages,

your paragraphs, your clauses, your words, your letters, are not as confused and miswritten as you previously feared, and that a little polish is
all that is required to send your book toward the undusted desks of the
Oxbridge graduates who run the whole publishing business from their
Charlbury mansions, or so you assume. Your warm, dreadless feeling
starts to ebb away, some time around the eighth hour, when your mind
replays the typos, unfinished sentences, cries for help, and random expletives that pepper every page, and the slowly moving tickertape of
your utter incompetence at putting words on the page plays for days
and days, a constant rolling reminder of your constipation and desperation and madness, your creative nonability, your failure to devise one
recurring character or linear plotline or uninsane idea on any of the 339
pages, your nuclear annihilation of a novel, in twenty-six pointlessly
numbered chapters, one for every letter of the alphabet whose sanctity
you expertly mangle, destroy, and defecate upon, unspools slowly before
you, and you stand in the fire of your complete disaster, your pathetic
failure, your nonsensical nonentity of nonvel, and you start to cry copi-
ously, you cry like someone has stabbed your newborn in the nose, you
cry like you have fallen from your bicycle and crushed a box of baby kittens, you cry like you have seen the face of Jesus in your soup and that
face says "Go to hell, asshole", you cry like you are listening to any track
from Vashti Bunyan's *Lookaftering*, you cry like you have been told that
your waistcoat is too tatty for access to the Garrick club, you cry like
the abyss has opened up and swallowed you whole and spat you back out
again because you are too ugly, you cry like your blind girlfriend has told
you she never wants to see you again, you cry like it's 1993, you cry baby
cry and make your mother sigh, you cry like the risotto is riddled with
shorn-off warts, you cry like the end of the world has taken place and
then by some fluke restarted all over again with the same species, you
cry like encrusted milkshake stains remain on your favourite tumbler,
you cry like the Korean pop starlet has snubbed you outside the recording studio, you cry like the vicar has sternly told off a raucous toddler

for whooping during his rousing dénouement, you cry like the hosepipe has flailed wildly and strangled the retired old codger like at the start of *Blue Velvet*, you cry like your brother has ridiculed your statement that "we should fight for the NHS", you cry like the student reader upon glimpsing the font size in *Dombey & Son*, you cry like the Arab in your oxtail soup, you cry like a broccoli salesman upon being told that broccoli is loathed by every sentient mammal in the universe with a violent burning hatred, you cry like the moon in silhouette behind the showy scene-stealing sun, you cry like a forty-three-year-old five-year-old in the strenuous act of collywobbling, you cry like an unheeded Belgian assertion, you cry like the keys that will not fit the keyhole that is you, you cry like the blushing chin of a drowsy dowager en route to view a special pie, you cry like the affixed stamp on a letter to a pre-fried ex-prisoner, you cry like the balloon soon to pop in the hands of a phono-phobic toddler, you cry like the indefinite article in an article about the definite article, you cry like a pampered janitor unable to unpeel the satsuma in his right hand, you cry like the bottle unfilled with pebbles on the outside mantel, you cry like the pawnshopped artichokes of Alexis Arquette RIP, you cry like the ogled bride at a Tyrolean ceremony of undisclosed miscellany, you cry like the botoxed woolly mammoth returning to her mirrorless enclaves, you cry like the floating amendment unwooed by the impudent lawmakers, you cry like the beetroot lumps on the ankles of a polyoctoroonish male, you cry like the sense of senescence in a sentence on senselessness, you cry like a kink in a knot on a Welsh Tuesday, you cry like the air steward caught lollygagging in a lounge fat with lithium, you cry like a loose screwball in a comedy of errors, you cry like a wink unheeded by a lumpen school teacher whose eyes scan the room in search of a pink everafter, you cry like the immaculate moment before a dragoon passes wind in a box in a sort of place, you cry like the vanishing draught in a room where the formerly alone perch with pecans, you cry like the unalliterative sentence in a boggish line of artless prose, you cry like the reptile compartment in Susan Allbright's wicker replica of Iraq, you cry like the stammering Hector in an undulating copse, you cry like a sailor at sea with a novel to which he cannot relate a single detail without derisive stares, you cry like the councillor in command of a Short Kingdom in an Ultraverse, you cry like a crying you, you cry like a dying shrew, you cry like a crying you, oh, you cry, my sorry soul, you cry, cry, cry, because you are still you, you know, yes, you are, you are still you, and you know you are still you, and you know your knowledge that you are still you, that you you loathe, that you from whom you flee, that you that knows you, that lives in you, that breathes in you, that sleeps with you, that bathes with you, that screws with you, that chomps with you, that strides with you, that weeps with you, you know your knowledge of you in all your youness is keeping you trapped in your youyoulating youhood, in your sinking leaking youboat, in your youniversal youselessness, in your youniversity of youhoo, in your youyouing youniverse, in the you-certificate film that is you, and that every attempt you make to unyouyourself, to disyounify you, is youseless, for you are you, and that is a fact, a youniversal fact that you younilaterally youh-youh, that you cannot accept, as you crawl and sprawl across the Younited States of Your Face, you-ing and fro-ing across Alabamyou, Alaskyou, Arizonyou, Arkyousas, Californiyou, Colyourado, Connectyoucut, Delyouware, Floryouda, Geyourgia, Illyounois, Indyouana, Kansyouas, Kentuckyouy, Mayouine, Maryouland, Massachyousetts, Michyougan, Missyoussippyou, Missyouri, Montanyou, Nebraskyou, Nevyouada, North Caryoulina, North Dyoukota, Ohiyou, Oklahoyouma, Oreyougon, Pennsylvanyoua, Rhode Islyouand, South Caryoulina, South Dyoukota, Tennessyouee, Teyouxas, Veryoumont, Virginiyoua, Washingyouton, West Virginiyoua, Wisconyousin, Wyouming, You Hampshire, You Jersey, You Mexico, You York, Youdaho, Youisiana, Youtah, Yowa, and Youwaii, youtilising your youlbelt of anti-you putdowns to deyounify yourself, your youness, your you-that-is-you, your you-you-yes-youness, your youyouyouishness, your doubleyou doubleyou doubleyou dot forward slash youyouyou, your yep-that-is-youosity, because you are you, and there is nothing you can you, to stop you being you, and you have to live with you, only you, in your youseless little youzone, until the end of you, and you know what, that is making you sad.

[ ]

Your novel has killed you. Your novel, that slow-acting virulent bacteria of a novel, has worn away at the thin tissue of sanity you possessed in the first place, multiplied its miseries until your tender, fragile little heart has snapped in two, reproduced its rot in your sallow, weak little soul, and devoured your hope completely. The novel inside you is dead, and you are extremely embarrassed, ashamed, and humiliated by everything you have become in that terrible, terrible year, and tidy the manuscript hastily away in a drawer. You'd better read Gillian's letter.

M.J. Nicholls is the author of *Scotland Before the Bomb*, *The 1002nd Book to Read Before You Die*, *The House of Writers*, *The Quiddity of Delusion*, and *A Postmodern Belch*. He lives in Glasgow.

[BUCKINGHAMSHIRE]

NAME: SORGHAM OPEN

AGE: 17

SENTENCE: 31 WEEKS

CRIME: OVERFEEDING THIS MAN'S BLUEBOTTLE

Kathleen Nicholls is an author and illustrator, best known for *Go Your Crohn Way*, the first of three books loosely based on her own experiences with chronic illness. Kathleen lives and works in central Scotland with a blossoming Nutella addiction and a mountain of cat hair.